I0633574

HIGH
COURT
Bully
KING
NEW YORK TIMES BESTSELLING AUTHOR
JA HUSS

ISBN: 978-1-950232-52-9

Edited by RJ Locksley
Cover Photo: Wander Aguiar
Cover Model: Andrew Biernat
Cover Design by JA Huss

Bully boys.
Arrogant tyrants.
Blue-blood bastards.
Call them whatever you want.
Around here, we just call them Kings.

Fancy boats.
Lakeside mansions.
Luxe watches and bespoke suits.
The Kings of High Court College act like Gods.
And Cooper Valcourt is the worst of them.
He is the bully king.
His family owns everything.
And his mission is to put me in my place and send me packing.

But Cooper and I have a history filled with secrets.
And everyone knows that power doesn't come from having money.
It comes from holding secrets.
And I'm holding one of his.
A very dark secret that can bring him to his knees.

***Bully King* is new-adult, dark, bully romance from New York Times bestselling author JA Huss featuring boys with power and girls at their mercy. It's a campus shrouded in lies and a summer rush into an elite society that can propel a poor girl straight into the ruling class.**
If… she's willing to pay the price.

CHAPTER ONE

"Do you know what your problem is, *Christopher*?"

I hate it when my father calls me Christopher. He only does it to be a dick. No one calls me Christopher. Not even him.

Except when he wants to be a dick.

And he always sneers it. Because my given name wasn't his idea. It was my dead uncle's name on my mother's side and she insisted on it. My oldest brother nicknamed me Cooper because my middle brother couldn't say my name right.

"Well? *Do you*?" There's a bulging vein sticking out the side of his neck.

"This a real question? You *really* want me to tell you what my problem is?"

"I asked"—he takes a moment to suck in air

through his flaring nose—"if you *knew* what your problem was."

I pull out my phone, bring up my notes app, and click on the starred title at the top. "My problem is"—I sigh as I read from the app—"I'm an inconsiderate little prick who thinks that this good life I've been provided is a right instead of a privilege. I'm also greedy, stupid, lazy, and will never amount to anything." I slouch in the chair in front of his massive mahogany desk. "Does that about cover it, *Dad?*"

He hates when I call him 'Dad.' It's only ever been 'Father' for him.

But hey, he called me Christopher first. So fuck it.

"I should throw you out," he threatens.

"Do it," I say back. I even narrow my eyes at him to put some threat behind the dare.

He won't. If he was going to throw me out of High Court College—the college my family *founded* nearly two hundred years ago—he'd have done it long before the end of junior year.

"You're on your own next semester. Do not expect that trust fund to mature upon matriculation."

Why he has to use words like 'matriculation,' I'll never understand. Can't he just say 'acceptance' like everyone else?

No. He's a pretentious bastard who feels the need

to rub everyone else's inferiority in their faces.

Like I even want to be a part of his stupid fraternity. It wasn't even my idea. I was forced into it.

"No money," he continues. "No cars. No boats. No trips. No—"

"I get it, *Dad.* I'm cut off. There are no favors from your criminal friends in my future. Are we done here?"

"Criminals!" He bellows a laugh up at the high ceiling of his office. "You're one to talk."

"So we got a little messed up. Who cares? That's what guys my age do."

"You were arrested!"

"It was a drunk-tank arrest. And we weren't driving the boat. She was." I almost manage not to laugh.

But not quite.

"This is funny? *Boy*?" And now he's growling at me so I know we're already done here. The growl is a sure sign he's about to lose his shit. "You didn't just get drunk. That girl's father called me."

"So? She *wanted* it."

My father just stares at me, his unblinking focus on me as he probably wonders how a boy like me could possibly be related to him. "Do you have any idea how many problems you caused for me because of your actions last night? You're not going to get away with it this time."

"OK. Fine." I throw up my hands and roll my eyes. "What's my punishment?"

I expect the usual. Some high-visibility community service so the masses might see me as some relatable, humble human being. Which is stupid. Very few people can relate to me. And I'm not very humble. Humble doesn't get you far in this life I'm living.

My father slides a glossy blue and gold folder across his desk. It slips right over the edge and I have to catch it before it drops to the ground.

School colors, ut-oh. I hold the folder up. "What's this?"

Winston Valcourt, Chairman of High Court College and Prep, AKA my *father*, grins like he just slipped something past me and I haven't realized it yet. "Your summer job, son."

"Job?" I laugh. "No. I've already got a summer job. I'm out of here this afternoon. I put in my mandatory family appearance at the Prep graduation last night and now I've got a ticket to New Zealand with my name on it."

"Not anymore."

"Like hell." I glare at him. "I'm not getting stuck here all summer. Ax, Lars, and I are all leaving for the airport in"—I look at my watch—"*three* hours."

"Cooper, when are you going to understand that unless you do as you're told, you have nothing in this world?"

"I bought that ticket with my own money. I worked for it." This is not entirely true. Ax worked for it. And he sold drugs, so that's probably not really considered *work*. But eh. Fuck it. It sounds good when you say it out loud. "You're not footing the bill for my summer holiday. So I don't get what the problem is."

He points at me. "That is the problem. You think you own this world."

"I wonder where I got that idea?"

"You"—he's still pointing—"do not. Own this world. *I do*."

I slouch even more in my chair and let out a long breath of air. "I'm not staying here."

"You are. And so are your friends. The Judge and the Mayor have both been contacted. You and your buddies have been grounded."

"Grounded? That's funny. I'm twenty-one years old, *Dad*. You can't *ground* me."

"The *plane*, Cooper. The plane has been grounded. Not you. *You*"—I have a feeling, if I were close enough, he'd be poking me in the chest right about now—"you will be spending the next eight weeks running the Fang and Feather Summer Rush."

"No. Fucking. Way. I'm not running that shit show. And you can't just ground some commercial airline."

"Can't I?"

Can he? He has to be bluffing.

My phone dings a text.

"Check it," my father says.

I slide my phone out of my pocket and glance at the screen. It's an alert from the airline. My flight has been canceled. I mutter, "Fucking. Prick," under my breath.

"As I was saying." My father leans forward, his elbows on his desk, and he steeples his fingers under his chin. "You will run the rush this summer. Your brothers did it before you. And believe it or not, Cooper, this year's pledges are expecting you."

"You mean their fathers are expecting me."

He just continues like I didn't even speak. "They know that you are a symbol of what Fang and Feather stands for."

"That's fucking sick, and you know it. I'm not babysitting incoming minions!"

"You absolutely are. You and Isabella are going to run the entire camp all summer long."

Fuck. He got Isabella mixed up in this plan? This

makes me hesitate. "And if I don't?"

"Walk out, Cooper. Go ahead. I dare you. Walk out. Walk away from all of it. Isn't that your favorite threat? Isn't that your dream? Tell me to just go fuck myself, slide your sunglasses down your face like you're some hotshot with power, and walk off into the sunset?" He laughs. "I'm going to make it very easy for you to do that now, son. You're nearly a grown man. Might as well let you make these decisions for yourself. But if you walk out, you take nothing with you. Your entire cottage was packed up last night while you were in the drunk tank. Your car has been taken to a secure location. Your bank accounts have been emptied. And you won't be able to go to Lars and Ax, either. I've already spoken with their fathers. They are in the same situation. Either the three of you show up at the Glass House for the rush, run it for the next eight weeks, and move forward in life humbled into submission—or all three of you lose *everything*."

Humbled into *submission*? Did he really just say that?

I open my mouth to reply, but he cuts me off.

"There is no discussion. This is not a deal to be negotiated. That part happened while you were sobering up this morning. This is an order." He leans back in his large, wingback office chair and smiles. "Do it. Or don't. And if your answer is no, then goodbye, Cooper. I wish I could say it has been nice knowing you, but the truth is, the last fifteen years were practically unbearable. You make me tired. And I'm done dealing with you. This is your last chance with me. And before you say no, understand this. Either all three of you show up and run the rush, or you, Ax, and Lars are all cut off. The deal has been made. And it's not just about money. I've already instructed your brothers that they will *never* speak to you again. If you walk away, you walk away from all of us. I will remove every picture of you I have. I will erase you from this family. Your brothers will forget you even *exist*."

"Bull. Shit. Maybe Dane. But Jack?" No. Jack would not do that to me. We're tight. *Aren't we*?

"Call him. Ask him. Trust me, Cooper. They signed on before you were even bailed out this morning. We're all tired of you."

I take a deep breath. I can feel my whole body heating up with anger.

My father, on the other hand, looks like he's been practicing that speech and waiting for this day since my mother died when I was five.

He has always hated me. Always *blamed* me.

"Say yes, Cooper. Say yes and run the rush camp, find the next crop of initiates, and I will give it all back."

"Where am I supposed to fucking live over the summer? What am I supposed to drive? How am I supposed to eat, for fuck's sake?"

"I didn't take the boat. That should suffice." I say nothing while my father smiles at me for a long moment. Then he goes all casual, leaning forward on his desk like he's about to chat up an old friend. "Can I give you a piece of advice?"

I scoff. "Better late than never, I guess."

"Always have a plan B, Cooper."

"What does that even mean?"

"Stash some money away for the next time you get caught and need to negotiate."

"What?"

"You are such a child. When Dane got this lecture, do you know what he told me?"

"Dane? When did Dane *ever* get a lecture?"

"He told me that if I cut him out, he'd have me arrested for at least fourteen felonies and I'd spend the rest of my life in prison wishing I could hang myself from the window bars using shoelaces."

"I'm sorry?" Like. Nothing he just said makes sense.

"He," my father says, "has balls. Unlike you. You're soft, Cooper. You don't do anything one hundred percent. You coast. You never plan for anything—"

"Hello? I have a job waiting for me in New Zealand! Just let me get on the plane and I'm out! I'll leave you alone forever!"

"No." He leans back again. "You don't get to simply walk away, Cooper. You have to fight your way out just like everyone else."

I throw up my hands. "I have no idea what you're even talking about."

"That's your problem. You have no idea about anything. Now get the fuck out of my office. I expect you and Isabella to join me for dinner tonight. If you don't show up, well—I'll just say my goodbyes now." He leans across his desk, stabs a button on his phone, and says, "Laurie, send in the next one. Cooper and I are done here."

"Yes, sir," Laurie squawks back from the speaker phone.

My father stands up, walks over to his bar cart on the far side of the room, and starts pouring a drink.

I just sit there for a moment, wondering what I should do. Argue with him? Apologize? Throat-punch him, steal his car keys, and run?

What? What should I do?

"Get. *Out,* Cooper."

I take my glossy blue and gold folder and get out.

CHAPTER TWO

Why would the chairman of High Court Prep want to speak to me?

Come on, Cadee. You know why. They are throwing you out!

I mean, your mother is dead. D-E-A-D. She was the only reason you got to live on this ultra-pretty, super-special, highbrow, blue-blood campus to begin with!

I never fully appreciated how lucky I was to live here until my dad died three years ago. Before that I existed in blissful ignorance, taking everything for granted, including our home. Which was reserved for the campus landscape director, who happened to be my father.

When he died, my mother and I had to move into an attic apartment above the Alumni Inn and she had to take a job as the head baker for the prep school cafeteria and catering department.

What will they make me do now? If I want to stay here?

Take over her job? Give me another one?

Do I want to stay here?

I never went to High Court Prep. I was educated at home by my mother and that was great. My non-traditional schooling fit me. I'm more of a loner. I like books, and going on nature walks, and painting with watercolors.

A gentle soul. That's what my father used to call me.

And I would not call a single child who ever set foot on the High Court Prep campus a gentle soul. Not even the artsy kids, which is the clique I probably would've ended up in. They are cut-throat creatives with dark souls that belong to the devil.

Not gentle at all.

That's why my parents didn't want me to go to Prep, even though at my father's level, we were entitled to an employee scholarship.

God, I miss him.

And now my mother is gone too. It hasn't truly hit me yet. Just how utterly alone I am in the world.

But I don't have time to dwell on it, because Chairman Valcourt wants to see me and I'm ninety-nine percent positive he's calling me into his office to kick me out of my attic apartment.

Then what will I do?

Where will I go?

I don't understand anything right now. The past two weeks have been a blur of denial and sadness. Denial, because I still haven't cried. Not even when I saw my mother in her casket at the funeral. I wanted to cry, I really did. But there are just no tears inside me anymore.

Something is wrong with me.

Focus, Cadee. You're about to get kicked out of your campus apartment. You need to come up with a plan. Something you could say to the Chairman to make him let you stay.

Do I want to stay?

These are not my people. I don't have a single friend on this campus. My parents were my friends and now that they're both gone, there is really nothing for me here.

But I don't have any plans, either. This feels like the path of least resistance.

So I keep walking towards my appointment with destiny because everything feels very much out of my hands right now.

The admin building is located on the north edge of the prep-school campus. The side facing me as I walk down the central gardens is bustling with parents and students as they wrap up all their last-minute details before heading home for the summer.

Then there are the seniors who will be going to High Court College next fall. That campus is right on the other side of the admin building. And these kids are having a party in the central gardens that includes water balloons, squirt guns, and cans of brightly-colored silly string.

They are targeting everyone walking by.

I would not say the kids at Prep *hate* me. That's a strong word. But I am not one of them. I'm the weird girl who lives in the Alumni Inn attic. And before that I was the weird girl who lived in the gardener's cottage.

When they notice me coming towards them, a few of them do target me with their pranks, but most of them just look sad. They feel sorry for me. And they stare.

One kid—not even a senior, so he shouldn't even be involved in the fun—takes aim at me. But I'm too far away to hit with his massive water gun. Then the other kids pull him back and start whispering in his ear.

I turn away before I can see the look of pity on his face.

Because today I am the girl with the dead mother.

I head towards the woods, taking the long way

around the art and lit buildings, and cross over onto the High Court College campus. The admin building intersects both campuses right down the middle. And while there is a high stone wall all the way around the college campus, there are also wide gates that allow access inside.

That's my route today.

And what the hell? I might as well enjoy the beauty of this place one last time before I have to move on. Because I know what's coming. Probably everyone knows what's coming.

My days here are over. They died with my mother two weeks ago in that car crash.

I pass through the wide gate that leads into the college side of the campus and let out a long breath.

There are far fewer people over here. The cottage houses that act as dorms for the college are all in the woods near the stadium. So while it's probably a madhouse in the parking lots, over here it's relatively quiet. Just a few dozen smaller groups hanging outside the admin building.

I climb the steps and I'm just reaching for the door when it comes slamming open and I jump back in surprise, stumble backwards, and then crash into a girl coming up directly behind me.

The cause of the crashing door is a tall student.

Big and muscular and smells like he slept in a brewery last night.

The girl I bumped into pushes me aside and then she and he are face to face, scowling at each other.

The muscular boy growls at her. "Watch where you're fucking going, *Mona.*"

"Suck my dick, *Cooper.*" She places one hand on his broad chest and pushes him out of her way, then disappears through the open door.

I stare at her back until the door closes and obstructs my view. Then I look up at the boy.

He is not a boy. Definitely a college student. Because he is massively tall and has enough scruff on his face to pass for an adult. And hey… do I know him?

"What the fuck are you looking at, you stupid whore?"

I step back from the venom in his voice and mumble, "Sorry," even though I have nothing to be sorry about. He's the one who came crashing through the door at us.

"Fuck off, *Cadee.*" He practically spits my name.

I'm so stunned that this hulking, handsome man knows my name, I start stuttering. "W-w-what?"

"Quit fucking looking at me. I told you I never wanted to see your face again, didn't I? Why the hell are you here in front of me?"

That girl—Mona—she called him Cooper.

"*Cooper*?" I say. Jesus Christ. He's… *changed.*

His hand comes out and pushes my shoulder so hard I stumble backwards again. "Get the fuck out of my way." And then he's hopping down the steps and heading towards the student cottages in the woods.

I watch him as he weaves his way through the central gardens—the gardens my dead father planted years and years ago—until he disappears into a crowd.

Holy hell.

That's Cooper Valcourt?

Damn. He grew up since I last saw him three years ago.

The door to the admin building comes crashing open again and I realize I've been standing in front of it for almost a full minute staring at a boy.

I collect myself, slip through the door before it closes, and exhale in a rush.

I will not think about Cooper Valcourt. Ever.

Especially not today, when my whole world is falling apart.

I push my way through the crowds in the lobby until I get to the stairs that lead up to the second floor, and then start climbing them.

The main reception area in front of Chairman

Valcourt's office is almost overflowing with waiting students. None of whom I recognize since they are all college-age and I have made staying out of sight a priority since the *last time* I bumped into Cooper Valcourt.

That was three years ago and didn't happen in front of the admin building—it happened in my brand-new bedroom in the attic of the Alumni Inn.

I snap back to attention when Laurie—Chairman Valcourt's assistant—calls a name out in a very loud voice. "Mona Monroe! Are you here?"

The girl who told Cooper to suck her dick pushes her way through the crowd. "Get out of my way, jerks. Do you mind? Coming through!" She has long, dark hair with wild, unruly curls that perfectly matches her dark eyes and black tank top. She's sexy. In every way possible. She's got the curves, the pouty mouth stained red with glossy lipstick, and the black stilettos that make her look more like a stripper than a student who graduated high school last night.

I don't know Mona Monroe, but I've seen her around, of course. She went to Prep and the Monroes own one of the lake mansions. The one next door to Cooper, now that I think about it. One of the three you can actually see from the window behind Laurie's desk.

"Jesus H freaking Christ! Can you get out of my

way?"

She was the best athlete on the swim team and was probably on her way to the Olympics—because that's what kids with her family status do when they're good at something. They take it all the way—but she got caught doping in her sophomore year of high school and was pretty much banned from the sport.

She's been something of a clichéd rebel ever since.

Anyway. Mona opens Chairman Valcourt's office and slams the door closed behind her with such a bang, the entire packed room goes eerily quiet.

We all stand there, kinda stunned. And then the screaming starts on the other side of the door.

"Cadee Hunter! Are you here?"

"I'm here!" I call out to Laurie, and then push my way through the crowd like Mona did, minus the harsh language.

The screaming on the other side of that door is still happening when I finally make it over to Laurie's desk. And it's not Valcourt yelling.

It's Mona.

I look at Laurie. "What is going on?"

"Mona," Laurie says. She's a middle-aged woman who collects pencils in her bun the way other people collect pens in a drawer. She currently has four of them sticking out from her head in various directions.

"Those two will never see eye to eye. If she were smart, she would've gone somewhere else for college."

"Hmm." I don't have a lot of opinions on the college plans of the High Court Prep rich kids. I can't even get into the local community college unless I take the GED because they are refusing to accept my mother's homemade high school diploma. So I have zero feelings about Mona's decision to stay here.

But, if you think about it, why would she go anywhere else? Her family legacy at High Court goes all the way back to when this campus was nothing but a one-room schoolhouse on the edge of Monrovian Lake.

Take the path of least resistance, right? Why not? That's what I'm trying to do too. *No room to judge, Cadee.*

Something crashes on the other side of the door and everyone goes still again, watching. Waiting to see who emerges from the office.

The door opens and Mona appears, scowling at everyone. "What the hell are you all looking at?" Funnily enough, and without realizing it, echoing Cooper Valcourt's words to me just a few minutes ago.

She storms past us and then disappears in the crowd.

"You're up!" Laurie says.

"What?" I turn to her. "Now? After *that*?"

"You'll be fine. He's always liked you, Cadee."

"Liked me? He doesn't even know me."

Laurie points at the door—still open. "In, young lady. We have thirty-seven more kids to discipline this morning. That party last night was one for the books." She winks at me. "That's not why you're here, honey. Don't worry."

Of course, that's not why I'm here. I've never gone to one of the infamous graduation parties. "Do you know why I'm here?"

She's just about to open her mouth and answer me when Valcourt bellows, "Cadee Hunter! I do not have all day!"

"Go," Laurie says. "You'll be fine."

I don't know about that.

After my mother's death two weeks ago, I doubt I'll ever be fine again.

CHAPTER THREE

I have feelings for Cadee Hunter right now.

Hateful ones.

Jesus Christ. I haven't been face to face with that girl since I was a senior at Prep three years ago and she was the last person I wanted to see coming out of my father's office this morning.

Forget it. Put her out of your mind. Because, Cooper, you have bigger things to deal with.

Like the fucking truck parked on the front lawn of my small three-room red-brick cottage and the half a dozen huge men who are currently removing my furniture.

I start running through the woods, yelling. "Hey! What the hell?" I stop right in front of the biggest one, a huge dude with cannons for arms who is currently holding up his end of my fucking couch. "Put it back!

Right now!"

"Cooper?"

I whirl around and find Sheriff Woods walking up to me. He's a short, middle-aged man with a bushy handlebar mustache you mostly find on throw-back cowboys. And he's mostly a nice guy, but he's also one of the High Court cronies—i.e. he works for my father. "Make them stop."

"Your father called me this morning—"

"I don't care. This is my stuff. Not his."

"Do you have receipts?"

"Receipts? Are you fucking kidding me?"

"Look, son." Woods places a hand on my chest and I'm immediately reminded of how Mona pushed me in front of the admin building.

I look down at his hand. Take a breath. And then slowly track my eyes back up to his.

He removes his hand from my chest. *Wise choice, asshole. Because I'm not in the mood.*

"You've been kicked out. I have the eviction notice right here."

I snatch the piece of paper from his hand and scan it, then crumple it up and toss it aside. "Eviction notice? Tell me, Sheriff, how does one go about getting an emergency eviction notice for student housing without the occupant even being served?"

I'm gonna lose my shit. I can feel the anger inside me ready to explode.

Woods, to his credit, looks ashamed. Because we both know this so-called eviction notice might have the Judge's signature on it, but it was obtained in secret, during the early morning hours, probably in the Judge's fucking kitchen, without due process, and in exchange for either a healthy sum of money or the promise of a future favor.

"I thought you were better than this." I figure it doesn't hurt to shame the sheriff. He did take an oath to protect and serve.

"Son," Woods says calmly. "It's done. He wants you out."

"He wants me to move *home*. You *know* that's what this is about."

Sheriff Woods looks out across Monrovian Lake. Right at the Valcourt family mansion on the opposite shore. It's an imposing home, even from this distance, which is a good half a mile away. Then he looks back at me. "Cooper, if you're this pissed off because your father is going out of his way to make you move back in the family mansion, then—"

"You don't understand—"

"Shut up." He pauses so his sharp words can sink in. "Just go home. Your personal things are already there. This is just… stuff. And it's going into storage. I'm sure you'll be back at the end of the summer." But then he stops and shrugs. "Or not. I don't really give a shit if you're coming or going. But you need to get the hell out of my face or you will be spending the day in lockup."

My own words to Cadee Hunter thrown back at me. And it feels like karma. I run my fingers through my hair and turn away. "Fuck this shit."

I'm just about back to the central gardens when I spy Ax coming towards me. His mouth is moving long before I can hear his words. So when he's finally in earshot, I get the middle of his monologue—

"… and you know the worst part? He took my fucking bank account! My bank account. With my name on it! Filled with money I earned! He can't do that, Cooper!"

Ax is tall, broad, and tatted up from shoulder to wrist with images of demons. Lots of fangs, and horns, and hooves on his arms. His head would normally be covered in light brown hair, but he started shaving it back in ninth grade and never really stopped. Right now, it's about a quarter-inch long. If the sun hits his green eyes at just the right angle, they turn yellow. He looks… evil. But he's one of my best friends and we've been in this shit together for so long now, there's no way to back out now.

I sigh, feeling pretty defeated. "To be fair, Ax, it *was* drug money."

"Not the fucking point!" He yells this. "And what the hell is going on here?"

I look over my shoulder at the movers. Then turn back to Ax. "Apparently the Judge signed an eviction notice for my father while we were sobering up."

"What?" He grabs his head with both hands. "But—"

"Hey!"

We both turn to find Lars, the other leg of our tight trio, jogging across the gardens towards us. Lars just looks like a Lars. He's tall, and lean, and well… just think Alexander Skarsgård. That about sums him up. "What the hell is happening? I just made bail and the Mayor called saying we were kicked out or something and—" He stops mid-sentence. Presumably because he's spied the movers.

I press my fingertips to my forehead, then cover my eyes with my whole hand. My head is pounding so hard. "They really have kicked us out."

"What's that?"

I remove my hand from my eyes and find Lars pointing at the folder in my other hand. "This?" I sigh. "This is my new job packet."

"What job?" Ax says. "We're on a fucking plane in three hours to goddamned New Zealand. Please tell me that's a job in New Zealand, Coop. Or I'm gonna lose it."

"Yeah. We're not going anywhere. It seems our fathers have managed to ground the plane."

"No." Ax grabs his head again. "No. No. No. I'm not staying here."

"We're supposed to move home."

"No." Ax is turning in circles now. "No fucking way. I'm not going home. I don't care anymore. I'm so done with this place."

Lars puts a hand on his shoulder. "You can crash at my house."

"You're going home?" Ax is stunned. He looks at me. "You're going home too?"

"What choice do we have? They took everything from us, Ax. We have to run the Fang and Feather rush to get our shit back. The Chairman wants me to choose the next crop of initiates."

Lars bellows a laugh. "Oh, that's funny." He points at me. "That's actually funny!"

"It's not a joke. And you two are stuck with me. Guilty by association, I guess."

"Cooper!" Ax puts a hand on my shoulder. "No. You need to go back and talk to him. Apologize."

"For what? That girl was begging me last night. I wasn't gonna tell her no. Fuck that, I'm not apologizing."

"You have to." Ax is pleading. "I'm not going home."

"You can stay with me, dude," Lars says. "It's cool. The Mayor won't mind. Hell, sometimes I think he likes you better than me."

That's probably truer than Lars would like to admit, but it's not something we talk about.

"Cooper," Ax says. "Dude. I don't ask for much. You know that. I take my licks. I deal. I'm not complaining. But I am not going home. Ever. Can't you at least… I don't know, beg? If we have to run the rush, you need to beg for us to stay in one of the cottages. Because I'm done. I'm done taking it."

And he is. I can see it all over his face.

Fuck.

I turn my back to him and rub both hands over my jaw. "Fine. I'll ask." I turn back to him. "But he's gonna say no. And when that happens you will just go home with Lars, bite your fucking tongue, and play nice for the summer. You don't even have to run the rush. I'll cover for you, Ax. But you will show up at least and make them think you're on board."

I see the rebel in him. I see that fire inside that

wants to tell me to go fuck myself.

But he knows I'm right.

"We have one more year," Lars says. "Just *one.* More. Year. And then we're out, Ax. It'll be over."

Ax looks at me and I give him a small nod.

But I don't believe it any more than he does.

When your fathers are the Chairman, the Mayor, and the Judge—well… you don't walk away from that.

There is no out.

My friends follow me back towards the admin building, keeping a few paces behind me, very quiet now. The time for protest over.

If I had known what the consequences of last night would be, would I have thought twice about what we did?

I crack a smile as I climb the steps to the admin building.

Nah.

CHAPTER FOUR

I swallow hard as I walk into Chairman Valcourt's office.

"Close the door, please." He's a very tall man. Nice head of thick, silver hair. Broad shoulders filling out his expensive dark gray suit. Straight posture, hands in pockets. And a nice face that is very reminiscent of his oldest son, Jack. He's not looking at me. He's standing in front of the window gazing out at the central gardens of the college campus that end at Monrovian Lake.

Or maybe his expansive mansion directly across the water?

When you picture a huge mansion in your head you probably see a large white home with columns. Very symmetrical. Maybe some black shutters and a grand semi-circular porch.

But that's not what his home looks like. It's a Tudor, made of dark gray stone with severely pitched rooflines. There are more tall, skinny windows and arched doorways than I can count, and there's even a turret for added effect.

I'm pretty sure it has historical value because important people, like himself, have lived in it for nearly two hundred years. Long before this school even existed.

I close the door quietly and the bustle out in the reception area recedes, creating an uncomfortable silence in the room.

"Um…" I don't know what to say. "Hi… you wanted to see me, Chairman?"

He turns around slowly, his mouth a flat line of… I dunno. Lack of interest? Anger?

Mona Monroe did just leave here. She lives to piss people off. Just my luck to get the appointment right after hers.

"Sit," he says, pointing to a small table in the corner of the room that appears to be set for tea.

I walk over to it and take a seat, feeling self-conscious about not touching any of the beautiful china or tableware laid out on the white tablecloth. He watches me do this with an intense focus that immediately makes me uncomfortable.

I let out a long breath and wait.

"Would you like some tea?" He doesn't give me a chance to answer, just stabs a button on his phone and says, "Laurie. Pour us tea, please."

Moments later Laurie appears, smiling. She pours me a cup, then fills the other cup, even though the Chairman has taken a seat at his expansive desk.

"Thank you, Laurie."

She smiles at him as she leaves the office, pulling the door closed behind her.

"Go ahead," the Chairman says, motioning to the table. "It's good tea. I don't really care for tea but people buy it for me all the time. I'm a hard man to buy gifts for, I suppose." He pauses to contemplate this idea. "Still, I do enjoy serving it."

"O…kay." I use the tiny tongs to drop two raw sugar cubes into my cup, and stir it up with an equally tiny spoon. Then I take a sip. "Mmm." I fake-smile at him. "I like it."

Not a lie. But not entirely true either. I'm just… *why am I here?*

"Good. I'm glad." He folds his hands on his desk, smiles at me.

This is so weird. There are dozens of students out in the reception area waiting their turn for a meeting with him, and yet we're in here just staring at each other.

His smile falls. And then he's frowning at me.

"I'm sorry. Did I do something wrong? Is that why you wanted to see me?"

"Wrong? Dear, God, no. You didn't do anything wrong. I'm so sorry about your mother, Cadee."

"Oh." I shrink a little. Kinda go inside myself with the reminder of my recent loss.

"I wanted to make sure you were OK. You have a place to stay?"

And here we go. I knew this was why I was here.

"I know you're living in the attic apartment. But you and your mother were getting ready to move today, so I just want to make sure—"

"Wait. What? What did you just say?"

He looks confused for a moment. "Moving?"

"We weren't moving out today."

He cocks his head at me. "I'm fairly sure you were. Your mother put in notice two months ago."

"Notice for what?"

"She quit."

"She… *quit*?" These words do not make sense to me.

"Oh." He pauses, frowns sadly at me with tight lips. "You didn't know."

"No. I had no idea."

He draws in a breath and squints at me. "There are movers at the inn."

"No."

"Yes."

"No!" I say it forcefully. "I was literally just at home an hour ago. We weren't packing. We're not moving!"

"I…" He hesitates. "I got a call from campus security. The movers arrived thirty minutes ago and no one was there, so he let them in. They are packing up your apartment as we speak."

"What?" I stand up.

"Sit," he commands. "We're not done here. And as you can see by my reception area, I have a lot of other issues to deal with this morning."

"But my stuff is—"

"I'll make a call." He slides his hand inside his suit coat, pulls out his phone, and taps the screen. "Yes. Can you please tell me what is happening at the Hunter apartment?" He nods to whatever the other person is saying. Looks at me. Looks away. "Thank you." He ends the call. "I'm afraid it's all loaded on the truck. They just pulled away."

I laugh. I can't help it. "That's not possible! No one can pack up an entire apartment in thirty minutes."

"You didn't own the furniture. It was just clothes

and such?"

"Yeah, but—"

"I'm afraid it's gone. Your mother did have plans." He shrugs. "I'm sure it will all arrive safely."

"Arrive where?"

"I don't know." He must see the panic on my face because he says, "I'll make a call and find out for you. Don't worry."

"What? No! This is not happening!"

He holds up a finger. "Give me a moment, please." He makes his call without waiting for my approval. "Sheriff, can you run down a truck for me? It just left the Alumni Inn with Cadee Hunter's things inside it." He listens for a moment. "Oh."

"What?"

"Oh. I see."

"What? What is he saying?"

The Chairman hushes me with a sharp look. "OK. I will let her know. Thank you."

"Let me know what?"

"Well, apparently you were moving to North Dakota."

I laugh. There is simply nothing else to do.

"I'm serious, Cadee. That truck is on its way to North Dakota. The sheriff already looked into it. He thought it was suspicious as well, but they produced paperwork. Your mother bought a house there."

"In North *Dakota?*"

"Yes." He looks concerned for a moment. "It's an odd choice. Isn't it?"

"Odd? No. This is crazy. None of this is happening. Tell the sheriff to make them turn around."

"I'm afraid I can't. There is no legal reason."

"The legal reason is that they stole my stuff!"

He frowns at me. "Cadee, I have to say, I wasn't expecting you to be so… combative. You've never been a problem before."

"What?" I just blink at him.

But before I can string together some sort of cognizant response to that completely bizarre statement, he says, "Your things were not stolen. The movers and packers had a work order. It was all done in good faith."

"Chairman Valcourt, respectfully, my mother is dead! Her orders don't matter anymore."

He walks across the room and takes the seat across from me at the tea table. "I didn't want to bring this up, but this move was spelled out in the will."

"What?" I just stare at him. "No. It wasn't. I went to the reading a few days ago. I was there. I inherited… well, nothing. We didn't have anything. But—" I shake my head, trying to gather my thoughts. "That doesn't even make sense. Why would—”

“Listen, Cadee.” He makes one of those smiles that is nothing but clenched teeth. Like he’s got something to add to that, but he doesn’t want to. Then he inhales quickly and reaches across the table and takes both my hands in his. I’m so startled, I pull away. But he just grips them tighter. “I’m not sure any of this matters.”

“What are you talking about? Of course it matters! You’re telling me that my life was just packed up in a truck and it’s now on its way to North Dakota!”

“Perhaps you have relatives there?”

“I do not!”

“Stop it now, Cadee.”

A chill runs down my arms. I don’t like the way he’s saying my name.

“You’re going to work yourself up into a frenzy, Cadee. And there is no point in that.”

“I’m— ”

He lets go of my hand and the next thing I know two fingertips are touching my lips. I’m so startled that he did this, I go quiet immediately.

“Shh. Stop talking, Cadee. I’m telling you, this doesn’t matter. You will not be leaving for North Dakota. In fact, you will not be leaving this campus.” He pulls his fingers away.

"I won't?"

"No. I called you here to make you an offer."

I blink at him. Stunned. Desperately trying to catch up with this conversation because I feel like I'm still stuck on the words 'North Dakota.' "What kind of offer?"

"School, of course. I heard some rumors that you were having trouble getting accepted into the community college?"

"Oh." I sigh, then look down and realize he's still holding one of my hands. And his thumb is caressing my wrist. I swallow and look up. *What the hell is happening*?

"You don't need community college, Cadee."

"I don't?"

He's still caressing my wrist and I'm trying to come up with an idea to make him stop when he says, "No. You're going to college here."

"I am?"

"Yes. We have a special scholarship program. A summer internship. In the kitchen of the Glass House."

"The what?" I've never heard of this place. And I've lived on this campus my whole life.

"There is a lake across the lake." He smiles at me. I want to pull my hand out of his, but it's like he's reading my mind and grips just a little tighter. "Behind my mansion. You've probably never been over there."

"I haven't," I admit.

"And a really interesting club house for the residents of Monrovian Lake Estates. We call it the Glass House because, well, it's made mostly of glass. That's where the job is. Would you like it?"

"The job?"

"All of it." He finally lets go of my hand and leans back in his chair. Smiles at me. "The job, the scholarship. The education that will propel you into a completely different life."

"Well… um. I guess? I mean, I wasn't expecting this when I came up here, so I don't quite know what to think about this."

"Say yes." He smiles again. "And then we're done here. Your life is settled. I'm truly sorry for your loss, and I know this won't make up for it, but anything I can do, just ask. I feel like you're… one of mine. I've known you since you were born."

Hmm. I think about that for a moment. It might be true. I have lived here all my life. But… before this meeting I can't say that I have ever even been in the same room as the Chairman. He feels like a stranger to me.

"Now," he continues. "The only thing left to

settle—"

But he's cut off when his office door swings open and crashes against the polished wood paneling behind it with a bang.

And Cooper Valcourt—his fuck-up son—stands in the doorway.

He throws up his hands. "I'm sorry, OK? Is that what you want to hear? My apology? Happy now? Can you just… please be a decent fucking human being for a moment and give us back our cottage for the summer? We'll do your stupid job, all right? I'll get it done. And you don't have to hear from me at all."

"Cadee," the Chairman says, standing up and buttoning his coat. "This is my son, Christopher. Christopher, this is Cadee. She's going to be living with us this summer."

"What?" Cooper and I say it at the same time.

"Escort her over to the mansion. Show her into the southeast guest suite and help her get settled."

"*What?*" we say again. This time, Cooper and I are looking at each other with a mixture of confusion and fear.

"And the answer is no. You will not get that cottage back. You will live at home like your brothers did when they were in school."

"But—" Cooper makes to protest.

The Chairman stabs the phone and barks, "Send in the next one, Laurie," even though the door is wide open and everyone in reception just heard that entire exchange.

He turns to us. Frowns at Cooper. Says nothing to him and instead redirects his attention to me. "Cadee." He walks over to me and offers me his hand.

I don't know what to do except take it and allow him to help me up.

He kisses my knuckles and I hear Cooper breathe, "What the fuck is happening right now?"

I wish I had an answer for him, but I don't. And he just saw his father—a man I do not know. Like *at all!*—just kiss my hand and invite me to live with them.

Like… is that… what basically happened here?

"Once again," the Chairman says, "I'm truly sorry for your loss. I'm sure we'll get that truck back eventually. In fact, I'll make it a priority." He holds my hand in both of his. Pats it. "We'll get your stuff back. But in the meantime, you make yourself at home in our guest suite and Cooper here will fill you in on your new job. In the fall, my dear Cadee, life will look completely different than it does now. And you will be getting ready for your freshman year at one of the most elite private colleges in the world. Congratulations."

Then his smile disappears just as quick as it

formed. He turns to Cooper and growls the words, "Get the fuck out," between clenched teeth.

I don't even know what's happening, but I'm *so* done.

I'm trying to leave, but there's a girl waiting in the doorway for her… meeting? Hell, maybe she's getting an invitation to be the Chairman's… what? What was that?

Did he *come on to me*? In front of his *son*?

Oh, my God. No. Oh, my God. This is *not* happening.

I almost knock the waiting girl over as I push past, and then I have to jostle my way through the crowd of kids—who just heard everything after Cooper entered the office!

I'm so… I don't know. Humiliated? I'm not sure.

I just head for the stairs and start down them, trying to make my escape as quick as I can.

I'm just about to head for the doors that lead outside when Cooper Valcourt grabs me by the arm, swings me around and pushes me into a little alcove under the stairs.

"Oh, no, you don't. Fuck that." He pushes me against the hard, stone wall and leans down into my face. "You're not walking out of here until we have a little chat, *Cadee*."

CHAPTER FIVE

I seethe down at her. "What did you tell him?"

"Nothing!"

"You lying little bitch! You *told* him!"

"I did not!"

"Then why was he all over you like that?"

"I don't know! He called me in for a meeting and… there was tea, and talk of North Dakota, and then…" She throws up her hands. "He invited me to live with you guys!"

"*Why?*"

"He didn't say!"

"Jesus fucking—" I turn around and scrub my hands down my face. Can this day get any worse?

"He gave me a job. That's it. A job, and a scholarship at the end."

"No." I'm shaking my head as I turn back to face her. "This is not happening." *Calm down, Cooper. You don't have any of the facts yet. Let's get the facts.* "What job?" I growl.

"Some… lake house. Glass place?"

"Fuck."

"What?"

"What did your mother know?"

"Nothing!"

I lean down into her face and hiss, "*Liar.* You're such a little fucking liar! You told her, didn't you?"

"Cooper." She grits her teeth and sneers at me. "I *did not.* Tell her. Trust me. The last thing my mother would've wanted to know was that I got a secret abortion when I was *fifteen*! It would've devastated her. I did it for *you*."

I hate Cadee Hunter. "I wish I'd never fucking met you."

She slaps me. Hard. I reach for her, but she ducks under my arm and starts running for the door.

I chase her. But she pushes through the doors and by the time I'm outside, she's already down the stairs, sliding into a crowd.

"Over here!" Lars calls from off to the left.

"Grab her!" I call, pointing at Cadee, not even caring that there are dozens of people around. They are all busy with their own move-out day problems, anyway. They pay no attention to me, or the fleeing

Cadee Hunter, who now finds herself running straight towards Lars and Ax.

She either doesn't believe that they will grab her for me or she didn't hear me. Because she practically walks right into their waiting grips.

"What the hell!" She whirls on them, like a ferocious little rat.

God, I hate this girl. She almost ruined everything three years ago. It took me weeks to convince her to shut her fucking mouth and do what I said.

"Let go of me!"

But they don't let go. Lars grips both her arms behind her back and Ax gets that gleam in his eye that means he's found a target. Someone to unload on. He leans into her ear as I come up behind them and says, "Be a good little girl now, Cadee. Or I'll put a leash on you and walk you through the gardens like a bitch."

She recoils from him.

"All right," I say, knocking him off her. "That's enough." But then I take Cadee's hand and squeeze it. Hard. As I drag her into the gardens with me.

She tugs, and resists, and digs her feet into the gravel. "Let go of me! Let go!"

I jerk her towards me so hard, she does a little twirl and her back crashes into my chest. I hug her. Tight. Almost bear-hug her from behind. So that we almost look like a couple who stopped in the garden to gaze at the roses.

But I hiss my words into her ear. "You will calm the fuck down and be rational, do you understand me? There's a lot more at stake here than you can possibly realize."

She growls back. "Let me go. Right now. Or I will scream so loud—"

I let her go. But I push her away from me. Just in case she goes through with her threat anyway. The last thing I need is stupid Cadee Hunter fucking my day up even worse.

She whirls around to glare at me. "I'm going home."

And then she turns in place a few times, like she's confused as to where she is. Which might actually be the case, because we're on the college side of campus and she must not come over here much. That's why I haven't had to look at her stupid face for three years.

But she figures it out and starts heading back towards the Prep side of things where the Alumni Inn is located. And her tiny attic apartment.

"Great," I say, throwing up my arms and looking at Lars.

"What the hell is going on?" he asks.

"My father. That's what." Then I glare at Ax.

"Great idea, by the way. Telling me to go back up there."

"What happened?" Ax asks.

"He…" But I don't actually know how to explain it. "She… she's supposed to move in to the mansion. And I was ordered to get her settled."

Lars bellows a laugh. "Holy shit. That's funny. Crazy Cadee is moving in with your father?"

"No," I scoff.

But then… maybe? Maybe that's what that was? He did like… kiss her hand. In front of me. That's fucking weird.

But I do have to admit that it would still be better than him finding out I talked Cadee into getting a secret abortion three years ago.

My phone dings a text in my pocket and when I pull it out and look at the screen, it's from my father: *I want a picture of Cadee settled into her suite in thirty minutes.*

I turn around and look up at his office window. Find him standing there looking at me. Then I whirl around and start walking towards the gate that leads to the Prep side of campus.

"Where are you going?" Lars jogs to catch up with me and Ax comes up on the other side.

"To get her."

I can sense that Lars and Ax are as confused as I

am. But they don't say anything else.

I start jogging and they keep pace. And when we finally make it over to the other side of campus where the inn is located, we spot Cadee opening the back door of the old brick building and disappearing inside.

When we get to the door, I put a hand up and stop Lars and Ax. "Wait here. I'll get her."

"Should I find a leash?" Ax asks. "Just in case."

I almost laugh. "Maybe?"

This makes Ax smile. Which is good. He's having a bad day too. We're all having a bad day. And Cadee seems to be doing her best to make it worse.

"I'll be right back." And then I go after Cadee Hunter.

The back door leads to a stairwell and I go up three steps at a time until I reach the landing of the fourth floor. Then push through into the hallway and travel down to the end where the door to her apartment is wide open.

When I reach it, I listen for noise. But it's completely quiet.

Just great. If she's not here—if she went out the front instead of coming upstairs—I'm fucked. And there's no way to tell if she will keep her mouth shut about everything that happened three years ago or not.

I don't know what's going on with her and my

father. Hell, maybe he *is* infatuated with her? Maybe that's all this is? Some dirty old man who wants a sweet young thing?

Jesus. That makes me want to barf.

"Cadee!" I call up the stairs.

No answer.

I go up. Find her standing in the middle of the living room. Not an empty living room, but… it's definitely been emptied of her things. The way my cottage was this morning.

Is there a connection?

But before I can try to convince myself there isn't, Cadee whispers, "It's gone. It's all gone. He wasn't lying."

"Look," I say, sighing. "I don't know what's going on. But—"

"My stuff is gone! All our stuff is gone! He put it on a truck to North Dakota!"

"What the hell are you talking about?"

"This was not my mother's idea! We had no plans to move!"

I think she might be getting hysterical. And the last thing I need today is Cadee Hunter getting hysterical. Not after what happened last night. I can only take so much.

"Cadee," I hiss, "I have a fucking hangover. My

head is pounding. I got no sleep last night, I'm *not* on my way to New Zealand for the summer, I got kicked out of my cottage, and I have to move home. I really… like *really* do not have space inside my brain for your petty little problems."

She turns to me with a look of complete disgust. "Fuck. You."

"That's it." I look around, find a piece of orange baling twine discarded on the floor, and pick it up.

She smirks at me. "What do you think you're gonna do with that?"

I don't answer her. I attack. Grab her by the shoulders, push her down on the couch, pin her in place with my knee on her ass, and tie her fucking hands together.

She screams and wiggles the entire time, but I don't care. I'm done. I pull her up on her feet, take my shirt off, and then stick it in her mouth like a gag.

Her eyes are wide and her feet kicking. Which is not a smart move on her part, because she falls to the floor. And then, finally, she stops being a problem. Because she gives up and starts crying.

I need a minute, so I go back down the stairs, pull the door closed behind me, lean my back against it, and sink down to the floor so I can text Lars.

He and Ax appear through the doorway at the

other end of the hall a minute later. "What's going on?"

"She's being a bitch," I say. "So I tied her up."

Ax laughs, then holds up another discarded string of baling twine. "Great minds," he jokes. "I was ready."

"Can one of you just…" I massage my temples with my fingers, trying to will this hangover headache into submission. "Just… go talk some fucking sense into her? Please. She needs to do what she was told. We *all* just need to do what we were *told*."

Ax's smile falls, his jokes gone. "Fuck. I'll do it."

He's probably not the right choice. But I'm not going back up there. And Lars doesn't volunteer.

I move aside so Ax can get through the door.

"What the fuck happened to your shirt?"

I look down at the Valcourt lions rampant tattoo that spans my entire chest and briefly wish I could go back to that day and never have it done. But wishing doesn't change anything, so I just look up at Lars. "I gagged her with it."

We both laugh. We can't help it. It *is* kinda funny.

He slumps down next to me, sighs. "Are we fucked? Or what do you think is happening?"

I side-eye him. "Did you really think it was going to be that easy to get out of here?"

He shrugs. "I was kinda hoping, ya know?"

"We should've seen this coming. There's no way you're getting out. You're an only child."

"Am I?" he huffs.

"And Dane. I think he's the one behind this."

"What do you think he knows?"

"No clue." It's only half true, of course. My father might know about Cadee's abortion. I don't know how. But that's the only way this day makes sense.

We sit in silence and then quickly get to our feet when we hear Ax stomping down the stairs. A few seconds later the door swings open and Cadee steps out. She looks like she's been crying and her hands are still tied behind her back.

I put a hand up to my mouth to hide my smile when I see the second length of baling twine has been tied into a slip knot and is now around her neck. My t-shirt is still stuffed in her mouth.

"OK, then," Ax says, kinda puffing out his chest with pride. "We're good."

"What the hell is this?" Lars laughs. "She can't walk through campus like that!"

"Oh, she can. And she will." Ax growls these words into Cadee's ear and she furrows her brows and shrugs her shoulders to make him back away from her neck. "I warned her. If she needs a leash, I can provide."

She starts protesting through the gag.

I reach over and pull it out of her mouth.

"This is kidnapping! I'm pressing charges!"

"Good luck with that." Ax laughs. "The fucking sheriff works for my father, Cadee. They only send us to jail when they want to teach us a lesson. You're not part of today's lesson. You're just a task to check off our list. You're going over to the Chairman's house. How you get there is up to you. I thought I explained this upstairs?"

"You're a bunch of animals!"

"Listen." I sigh. "We can do it the easy way. Unbind your wrists, take off the leash. Or we can do it this way. You'll be just another move-out day prank, Cadee. No one will care."

Lars is nodding his head. "Yup. That's pretty much it right there. So decide. Easy way? Hard way? We don't really give a fuck."

She huffs.

"Is that acceptance I hear?" I cup my hand to my ear to be an extra-special dick about this whole thing.

"Fine."

"Oh, no, that's not good enough," Lars says. "We're kinda pissed off at this point. Hell, who am I kidding? We're definitely pissed off. We're having a bad day, Cadee. And you're very much a part of that.

So get on your fucking knees and apologize for making things worse."

Cadee looks at me, her eyes begging me to take pity on her. But I shake my head. Because I like this idea. Humiliating Cadee Hunter might not fix anything, but that old saying—'misery loves company'—is so very, very true.

I narrow my eyes at her. "Knees. *Now.* Someone has to teach you a lesson."

CHAPTER SIX

Eleventy-billion terrible, evil things run through my mind in this moment.

I thought Cooper was the worst? Uh… no. Ax Olson is *the* worst!

I look at him. Not Cooper. I'm done with Cooper. How dare he accuse me of telling my own secret?

"First of all," I say, looking right at Ax, instead of Cooper, "it's not your secret."

"W-what?" Ax laughs. Looks nervously over at Lars.

"It's not your secret to hold close or spill like an idiot. It's mine." I practically spit the words at him.

"Uh… what the hell are you talking about?" Ax says.

"And," I continue, still *not* looking at Cooper, "if you ever"—I lower my voice—"*ever* touch me again, I will have you arrested."

"Um… Jesus, dude," Lars says. "What the hell did you do to her upstairs?"

I whirl on Lars. "And you—"

"Me?" He points to himself. "What did I do?"

"Do the words 'willing accomplice' mean anything?"

"Clearly she is losing her mind."

Oh, Cooper Valcourt. You did not just say that.

But I will not look at him. I refuse to look at him. Not after what he did. "My mind is not lost. But one word from me about my *secrets*"—I'm staring Lars dead in the eyes—"and you. Go. *Down.*"

"Cadee," Lars spits. "What the hell are you talking about? I haven't even talked to you in three years! Whatever fucking trip you're on, it's got nothing to do with me." He looks at Ax. "Take that fucking thing off her neck. And untie her, for fuck's sake. We're not walking her across the campus like that."

"You're not walking me anywhere. I'm staying right here."

Ax sneers at me. And for a moment I wonder if he's going to actually do something stupid. Like choke me out. Because he's *that* kind of guy. Angry. Unstable. Violent. Even now I can see the greenish-yellow stain around his eye. He wears bruises like badges. That's how many fights this boy gets into.

"Go downstairs," Cooper says.

"What?" Lars asks.

"Just… both of you. Go downstairs and give me a minute with… *Cadee.*" He sneers my name like it is something truly disgusting.

"Gladly," Ax says, eyeing me up and down in a threatening way. "Fuck this bitch."

Lars follows him and Cooper waits until they are through the door at the end of the hall before he reaches for my wrists. "What the hell was that?"

"That was a threat."

He pulls a small folding knife out of his pocket, cuts the twine around my wrists, and then reaches for the noose around my neck.

I swat his hands away and remove the twine myself. "And if you don't think I'll do it, you have severely underestimated me." I try to say it with as much conviction as I can, but my voice cracks. And I know if I say much more I will probably start crying.

Cooper sighs, puts his hands in his pockets, then leans against the wall. Like he needs something to hold him up right now.

I don't mean to stare at the giant fighting-lion tattoo that spans his entire chest—or the muscles underneath it. He didn't have either of those when we were last together.

You were never together, Cadee. He bullied you. Relentlessly.

Right. Let's try to keep this day rooted in reality.

But holy hell. The last time I saw this much of Cooper Valcourt, he certainly didn't look this good.

I pull my eyes away from his chest and refuse to admit I like the tattoo and the muscles, because Cooper Valcourt is evil. All the Valcourts are evil. Which means… his father's offer might be…

"Look." Cooper sighs. "If you help me out, I'll help you out."

"I don't need your help."

"Don't you? Looks like he stole your life, just like he stole mine."

Now I do look up at him. "And whose fault is that?"

"Not mine."

"Wrong. Everything is your fault. Even when it isn't."

"Childish much?"

Air blows past my lips. "You are such a piece of work." I turn my back to him.

"Listen to me." He grabs my shoulders, spins me around, and pushes me up against the wall. Not only that—he pushes himself up against me. So his chest is pressing against my breasts.

Do. Not. Look at him. Do not!

"Look at me, Cadee."

Stay strong.

"Look. At. Me. Cadee." He pauses. Then his voice softens. "Please."

Fuck. I look. And man… why? Why does this *animal* have to have those eyes? Piercing. I know. It's overused in books. Every blue-eyed man has a piercing gaze. I get it.

But it's just true with this one. These blue eyes of his are not reminiscent of the sky or the long, brilliant feathers of a peacock. Oh, they're that color. An intense, almost surreal blue. But they are dark. They are the depths of despair. Lightning in a thundercloud. The flame of a gas fire. They are poison. Pure poison.

"I don't know what he's doing. I swear to God, I do not know. And I don't understand why he's gotten you involved. If I could stop it, I would."

"Then do it!" I yell it. Right up in his face. "*Tell* him."

He sighs and runs his fingers through his hair. "That's not going to help anything. What's done is done. He doesn't need to know about it."

"You would say that," I whisper. "Because you made this happen. You did this to me."

He walks away.

"All of it! This is all your fault. You killed my dad, you killed—"

He spins around and yells, "What the fuck are you talking about?"

"You are everything that's wrong in my life, Cooper Valcourt! Everything! It's all your fault."

He actually laughs and throws up his hands. "Fine. You want to make it all my fault? It's all my fault."

"'Get on your knees, Cadee!' You'd like that, wouldn't you? You and your bully friends! You made my life miserable that year. Do you have any idea what you did to me?" I scream it. So loud he rushes forward and cups his hand over my mouth.

"Shut up!" he growls down into my face. He grabs me by the hair and twists it up in his fist until he's pulling on my scalp. "Just… calm the fuck down."

I breathe hard into his palm, my chest heaving. And then… that's it. I have reached the end of my self-control and the tears spill down my cheeks and slide over his fingers.

All that sadness I've been holding in for the last two weeks suddenly comes pouring out. And this is the worst time. I don't want to do this in front of anyone, let alone Cooper Valcourt.

But I can't stop. And then I'm sobbing. Like

gasping for breath sobbing.

And what does Cooper do? Just… *stares* at me. And that look. I swear to God, I want to slap his face again.

"I'm going to take care of things. Do you understand me?"

I shake my head as I wipe my eyes and try to breathe past his hand.

"Wrong answer." He pushes his body against mine again. "Wrong answer, Cadee! You're coming home with me. I have fifteen fucking minutes to get you there and take a pic of you in your new room or—"

I force his hand off my mouth and suddenly the tears are gone, but the anger is back. "Or what?" I take a step forward and he takes one back. "Or what, Cooper? I'm not going home with you! I'm not! Whatever your father is up to, I don't want any part of it!"

And then—I don't know quite what happens—he picks me up and throws me over his shoulder. I don't even understand how he managed such a complicated move in the span of one moment.

"I'm done trying to reason with you," he growls, walking down the hallway.

"Put me down!" I grab the flesh just above his hip

and dig my nails into his skin.

He slaps my ass. Hard.

And then we're in the stairwell and he's practically running down the stairs. He kicks the door open at the bottom and doesn't stop.

Ax and Lars follow us. I can see their feet.

"What the hell?" Lars laughs.

"She's unreasonable. I don't care what anyone thinks. We'll cut through the woods and hit the lake that way."

"You're kidnapping me!" I scream. I catch the eye of a group of people. All high-school students. "He's kidnapping me! Call the sheriff!"

They… *laugh*.

"This isn't a joke!"

"Hey, Cooper!" some girl calls. "You can kidnap me instead, if you want. I'm willing!"

"Call the sheriff!" I yell again.

Ax leans his face down so I can see him. Smiles at me. "No one's calling the sheriff, sweetie. And even if they did, he wouldn't dare interfere. Orders of the Chairman. Don't you know what this place is yet, Cadee? You've spent your whole life here. They're all dirty. They all work for him. And if he wants you to live in his house, that's where you're gonna live, little girl. Better get used to it."

Then we're in the woods and Cooper does not slow his pace or put me down. Just carries me down a well-worn bridle path towards the gate that leads to the student cottages.

I go quiet. Mostly because being carried over a man's shoulder is pretty high up there on the uncomfortable scale and a sharp pain shoots across my ribcage with every step and it's pretty hard to breathe.

But also because Cooper's hands are gripping my ass and the back of my thighs. And even though it's super inappropriate and I should not find certain spots on my body all afire with tingles from his touch—that's exactly what's happening.

"That's better," Ax says. He's walking behind me.

I swipe my unruly hair out of my face and tilt my head up so I can see him. "What's better?"

"You." He flashes me a wild grin that makes him look even crazier than I know him to be. "All quiet and tame." He's whispering. Not so Cooper and Lars can't hear him. Just because that's what he does when he's being a dick.

I know this because…

"Don't talk to her." Cooper cuts off my thoughts.

Ax jogs a few paces until he's standing directly to my right. "But I think I might like to do nasty things to her, Coop."

"No. She's not one of us. She's a…" He stops.

"I'm not *one of you*?" I should not feel slighted because Cooper thinks Ax can do better than me, but screw them! "Not a whore? A slutty little puppet you can control?"

"Aren't you?" Cooper says.

"Whoa." Lars laughs. "Burn."

"Well, are you?" Ax whispers into my ear. "Or aren't you?"

"Fuck you, Ax!"

I'm not normally the kind of girl who swears. Also not the kind of girl who gets carried over the shoulder of a man in the woods. But this walk is so long, I'm starting to get used to the idea of being both.

Ax drops back so he's behind me again. "You sure about that? You're flashing your pussy at everyone right now. Those shorts you're wearing?" He winces, then holds his thumb and forefinger about half an inch apart. "Little bit too short for the over-the-shoulder carry, sweetheart."

I struggle and squirm in Cooper's embrace. "What?"

"Ax." Cooper's voice is loud and commanding. "Don't rile her up. We're almost there."

"Well, she *is* flashing her pussy. Not something nice girls are known for."

"I am not!"

"Take off your shirt, Ax."

"What?" He laughs.

"Take off your shirt." Cooper is growling. He's in a very bad mood. And he's starting to tire from carrying me, huffing a little more with each step. He might be big and muscular—yes, he is definitely big and muscular—but you can't carry a hundred twenty pounds over your shoulder for this long without feeling it. "And drape it over her fucking ass so no one can see her damn pussy."

Oh. My. God. "Can you please stop talking about my private parts like I'm not even here?"

Lars chuckles in front.

But Ax's face goes serious. "I'm not taking off my shirt. Lars, you do it."

A few seconds later someone's shirt goes over my ass, Cooper readjusts his grip on me, and the whole thing starts to feel very… stupid.

"Can you just put me down? I'll walk. I'll go wherever you want."

"Fuck you, Cadee." Cooper's words are low. And final. Like this is the last thing he's going to say to me. Ever.

And everyone goes quiet after that.

Finally, after what seems like forever, we're at the

marina. He carries me all the way down the dock, under the canopy of his slip, and then jumps into his flashy red speedboat.

With *me* still over his shoulder.

"Ughhhh," I moan. Because that hurt! My ribs are so sore.

Then he flips me over so fast my head spins, and before I can find anything to hold on to, I tumble over and land on the floor.

Lars and Ax stand over me while Cooper starts the boat. And before I can even get back on my feet, he's backing the boat out of the slip.

"Sit down, Cadee," Ax seethes. "*Now.* And I'm only gonna warn you once. If you do something stupid, like jump out of the boat? I will go in after you. And trust me, you won't enjoy what comes next."

I fall to the side—right into Lars. And his very muscular *bare* chest. He wraps his arms around my middle and plops down on a long bench, pulling me into his lap.

I elbow him in the neck and scoot over, getting as far away from them as possible.

Then I hear screaming on the docks behind us and… what the hell?

Lars laughs. "Looks like Mona got kidnapped today too."

And sure enough, one of those weird, hulking bodyguard men who are always following Mona Monroe around is carrying her to a boat as well.

We lock eyes for the briefest of moments, but… I see it. I see inside her in that moment.

She nods to me.

I nod back.

We're both part of something beyond our control.

CHAPTER SEVEN

The boat is loud and the engine whines as I increase the throttle. I have five fucking minutes to get her in that room and send my father a picture and I'm not going to make it.

I wish I could say I didn't care. I wish I could say he can't control me like this.

But it would be a lie.

We're crossing the lake going ninety and the water is a little bit choppy, so we bounce into the waves. Cadee squeals each time. Lars and Ax are yelling. Enjoying themselves.

Why can't I let it roll off me the way they do? Why do I always get so invested in things?

This is all part of his plan. I don't know what his end game is yet, but everything about this day is part of his plan.

Maybe he's infatuated with Cadee?

I mean, she's not bad-looking. She's actually kinda… cute. I guess. Not sultry and dark like Mona. Not confident and bitchy like Isabella. Who, by the way, I need to get in touch with about dinner tonight. Cadee's not even really bookish and quiet the way… well, I'm sure High Court has some bookish, quiet girls around here somewhere. I just don't know their names.

Cadee is a little mixture of all three.

She has lived through some dark times. No doubt. I've seen that first-hand.

And she's got a mouth on her when you piss her off. So even though she pretends to be all bookish and quiet—spying on students from the safety of the woods all these years—she's not.

It's an act.

She doesn't belong here and everyone knows it.

If she had gone to Prep like the rest of us, instead of being homeschooled by her mother all these years, she would've adapted. Conformed to one group or the other. She would know her place.

But she didn't go to Prep. And she doesn't know her place.

And yet she *is* here. Has always been here.

She's moving into my house today. Like… what the fuck?

Why?

Maybe that's what my father wants? To put her in her place?

I would be more than happy to knock Cadee Hunter down a few rungs. She holds a secret of mine. And even though outsiders think that money is what drives us, that's simply not true.

Secrets. That's the currency of the über-rich. We deal in secrets.

And she's flush with secrets right now.

This has to be why my father has taken such an interest in her. There is no other logical explanation for why he's keeping her around and forcing me to stay here this summer.

He has a secret of mine now too.

He knows. He has to know.

I swing the boat sideways and splash what amounts to a small tidal wave over the dock out in front of our family mansion. Lars jumps out before we've even settled, and Ax hands him the rope to tie up the boat.

I turn and point to Cadee. "Do not give me any trouble. Hear me? Let's go."

She opens her mouth to protest, but I grab her by the arm and tug her to the side of the boat. Lars reaches for her, pulls her out, and then we're walking down the dock towards the house.

The side of the mansion facing Monrovian Lake is technically considered the back of the house, but it's really the only side that counts. The only side people can see. The side meant to impress. And in that respect, it does its job.

The Valcourt Mansion was first built in 1821. Of course, it didn't look like this. I've seen photographs from as far back as 1832 and while I'm sure it was nice for the time, I would not call it stylish—an imposing Tudor made of dark gray stone with the characteristic half-timbers on the second floor filled in with dark gray stucco.

I love this house. I have always loved this house. And when I was a kid it made me feel like a king—or at least a prince—because the elaborate gables, severely-pitched roofline, arched doorways, and stone chimneys really do make it look like a castle.

The real front of the house is on the other side facing the narrow black-top road that weaves through the forest of old sugar maples and tall tulip trees. But this is a gated neighborhood of only two dozen sprawling mansions that all face the lake like our place. So no one gets to see that side, except for the kids in the club.

I drag Cadee through the high archway that leads

to the main door and hold it open to let everyone pass through before closing it behind me.

"This way," I say, once again grabbing Cadee by the upper arm. I'm late. There's no way to fix that. I just want to tick this task off my list and forget about Cadee Hunter until I'm forced to consider her again.

I drag her down the long hallway that leads to the guest suite at the end of the southeast wing and then throw open the door to the suite and shove her inside.

"Stand right here." I push her until she's in the middle of the room and then take out my phone to snap a pic. I send it to my father via text message.

He replies a few seconds later with the message: *That took forty-seven minutes.*

I don't reply. Fuck him. Deed done. Task over. "Listen to me very carefully, Cadee Hunter."

She's looking around the room. Taking it all in. But when I snap at her, she finds my gaze. "What?"

I point at her. "Stay here. Do not leave this room. If I see you in the hallways, or the kitchen, or anywhere inside my fucking house but this room right here, I will end you. Understand me?" I don't wait for her answer. I just turn around and start heading back to the other side of the house.

Ax and Lars didn't follow us. They're probably in the kitchen.

"Wait!" Cadee calls. "What am I supposed to do here?"

"Don't ask me," I growl. "You're not my problem anymore."

"Cooper!" My brother Dane's voice bellows through the house.

"Shit," I whisper. I stop in the hallway and look back at Cadee. "Do not fucking move. Do you hear me?"

She looks… scared. Terrified, actually. The reality of her situation finally kicking in. But she nods, suddenly compliant.

"Close the door, stay quiet, and do not leave that room."

She nods again. And she closes the door.

The lock is clicking when Dane rounds the far corner of the hallway. "There you are. What are you doing here? I thought you were on your way to… where were you going again?"

"Fuck you. Go home, Dane. Your wife is waiting." I make sure to bump his chest with my shoulder as I pass and then head towards the kitchen to find Lars and Ax.

"Hey. I'm talking to you." Dane catches up with me and grabs me by the arm. Exactly the way I was grabbing Cadee.

I stop and look down at his hand. Then my eyes track up to his face. We're the same height now. I finally caught up to him. Dane and Jack are only one year apart so they have always been equals. But I am three years younger than Dane and four years younger than Jack. And while Jack and I have always gotten along, things between Dane and I have never been equal.

Middle-child syndrome?

No. He's just an asshole.

He doesn't let go of my arm even though he must surely see the anger in my eyes. "Why are you here?"

"Ask Dad." I pull my arm out of his grip and turn back towards the kitchen.

But he grabs me again. And this time I don't hold it in. I let that anger out through the end of my fist. It crashes into his face, and then we are in a full-on brawl right there in the hallway.

He grabs me around the middle, hoists me up, and then throws me down onto the dark-gray slate floor so hard, I think the slate tile cracks underneath me.

He's swinging at my face and I've got my hands around his throat, ready to choke him unconscious if I have to, when Lars and Ax appear and start pulling us apart.

I get to my feet first because Dane is too busy

trying to swing at Ax, but Ax won't take that shit and he swings back, chopping Dane in the throat so hard, he stumbles backwards gasping for air.

We watch him for a few moments, all of us waiting it out to see if he's really gonna die from that blow, or just cough and wheeze his way into submission and eat his humiliation.

It's the latter. Thank God. Because if he truly needed saving, I don't think I would do it.

"You're gonna… pay… for that." Dane croaks the words out between gasps of air and points to Ax with an accusatory finger while his other hand holds on to his throat like that's gonna help.

Ax makes a move, always up for some violence. But Lars and I pull him back. "Fuck you, Dane," Ax spits. "Any time you want more of this, you let me know."

Dane looks at me as I push Lars and Ax back towards the kitchen. "You're gonna pay for that too. I know what you were doing last night. I know more about you than you think, *Christopher*."

"Right back at you," I snarl. I back away. I'm not afraid of him. We can do this all day if he wants. But I'm not about to turn my back on this asshole. "I'm here. Under Dad's orders. So if you don't like it? You take it up with him. Otherwise you better keep your distance from me. I'm not that kid you used to beat up anymore. And trust me, brother. You've got payback coming."

He glares at me, then squints a little, maybe trying to figure if that threat is real or not. But the important thing is that he says nothing. So I just back around the hallway where Ax and Lars are waiting.

We walk backwards a few paces, waiting to see if Dane will follow us. He stops in the entrance to the hall we're standing in, wipes some blood off his lip and says, "You better watch your backs." But then he continues down the hallway towards the other side of the house and disappears from view.

We turn and walk towards the kitchen.

"Jesus Christ." Lars laughs. "You two haven't changed a bit."

"Watch my back?" Ax seethes. "I fucking hate that asshole. He better watch *his* back."

I pace the length of the kitchen, which is located on my end of the great room that faces the lake. One side is all high-end industrial appliances, black soapstone countertops, and gray cabinets and the other side is the sitting area with a massive stone fireplace flanked on either side by built-in bookshelves with several seating areas in the middle.

There is an entrance to the main part of the house

on either side of this room. And that's what I'm focused on as I pace. Checking to make sure that Dane doesn't go back to the wing where I put Cadee.

He doesn't. And finally, after about ten minutes of this—long after Ax and Lars have made themselves at home with snacks and are watching a baseball game on the huge ninety-eight-inch TV mounted over the fireplace—I hear the front door slam and I take a seat in a chair.

I sit on something, realize it's the glossy blue and gold folder my father gave me, and pull it out of my back pocket.

"What's in there?" Ax says, stuffing cheese puffs in his mouth.

I slap the folder onto the coffee table in front of me, then smooth the crease down and open it up. Lars plops down on the couch opposite the table and Ax joins him.

We study the papers.

"Well, this doesn't look good," Lars says, probably thinking about our own rush three years ago.

It was a fucking nightmare. Dane was running it that year. He was King and I was just a little princeling who needed to be put in his place.

"No," I agree. "It doesn't."

Ax leans back into the couch cushions with a sigh.

"I thought that shit was behind us."

"Apparently not."

"So where's Cadee fit in?" Lars asks, taking the folder and shuffling through the papers.

"I think she works for us. Kitchen help? I think."

"Oh, hell yeah." Ax perks up. "I'm gonna have some fun with that little tart this summer. If I have to be stuck here, I will make everyone pay for it. It's gonna be senior year of high school all over again."

Lars chuckles, then slides the packet over to me. "Could be fun. How many?"

I pick up the folder and scan the names of the incoming college freshmen. "Dude. Mona is on here."

"Ah," Ax guffaws. "So that's why her ass was dragged back too. Good. I'm glad. She deserves a summer like that."

But Lars laughs. "Mona? A *Swan*? That's hilarious. Whose practical joke is that?"

I laugh too. Can't help it. The Swans are the Feather side of the Fang and Feather Secret Society at High Court College. The Fangs are… well. Us. The Kings. "That's actually funny," I say. "She's probably sitting next door right now going, 'Ax, Lars, and Cooper? *Kings*? Never!'"

We all laugh. We have to laugh. It's the only way to cope with the punishment we've just been handed.

Then, as if on cue, Lars and I both look down at our bare chests, both of our shirts lost some time during the Cadee Hunter kidnapping. We have the same huge tattoo spanning the entire width from pec to pec. A double lion rampant—mouths open, hind legs clawing at the enemy, facing each other—with the High Court coat of arms between them.

It's all very… whatever. Ruling class? Pretentious? Necessary? All of the above, I suppose. Because secrets, man. They make the world go round.

Even though it's called Fang and Feather, there's a subgroup called Fang and Claw for men only. Then the girls—the Swans—they have their own little club within the society too. We call that Wing and Feather. Their mascot is a swan with upstretched wings and long, arched neck.

Fang and Feather is secret only for what's kept inside the tomb out in the woods, because everyone at High Court College knows this society exists.

I'm already a member. Technically. And so are Lars and Ax. But initiation is a full, four-year process and you're only truly inducted—meaning you don't get access to any real society secrets—until after graduation in senior year when you go through the final rite of passage.

Which, for us, is next spring. And that's

something I do not want to think about.

Lars blows out a breath. "It's only eight weeks. We'll have almost a whole month at the end to do something fun."

Ax sneers at him. "Always Mr. Brightside."

"What else are we gonna do?" Lars says. "Might as well make it a glass-half-full kinda thing."

"We should've just… pretended. Ya know?" I look at Lars and Ax. Picture all the ways we've been rebelling against our lot in life through the years.

Ax and his violence and drugs. He's been in rehab six times since he was thirteen. Only two of them were actually about the drugs. The rest were just a way out of juvenile lockup, thanks to his father, the Judge. He's clean for now. But for how long?

Lars and his suicidal antics. He's been in the hospital for dirt bike stunts, jumping into pools from third-floor rooftops, and waterskiing wipeouts more times than I can count.

Me and my careless indifference about… well, pretty much everything. Grades, people… *sex*.

"That's why we're here," I say. "We should've played the game from the beginning. Kept our heads down, did what they wanted, and then we'd be free now. They would've just assumed we'd go along in the end."

"Fuck that," Lars says. "We'd be in deeper."

"Yeah," Ax agrees. "We'd have fallen for it. We'd have given in by now if we'd played the game. Just like everyone else."

"But now they have their eye on us," I counter. "We've done nothing but put a target on our backs."

"We just do the job," Lars says, sighing. "Be the bully kings and in eight weeks they'll have their new crop of minions and we can take off for a little bit. Then one more year, you guys. One more year and we get the trusts. Then we're free."

Ax and I both look at each other.

We don't believe it.

Oh, that's the stipulation in the contracts. All we gotta do is graduate High Court College as members in good standing of Fang and Claw and we get the money.

But it's just never that easy.

It won't be that easy.

CHAPTER EIGHT

When they start fighting out in the hall I just back away from the door until I bump into the bed and have to take a seat. I stare at the door, wondering which one of them will win.

But then I hear Lars and Ax and it's pretty clear that Dane will have to back off or risk getting his ass kicked by all three of them.

I mean, that's the whole point of having friends like Ax and Lars, isn't it? So you can't get jumped in a hallway. You can't ever be outnumbered. Someone always has your back.

It's a good plan. I have to admit that much. And if I had known how things were going to turn out, I'd have formed my own tight-knit circle of back-havers.

But I'm starting to wonder about my life. Have been wondering for the last two weeks. I am not naïve.

I know what people think of me. I'm the good girl. The smart girl. The weird girl who used to live in the gardener's cottage in the woods and now lives in the attic of the Alumni Inn.

But I grew up at High Court. Maybe I didn't participate in all the wild things the girls my age have done over the years. But I saw it. I watched it from a distance. So I have an idea of what the outside world might be like.

Ruthless. Cutthroat. Runs on status and money.

Yeah… I sigh. I'm not gonna lie. That scares me. So even though that whole meeting with the Chairman was weird—and that's putting it mildly—and even though I suddenly find myself in the lair of the enemy, I'm gonna stick it out and see where it goes.

Because I don't have much choice.

All my things are gone. That makes me sad.

I turn and look at the room. It's all very nice. A large queen sized canopy bed with a lavender velvet duvet and matching curtains hanging down the sides. Which is kinda cool. Very… royal treatment. There are a lot of pillows on the bed, both the kind you use for sleeping and the pretty, decorative kind with beaded designs depicting medieval scenes and gold tassels hanging from the corners.

The curtains covering a set of French doors are

really drapes, very heavy and pulled aside with more gold tassels, and sheer white ones underneath. The walls are a light gray, the floors are dark slate with a large room-sized carpet in the middle, and the trim is black. Very nice. Very high-end. Very… not me.

There's a loveseat, a chair, two bedside tables, and a small writing desk with a computer on it. Glancing to my left I spy an en suite and a closed door, which is probably a closet. I can't resist flipping the light on and taking a look at the bathroom.

And… yeah. Jaw-dropping. The bedroom design continues with the same floors, paint, and trim colors, but the sink and all the finishes are gleaming gold. Which normally I find tacky, but rich people always seem to be able to pull it off.

The soaker tub is freestanding on the far side and there's a walk-in shower too.

I back out and take a long breath. Things have quieted down in the hallway and all the men have moved to other parts of the house, so I allow myself a moment to just… let my guard down and lie back on the bed.

Mona.

That's the name that comes to mind right now. She was being kidnapped too. Not that I've actually been kidnapped. I glance at the French door that leads… well, somewhere that is not here. Outside, from the look of the sunshine filtering past the semi-sheer white curtain over the window. I could just leave.

And go where?

I literally have nothing. The Chairman took my whole apartment. My entire life was just stolen from me. Isn't that what I heard Cooper say too? I think back. Yeah. He said, *Looks like he stole your life. Just like he stole mine.*

So where the hell am I going to go?

I know all the girls my age who go to school at Prep, but they're not my *friends.* I've never actually needed friends. I had my parents. I'm a loner.

I *like* this about myself and I don't want to change that.

But I might have to if I want to survive.

Because up until two weeks ago I have never been alone. I did have someone on my side. My mother. And my father before he died.

But she's gone now. So I am truly and utterly alone.

I need to change that.

I get up and walk over to the French door, try the handle, find it locked. But it's a stupid lock, just one of those twisty things on the knob, which twists and unlocks.

So I open the door and find myself on a cute little patio facing an expansive green lawn. Through some trees I spot the side of the mansion next door. I look left and right, see nothing and no one, then close the door behind me and start walking towards the other mansion.

I know Mona lives next door to Cooper. I can't say how I first learned this fact, and I have certainly never been to one of her infamous parentally unsupervised parties. But I know that Lars lives on one side of Cooper and Mona lives on the other.

This house I'm creeping towards might be hers and there's only one way to find out.

I can hear her yelling long before I stalk up to the closest window and peek in. She's not in this room, but her bellowing is loud and filled with threats. So. Good. My fifty-fifty chance panned out.

Now what?

She's obviously still in the middle of her crisis and mine seems to be on hiatus.

I shuffle in place for a few moments, then duck behind a line of shrubs when I hear Dane Valcourt's voice from behind me.

He's not close enough for me to hear his conversation, and I'm not the least bit interested in spying on him anyway, so I just stay hidden and go over my options.

I could break into Mona's house. Make her my BFF and get her on my side. But that's kind of a stupid plan.

Mona doesn't do friends either. But for the exact opposite reason as me.

Everyone hates her. I mean, don't get me wrong. They will still show up for her parties, drink all her booze, and smoke all her weed. But they don't like her.

They use her, she uses them. That's how it goes with Mona.

And while I will take some mutually beneficial arrangement over nothing, I need more than just a business partner right now. I need a friend.

And that takes time.

She must be going over to Swan Camp. That's why they dragged her home. That's why Cooper dragged me here. I've heard about Swan Camp. Everyone has. The secret society at High Court isn't much of a secret. I've heard girls talk about it through the years because I live on campus year-round and in the summers I used to help my dad in the gardens before he died. There are lots of kids who stay the whole summer. Maybe their parents are on vacation, or maybe they actually like staying here for the various camps. There's a horse camp. An art camp. A football camp. Lots of camps.

But I think they stay because their parents don't like them.

At least that's what I've told myself over the years. It's only natural to want to be the winner in some category, regardless of how small and meaningless.

And I won the jackpot with my parents.

Anyway. My point is that I know about Swan Camp.

And now I'm going too. Kind of.

As… the *help*.

But this is good. Because I'm pretty sure that Mona is going to Swan Camp too and that's why those weird bodyguards of hers dragged her home. And that means that Mona will be there all summer. With me. Plenty of time for me to get on her good side and prove to her that she needs someone like me—someone who can watch her back from the outside, while she watches mine from the inside—so that both of us can get what we need.

I know what she needs. I think. The Cygnet is in charge of all the Swans. She is the queen. She calls all the shots in the secret society they have in the woods. Just like the King over on the male side of things.

I don't know much about the Fang and Claw or Wing and Feather societies. I barely know anything, actually. But I know they are real and I know that a freshman girl like Mona would never be put in charge. There is, right now, some uptight girl calling herself Cygnet just waiting to make Mona's life miserable all summer.

I can help take the queen down.

Whoa. Easy there, Cadee. That's kind of diabolical.

This makes me smile. I'm learning. And this is definitely the offer I'm going to make Mona to make her help me… do what?

What will she help me do?

Do I need money from these people?

I mean, sure. I'm not going to turn down some free money. But I'm not going to break the law and bribe someone to get it.

The Chairman has already offered me a scholarship. I have no intention of accepting that. My dream has nothing to do with the drama of High Court College and the ruling class fighting for the crowns.

Maybe I can cash it in?

Somehow, I think not.

So what can I get out of these people?

Hmm. How about an apology?

Yeah, Cadee. Like that's going to happen.

How about the truth about what really happened when I was fifteen?

I would be satisfied with that.

So the truth. If Mona helps me shine light on the truth about the dirty tricks the Valcourt family deals in, then yeah, I'll help her depose the current Cygnet queen and do whatever it takes to put that crown of feathers on her head.

That's four years of power for Mona. Definitely more than I'll be getting out of it.

She will say yes.

She *has* to say yes.

But should I aspire to something higher? What if Mona laughs at my request? What if she thinks I'm simple and stupid for not wanting more?

Maybe I should get even? Make Cooper pay for what he did?

I realize it's not all his fault, but I don't care. I blame him anyway.

If his father is going through all this trouble to make him stay for the summer, then that can only mean one thing.

Cooper Valcourt is the heir to the High Court College Crown. He's a senior this year. He had to have known he would be put in charge. He might not want it, but it doesn't matter. It's his, like it or not. Taking it away from him would only make him happy.

So I'm not going to take it away.

I'm going to make *sure* he's crowned King at homecoming in the fall.

With Mona at his side.

I actually laugh all the way back to my door.

And I'm still giggling as I drift off to sleep in my new room inside this ridiculously luxurious mansion.

A knock on the door wakes me and I sit straight up in bed.

"Cadee?"

Jesus. What the hell? "Yes?" I call.

The door opens and the Chairman walks in. He looks over his shoulder, like he's checking for people, and then quietly closes the door behind him.

I get out of bed and stand over by the small desk on the far side of the room before he even turns back. No way am I going to be sending this man any mixed messages. I don't really understand why he's got me here, but having him sneak into my room sets off all kinds of warning bells. After my experience with his son three years ago, I don't trust him.

He's surprised to find me so far away when he turns back. But he studies me. Folds his hands in front of him. Kinda rocks back on his heels. "Are you comfortable here?"

"Mm-hmm." I nod my head and shoot him a tight-lipped smile. "Very. It's… a lovely room. With an en suite. Nice touch." *You're babbling, Cadee.* "Thank you. I appreciate it."

"Good." He keeps studying me. Kinda eyeballing my legs, actually. I suddenly find myself agreeing with Ax about the shortness of my shorts and wish I had put on sweatpants this morning. "Did you check your closet?"

"My… closet?"

He walks over to it and pulls the door open to reveal racks of dresses and shirts and stacks of sweaters and pants. How long does he expect me to live here that he purchased me sweaters? And how the hell did he do all this shopping before I showed up? "These belong to you now. So you can change."

"I… um…" *Manners, Cadee. Just remember your manners. This isn't weird. It's fine.* "Thank you."

"For dinner, I mean."

"Oh. OK."

"I don't know if you will like anything in here." He pans a hand to the closet.

"Oh, I'm sure—"

"No. I mean, all this belonged to my third wife.

She left them behind when I kicked her out."

"Ohhhhh."

"So you might not like any of it. She and you…" He tsks his tongue. "Let's just say you have much better taste. Let me know if you need anything. I just figured you needed clothes after the mishap this morning and there wasn't time to get anything else set up."

Well. Wow. I do not even know where to begin. Everything I thought was happening is suddenly up in the air. Several dozen new alternatives begin to formulate in my mind, and I find myself very unsure of which game we are playing here.

It has to be a game. Doesn't it? He can't just be a nice man who wants to help me?

If there's one thing I know about the Valcourts, it's that they are *not* nice.

"I'm sure it's fine. Thank you. I mean, truly. My whole life has flipped upside down since my mom died two weeks ago."

He frowns at me. Deeply. And nods. "I know. I liked your mother. A lot, actually. She made the very best little shortcakes for the cafeteria. Did she make those at home, too?"

I nod, suddenly feeling sad. "Yeah. She did. They were my favorite dessert as well."

We're silent for a minute. A *long* minute. So long it starts to become awkward and I want to say something. Anything to break this uncomfortable moment. But I don't even know where to start.

"She was my friend," he suddenly blurts.

"What?"

"Your mother." He pauses. "Yes. I would count her a friend. I was at the funeral."

"You were? I didn't—"

"No, I stayed in the back and left early."

"I'm sorry… what's going on here? Were you two having—"

"No." He puts his hands up, palms forward, trying to ward off my words. "No. It wasn't like that. She was… just a friend." Then he smiles at me with tight lips, the way I was smiling at him when he first entered. "She loved your father. Was devastated when he died."

"I don't really want to talk about this," I whisper.

"I know. I understand. But… what I really want you to know is this—they have a legacy here. The gardens are your father's work. The desserts the cafeteria will continue to make will remain your mother's recipes. You are a *legacy*, Cadee. I really want you to stay here with us."

"Here?" I point to the floor. I am not staying in this house.

"Wherever you're comfortable. I was busy this morning. I didn't have a lot of time to come up with solutions. And Cooper." He sighs loudly and rubs his temple. "That boy. Not to mention Mona." He spits her name out. "The point is… the garden cottage is vacant. I would like you to live there. If you stay. It's up to you. You don't have to take the summer job if you don't see yourself at High Court for the next four years." He reaches into his suit coat pocket and pulls out an envelope. "I have a severance packet for you. For your mother. And your father. They were loyal. Legacies, like I said." He stretches his hand out, beckoning me forward to take the envelope from him.

I stare at the envelope for a moment, but then step forward and take it. "Thank you."

"Do you want to stay?"

"Not here," I say too quickly. "But. Yes. The garden cottage." I smile. I can't help myself. "I grew up there."

He smiles back. "I know. I'm sorry you ever had to leave. It was Cooper's idea."

"What?"

"Yes. He talked me into it. He wanted it for the lacrosse team that year."

I *seethe* inside. *He's* the reason we had to move. *He* stole my home from me. Just one more reason to hate that asshole.

"So you'll stay? In the cottage?"

I nod before I even realize I'm doing it. "Yes. I would love to stay. And I'll take the job. And the scholarship."

"The two are conditional. I'm afraid that's the best I could do with the board on short notice. We reserve that job and scholarship for a needy Prep student. It was Lacy Pendleton's up until a week ago. Don't worry about her though. I'm sure her student loans will cover most of her tuition."

"Oh. Wow. Um—"

"It's fine. She completely understands."

R-*iiii*-ght. *Note to self. Stay the hell away from Lacy Pendleton. She's gonna have it out for me next year pret-ty bad.*

"Well, if that's your decision then my work here is done." He pulls a key out of his pocket and hands it to me. "For the cottage. It's partly furnished. But the severance packet"—he nods his head to the envelope in my hand—"should more than cover whatever you need to make it feel like home again."

I sigh. "Chairman Valcourt. I don't know how to thank you. For real. You've touched me with this gesture. And I want you to know how much I appreciate it."

He smiles. "It was my pleasure. Please change into

a dress and come for dinner. We eat at six. Dane and Jack won't be there, they're both busy at home getting ready for the summer trip. But Cooper will." He adds this like he's afraid I might think he was asking me on a date.

Gross. This is the first thing he's offered today that makes me want to say no immediately.

But it would be rude. And I can get through one hour of dinner if it means I can leave and go home to my cottage tonight. "Yes. Of course, I'll stay for dinner."

CHAPTER NINE

Isabella Huntington has her hands all over me on the dock in front of Lars' house. She and her Swans showed up to talk some business about the start of rush tomorrow and she's always been a hands-y girl. Not that I mind. Isabella is a girl I truly like.

We don't hang out much, but I always know if I need her to do something—anything—she'll be there. And parts of her are very easy. She tries hard, she's smart, beautiful, and even though most people think she's a bitch, I kind of like that about her.

Gives her depth.

But I'm stuck having dinner with my father tonight and he's already informed me that Cadee will be there too. Dane and Jack have other plans, thank God for small favors. So that's helpful.

But he said he wanted Isabella to join us. Which

can only mean one thing. Summer rush is actually a grooming exercise for Isabella and me. She will be the Cygnet and I will be the King next year.

I don't tell her that though. I'm sure she understands this—on some level. But she's not the kind of girl who likes to face reality. And that's fine. There's no need to think about the future—*yet.*

But I am kinda happy that Isabella will be my 'date' for dinner. Isabella and I are a team. And that means Cadee will still be an 'outsider', even though she somehow weaseled her way inside my house.

This makes me grin as we walk back to my house and enter the French doors that lead to the great room and family kitchen. The staff uses the catering kitchen on the lower level for food prep, so there's no one in here with us when I lead her across the room and into the hallway towards the formal dining room on the other side of the house.

"You're late," my father barks as we enter. But then he notices Isabella and forces a smile. "Why, hello, Miss Huntington. How delightful to see you again."

"Hello, Chairman," she quips, tossing her long, blonde hair and shaking her hips a little. My father admires the display, then gets to his feet and walks over to her. He extends his hand to take hers, then kisses her knuckles.

I don't really care that he does this with the girls I bring home because I don't really care about the girls I bring home. But with Isabella—and Cadee—it's fucking disgusting.

My father's chair is at the head of the table and Cadee Hunter is sitting in the guest-of-honor spot to his right. When I glance at her she's squinting her eyes at Isabella. Then they shoot to me and she scowls.

"Come," my father tells Isabella as he pulls out a chair directly across from Cadee. "Have a seat."

"Thank you, Chairman," Isabella coos up at him. She's learned to play the game these past three years and she's suddenly using every lesson she ever learned about how to get by, on my father.

"Have a seat, Cooper. The servers are waiting on you."

I resist the urge to roll my eyes and instead glance at Cadee one more time as I take the seat next to Isabella. It's just the four of us at the huge table that seats twelve.

I glance at Cadee again. Because she's changed her clothes since I last saw her and is now wearing a low-cut light blue dress that announces to everyone who cares to look that she is not wearing a bra. "What the fuck?" I mutter.

But no one hears me. My father is asking Isabella what she's been up to.

Cadee notices me noticing her and nervously clasps the silky thin fabric between her breasts together, like she's self-conscious. Then she glances around, trying not to look at me. Trying to look at everything but me.

I slouch in my chair as we're served a light soup as the first course.

Cadee has no idea which spoon to use, because she stares at them for like twenty seconds before Isabella says, "It's that one, honey," as she points to the soup spoon next to the knife. "Go ahead. Pick it up. Eat, sweetie. You're going to need your nourishment. I hear you're going to be working for me this summer. Is the rumor true, Chairman? Is Cadee Hunter our servling for this summer's rush?"

"Absolutely." My father beams. "She's going to be a wonderful addition to the rush camp. And at the end of the summer, she will be offered a full scholarship to High Court College."

Isabella places a hand over her heart. "My. What a generous offer!" Then she looks at Cadee, who is now visibly frowning. Probably wondering about that word. *Servling.*

Yes, honey. It means exactly what it sounds like.

I can practically read her thoughts. *Will I be serving cookies and tea to the Swans? Or be down on my knees in front of King Cooper's big fat cock?*

I laugh out loud and everyone turns to look at me. "Sorry," I mumble, then kick my long legs out under the table. But then my foot unexpectedly hits something on the other side. Cadee coughs and squirms in her chair, trying not to look at me as my father and Isabella discuss her role in the rush like we're not even here.

Well, that's fun. I slip my shoe off, angle my chair a little so Isabella thinks I'm trying to get close to her, and then rub my foot up and down Cadee's leg.

"Oh!" she exclaims, jumping in her chair, then blushes profusely. Jesus Christ. She is so easy to startle. I pull my foot back as the conversation between my father and Isabella halts at her outburst.

"What's that, sweetie?" Isabella asks Cadee. "Did you say something?"

Cadee shakes her head self-consciously. "No. Sorry. This soup is…" She looks down at the bowl of cold green sludge and hesitates. "Delightful. That's all."

"You haven't eaten any yet," I say, smirking at her. Hey, if this bitch gets to be in my house against my wishes, even if it is just for one night, then I'll make her pay for that. I told her three years ago to stay out of my face. She needs to learn that my commands are absolute.

Cadee, flustered and on the spot, picks up her dessert spoon and uses it to taste the cold cucumber soup, then says, "Mm," as she tries her hardest not to make a face.

"Oh, honey," Isabella says. "Stop. That's a dessert spoon. You do know how to properly set a table, don't you?" She looks at my father. "You know how picky I am about these things. We need to make a good impression on the swanlings. So we can set high expectations. Don't you agree, Chairman?"

"Of course." My father beams. He likes Isabella. Probably a little too much. "I'm sure she'll learn. You can learn, right, Cadee?"

She nods. "Yes, sir. I will study up tonight and be ready tomorrow."

My foot is sliding up her leg again and she squeaks a little.

"Are you OK?" Isabella asks.

"Fine," Cadee mumbles. "I'm just… not very hungry."

"Oh." Isabella looks at my father. "She should go rest then, don't you think? Tomorrow will be a very demanding day."

"I don't need to rest," Cadee interrupts. "And I'm not staying here tonight. I'm going to move back into my cottage."

"Nonsense," my father bellows. "It's too late to move in tonight. You will stay tonight and Cooper will help you move in tomorrow after your first day of work. But if you need to go lie down, we understand."

Cadee frowns, unsure if she's being dismissed or has a choice in this matter.

"Yes, Cadee," I say, once again sliding my foot up her leg. "You need your rest. Isabella and I will be putting you through your paces tomorrow."

"And you are to be there at five AM with the other servants," Isabella adds. "Cooper and I will be hosting the opening ceremony at eight sharp. And everything must be perfect."

"Go get your rest," my father says just as my foot finds Cadee's inner thigh.

She backs her chair away so quickly, it scrapes on the slate floor.

"Dear," Isabella says. "Do be careful. Slate floors are delicate. I hope you didn't scratch it."

I chuckle.

"Thank you for dinner," Cadee squeaks. Then she just stands there for a moment. Like she's not sure if she needs to say more or not.

"You're dismissed," Isabella says, waving her hand at her like the pompous queen she is.

My father chuckles like Isabella is just a delight and he can't imagine having dinner without her being present, acting like a snooty bitch to his house guest.

Cadee turns on her heel and walks out. But she's heading the wrong way. Dear God. This girl is going to be so easy to fuck with this summer. She flusters so easily.

"Other way," I call out. She turns and looks at me and I nod my head in the proper direction. "The servants' quarters are that way."

"Cooper," my father bellows. "That's uncalled for."

"As if." I chuckle. "Good night, Cadee. Rest well."

"You'll need it," Isabella calls.

Cadee turns and disappears through an arched opening in the wall.

We all pause in silence for a few moments, making sure she's out of earshot. Then Isabella whispers, "I don't know about her, Chairman. Lacy Pendleton would've made such a spectacular servling. I really wish she was still on my staff. And she really needed that scholarship. Not to mention she earned it. She put in her time. Cadee Hunter never even attended Prep! How will she ever fit in at the college?"

"Hmm." My father dabs his napkin at the corners of his mouth, considering this. "You might be right, sweetheart. What do you think, Cooper?"

"Me?" I point to myself. "Since when do you want my opinion?"

"Since you became the King-in-waiting. *Son.*" He kinda growls the word *son.* Like it's ironic or something.

"Please," I say. "Lacy Pendleton needs a scholarship because her father is sitting in prison for embezzlement."

"That's not her fault," Isabella counters, looking from me to my father, then back at me. "She's not responsible for the sins of her father."

"Isn't she?" my father asks.

Isabella pouts. This is the first time he's disagreed with her.

"She needs to learn a lesson. She needs to learn that we are all a reflection of each other. Don't you agree, Cooper?"

I don't say anything.

And thankfully I don't have to. Because Isabella says, "Oh, I do agree there. Absolutely. And if you feel Cadee is up to the job, well"—she beams a grin at my father and places her hand over his—"I totally trust your opinion, Chairman."

He looks down at it, then back up at Isabella to smile. He wraps his other hand around hers. "That's why I'm in charge, dear. But… I will keep your opinions under consideration. If Cadee doesn't cut it, we'll replace her."

"Replace her?" I grunt. "And take her scholarship away too?"

"Do you think it's unfair, Cooper?" my father asks.

"No. I actually think it's a great idea. You should do it tonight. Just kick her out. Send her on her way. We don't need her here. She doesn't belong."

"Let's not be rash, Cooper," Isabella sings. "Let's give the poor girl a chance." She looks at my father. "One week?"

"Sounds like plenty of time to me."

"Perfect." Isabella beams. And then squeals in delight and claps her hands when the soup is taken away and a plate of broiled lobster tail is set in front of her.

I endure the rest of the meal because I don't have any other choice.

But I spend most of it replaying the way Cadee Hunter blushed when I rubbed my foot up and down her inner thigh. And by the time my father excuses himself and the dishes have all been cleared, I have a raging hard-on.

As soon as I stand up, Isabella notices. "Oh, Cooper. You hot, sexy fuck of a man." She grabs my crotch and begins to massage it.

"Stop it. Jesus. My father's gone. You can quit playing now."

"I would just like to thank you for dinner." She winks at me. And man, she is trying way too hard tonight. "It was nice." She adds. Probably noticing the confused look on my face. "And you are my king now, right?"

"Right. You're OK with that?"

"Cooper," she sighs. "I would do anything for you. You know that. And I do mean… *any*. Thing."

Isabella is hot. Just... not the girl I was fantasizing about.

But she is the girl *here*.

Then I get a devious idea. A fantastically dirty and devious idea.

I take her hand and lead her down the hallway towards the stairs that lead up to my apartment.

"Oh… fun, Cooper. I wasn't expecting this, but—"

"Like hell you weren't. That's why you grabbed me. You want me to get you off, Isabella?"

She slaps me halfheartedly as I pass by my stairs, turn the corner, and keep walking to the end of the hallway.

"Where are we going?"

"Right here," I say. Leaning against Cadee's door.

"Here?" Isabella says, looking nervously down the long corridor. "Why can't we go upstairs?"

I turn us around so her back is against Cadee's door, slip my hand up her dress, and then slide her panties aside so I can finger her pussy. "Jerk me off, Isabella. Right now."

She moans a little. But not loud enough. So I push my fingers deeper inside her until she's writhing. I unbutton my pants and place her hand inside them. She grabs my throbbing cock and begins to stroke me.

"Fuck, yeah," I moan. "Squeeze it harder." She does, slipping my pants down my hips a little to gain better access. And it feels pretty good. I almost change my plan.

But I imagine Cadee Hunter on the other side of the door. Her face as she figures out what's happening just inches away from her. And then I turn the handle. The door bangs open and Isabella goes crashing to the floor of Cadee's room.

And then… Cadee Hunter gets a good long look at my rock-hard cock. I grab hold of it. Fist it a little. Smirk at her.

"What the fuck?" Isabella screams. "Did you just do that on purpose?" But she's not looking at me, she's looking at Cadee.

"You're a sick freak," I say, staring at Cadee's horrified face. Kinda jerking off as I do that. "If you wanted to join us, you should've just asked."

"What?" Cadee exclaims. "I didn't open the door!"

I help Isabella up from the floor, my dick still hanging out. Cadee's eyes drift down to stare at it, like she can't help herself. Then she whirls around, flings the French doors open, and disappears into the night.

CHAPTER TEN

I run across the wet lawn in bare feet, my ridiculous long, blue dress flying out behind me. I don't have a bra on—none of the dresses in that closet were anything close to something you could wear a bra with. And when I showed up for dinner wearing jeans and a sweater, I was told by the Chairman, in no uncertain terms, to change into a dress and try my entrance again.

At least Cooper and Isabella didn't see that part of the evening.

I keep running, unsure of where I'm going. I want to go to my cottage, but it's all the way across the lake on campus. I don't have a boat. So I can't get there.

And now I'm in someone's back yard. Some rich asshole's back yard. And Cooper and Isabella just—

Ugh. No. I will not picture that in my head again.

Who am I kidding? It's not the first time I've seen

Cooper's cock. But I never got such a good look at it before. Everything was dark when we were together last. Secret.

Everything about us was a secret. He was embarrassed to be seen with me. But that didn't stop him from wanting me. It just made me his target. He, and Ax, and Lars tormented me all through fall semester of their senior year of Prep. And then it all came to a head that New Year's Eve.

And still, to this day, I can't figure out if they liked me and were just acting like stupid little boys, or if they secretly hated me and only wanted to make my life miserable.

I wasn't a virgin when I had sex with Cooper for the first time. But I was very inexperienced and didn't realize that there are men out there—men like Ax, and Lars, and Cooper—who thought of women like a sport.

I dated all three of them that spring. It was nice. Having so many people care about me—that was a new feeling. I almost felt like I belonged.

Date? Date, Cadee? Are you kidding me? That wasn't dating.

They used me.

I run harder, looking over my shoulder, just to make sure Cooper and Isabella aren't coming after me, and then I smack right into the hard chest of a boy and fall ass-backwards into the grass.

And when I look up, who is staring back at me?

Ax Olson.

He scowls. "What the fuck are you doing here, Cadee?" Then he looks behind him. At the massive mansion. His mansion? Maybe? I wouldn't know. He never invited me to his house when we were… *dating.*

"Get up, for fuck's sake." He grabs my arm and pulls me to my feet, then starts dragging me down towards the lake. He pulls me along his dock and into the boathouse, then slams the door closed, not even flicking on the lights.

"What are we doing?"

"We?" He sneers at me in the moonlight. "*We* aren't doing anything. Just shut up and stay out of my way."

I can't see much since the lights aren't on. But when my eyes sweep the perimeter of the dock and get to the corner, I pause. "Oh, my God. Are you sleeping in here?"

"I said shut up, Cadee."

"Why did you bring me here?"

"I didn't want my father to see you."

His father is the Judge. Capital J. Just like when you say the Chairman's name, or the Mayor's name—

they all come capitalized. It's not just a title. They are proper names around these parts.

He walks over to the small window that faces the mansion and cautiously peers out.

"Are you… hiding from him?"

"Shut the fuck up."

"Well, then I'll just leave."

He crosses the length of the side dock so fast, I don't even have time to back up. And then he grabs my arm and shakes me. "You're gonna stay right here until I say you can leave, do you understand me? *Cadee*?"

"Fine. Whatever." And suddenly I feel like I'm back in time. To that year when these boys controlled me so completely, I lost myself and… made that one mistake.

Hell, who am I kidding? I made *thousands* of mistakes that year.

"Just…" He stares into my eyes. He's breathing hard. Unreasonably hard for the quick walk we just took. Then he points to the sleeping bag in the corner. "Sit down there and wait. Quietly."

I nod. Then he lets go of me and I slink to the back corner and kneel down on the sleeping bag. I want to ask him questions. But I know better. Ax is not the kind of guy who shares things.

He doesn't say another word to me. Just stands at the tiny window and stares out at the lawn behind his mansion.

I get tired and lie down on the bag. Yawn. Stretch out. And even though I plan on thinking about my day and how it all went sideways…

The next thing I know, I'm waking up to the rising sun.

And I'm alone.

"Where the hell—" It takes me a minute to realize where I'm at. Ax Olson's boathouse. I search for him, but he's gone. Probably left last night. And didn't bother to wake me.

Does that surprise me?

No. Like he gives a single fuck about me.

But then I remember what day it is. I start work today. And I heard everything that Isabella and Cooper said to the Chairman last night. They want me out.

I was hiding in the hallway because I knew they were going to talk about me when I left. And I was right.

These people—they are all cold, ruthless

predators.

I get to my feet, gather my long dress in the tips of my fingers, and then run out of the boathouse and back towards the Valcourt Mansion.

I'm just reaching for the French door that leads to my room when someone calls out, "You're late, Cinderella! The ball ended hours ago, honey!"

I turn and see Mona Monroe on a side patio of her mansion, smoking a cigarette, wearing a silky black robe and with her unruly black hair pulled back by a red satin headband.

She waves. "Better get a move on, sweetheart." She taps her wrist, even though she's not wearing a watch. "I saw all the servers heading towards the Glass House about ten minutes ago."

Shit.

I go inside, rip the dress off, pull on yesterday's clothes and then go back outside. And stand there.

I have no idea where this place is.

"It's a lake behind the lake," the chairman said yesterday.

I turn away from the lake and start walking towards the woods. I creep past the Valcourt mansion, crossing my fingers and praying to all the gods that none of the men inside see me.

They don't. Small miracles.

Then I cross a smooth blacktop road and head into the woods on an unmarked path.

It has to lead somewhere. And if there is a secret lake in this forest, it seems logical that there would be pathways right across the street that would take you to it.

I walk for a while and I'm starting to get worried—and scared about being lost, if I'm being honest—when I hear shouting ahead.

Happy shouting. Not screams or anything. Always a plus when you're walking through the creepy woods.

But that's bad. It means that the people I'll be serving are probably here already.

The shouting and boisterous laughter becomes louder, and closer, when I come upon a large stone… what is it?

There are weird markings on the door. And I stop in front of it, wondering if this is the place. It's not glass. More like a mausoleum, if I had to describe it.

But then I hear shouting again and keep going, pushing my way through the thick underbrush until I come to the edge of a clearing and find a massive glass house. Like a greenhouse. Except it's not made up of many small panes, but large sheets of glass that have to have cost a literal fortune to produce.

There are dozens of people here already. Some of

them servers, like me. I can tell because they are wearing navy shorts, gold shirts, and white aprons.

But not all of them.

I spy Ax first. Then Lars. And then… yes. There Cooper is with his future High Court Queen, Isabella.

"Psst!"

I startle at the interruption of my thoughts and turn to see a handsome man beckoning me towards him. "Come here," he whispers.

I do. Because he's wearing an apron, which means he's not one of the assholes, but one of the staff, like me.

"You must be Lacy," he says, pulling on my arm to make me follow him behind the glass building. "You're late. You're so lucky I was outside and saw you. They will crucify you, Lacy. You cannot be late. Ever."

"Um… thanks? But I'm not Lacy."

He stops and looks at me. "Then who the fuck are you? Everyone else is here already." He points at me. "If you're a fucking reporter—"

"I'm not a reporter, Jesus. I'm Cadee Hunter. I'm taking Lacy's place this summer."

"You got Lacy's scholarship? But…" He frowns at me, then looks around, like maybe Lacy is hiding somewhere in the trees, playing a joke on him. "That's not possible."

"Why not?"

"She worked her ass off for that scholarship."

"No. She's the daughter of an embezzler and was getting it as a favor."

He laughs. "Where the hell have you been hiding? Nothing's free. Trust me. She earned that spot you just stole."

"I didn't steal anything."

"Whatever. I don't really care. One more year of service and I'm done being a waiter. I will have all the right contacts to slide right into a very important position."

I side-eye him, not quite believing it.

"Well," he amends, "I will have more than I did when I came here. I've been inside the tomb. Once you get in, you're in. Keep that in mind, Not-Lacy." He taps my head for added emphasis.

"The tomb?" I wonder if that was the weird stone building I passed on my way over here?

"Never mind. You need to change into your uniform. Quick. They expect breakfast to be on time and they like to be served coffee first." He leads me inside, past a whole bunch of busy kids my age who are preparing breakfast, and then points to a door. "It's in there. Don't forget the shoes. They hate it when you try to work without the shoes."

"Thanks," I say. "But who are you? I've never seen you around before."

"I'm Victor," he says, reaching for my hand and holding it up so he can bump me in the knuckles. "Victor English. Lead servling to the heir apparent for four years running now and *not* at your service. You have nothing I need, Not-Lacy. So I won't protect you until you do."

"Why would I need your protection?"

"I know all the ropes. They can't hang you if you know the ropes."

Ominous. Like everything else since yesterday morning when my life suddenly went sideways.

I pass through the door, closing it behind me, and find myself standing in a locker room of sorts. I'm just about to go back out and ask Victor which locker is mine when I see the garment bag with a large piece of paper that says 'Lacy.'

Well, there it is. My uniform.

I sigh as I reach for the bag. Hmm. It's definitely not a pair of navy shorts and a gold shirt. It's bulkier than that. I sit down on a bench and wonder how bad it will be.

I figure it's a French maid thing? Maybe? If they want to sexually exploit me.

Or something ugly and demure. Very institutional in gray.

But never in a million years did I ever expect to see the costume I pull out of that bag.

CHAPTER ELEVEN

"What do you mean Cadee spent the night at your boathouse?"

The words are coming out of Ax's mouth, but nothing about them makes sense.

"I told you, I got in a fight with the Judge and bumped into her on the lawn. Well." He thinks about this for a second. "No, she bumped into me."

"Get to the part about the fucking boathouse and how you spent the night with her."

He shrugs. "I couldn't leave her there on the lawn. So I dragged her in there with me."

"Did you *fuck* her?"

"Fuck who?" Ax and I both turn to see Lars coming up towards the path in front of Ax's house that leads to Dragonfly Lake.

"Why do you care?" Ax says.

I turn back to him. "Because we had a fucking deal, Ax. You don't touch her."

"Touch who?" Lars asks.

"Cadee!" Ax and I both say at the same time.

"Hmm. Are we fucking and touching Cadee again?"

"No," I growl.

"Maybe." Ax shrugs.

"No," I repeat. "We are not. Stay the fuck away from her. She's trash."

"Huh. That's too bad," Lars says. "I kinda liked having her around yesterday. Fucking miss senior year of Prep. It was… hot."

"Shut up, Lars," I growl. "We're not getting involved with her. In fact, we're on a mission to get her fired today. Understand?"

"Why would we want to get her fired?" Lars asks. "She's not hurting us."

"She *could* hurt us," I seethe. "Everything that happened that year was…"

"Was fun." Ax fills in the blank.

Lars narrows his eyes at me. "What you guys did to her, you mean. I liked her."

"Yeah, and you know what?" Ax says, turning on Lars. "I'm still kinda pissed about that. Sometimes I think you want this life. Sometimes I think you like it too much."

"Hey." Lars shrugs with his hands. "I'm not gonna whine about my life. It's pretty damn easy, all things considered."

"Shut up, Lars," I say, pushing him on the shoulder. "Don't go soft now, asshole."

"You know what else?" Ax says, and I sigh. Because I can tell he's working himself up into one of those infamous tirades. "I'm super happy that your life is so awesome, Lars. But mine fucking sucks. And that's not fair."

"I didn't fuck up your life," Lars says back. "You did. All you had to do was follow directions and things could've gone easy. Even Cooper follows directions better than you do. So if your life is a shit show, that's your fault, not mine."

"OK, enough, you guys. Can we just concentrate on getting Cadee out of here?" I point to Ax. "Humiliate her today. Make her cry like a goddamned baby. She'll tell my father, he'll see she's someone he can't trust, and then she'll be gone and we can forget she ever existed."

"Don't worry about that." The three of us turn to see Isabella all dressed up in her garden party finery. I'm talking the wide-brimmed lace hat, the long, cream-colored dress with a pink satin sash around her waist, and white gloves. "I've already seen to her utter humiliation."

"That was fast," I laugh.

"Well." She shrugs and smiles. "I can't actually take the credit. They've been using this costume for three years now. But I signed off on it this morning."

"What uniform?" Lars asks.

But then an eruption of screams makes us all turn towards the Glass House to find Cadee dressed up in said costume.

"Oh, hell the fuck no! I am not wearing this!" Cadee is yelling at Victor English, who I kinda remember from our own summer rush.

"Oh, my God." Ax laughs hysterically. "That's so fucking wrong!"

Cadee Hunter is dressed up like a rubber duck. Complete with an orange beak hood, orange duck feet, and a wooden sign hanging around her neck from a chain that says, *Hi, my name is Fugling. How can I serve you today*?

I laugh. I can't help it.

And then everyone is laughing. Us. All ten of the wannabe princelings and swanlings. Even the staff has come out of the kitchen to point and chuckle.

"I'm not wearing this!" Cadee yells again. "You all can go—"

"Be careful," I bark, silencing everyone with my yell. "You better be careful how you speak to us, Cadee Hunter."

Isabella tsks her tongue. "Call her by her *name*, Coop."

Fugling. I sigh. But whatever. I need to keep Isabella happy this summer if I want her to be helpful. "You had better be very fucking careful what you say around here. One mouthy outburst from you, *Fugling*, and you're out. No place to live, no summer job, no scholarship."

"Which is probably a good thing," Ax says. He's made his way over to Cadee and he's circling her like a predator. He licks his lips, like he's going to be eating her for breakfast instead of the food the servers are preparing. "Just leave, Cadee. Why put yourself through this? You know you don't belong here."

Lars sighs.

"You got a problem with this, Lars?" I whisper it so Ax doesn't hear. I don't want him distracted. Cadee Hunter looks like she's thinking we might not be worth all this effort. And that's a good thing.

"She didn't do anything. It was us stalking her." Lars keeps his voice low.

"She agreed to everything we did that year. All of it." I stress this part. Just so we're clear. "We didn't coerce her. She wanted it."

"Right," Lars says. "And so did we. She never said anything, Cooper. She kept her part of the bargain. Just leave her alone."

"We have another year in this place. And then when we leave, she will be here, *alone.* Without us to run interference if she suddenly feels the need to put us in our places."

"If we're gone, who cares? So you guys bullied her a little? High-school kids who bully cute girls isn't what I'd call a career-ender."

Yeah, I sigh to myself. *Because that's not all that happened that year.* Lars has no idea how much shit I'm covering up. And I'm never going to tell him. Because he would take Cadee's side over mine without even blinking.

"Do we want her holding shit over our heads for the rest of our lives? And we won't be gone. We all know where we'll be."

"I'll be gone," Lars says. Then he looks at me. "I'm in finance. That means I'll get sent to the city no matter what. Not my fault you've been fucking off for three years and you'll get stuck here like your brother Dane."

"Fuck you." I point at him. "Do not compare me to Dane."

"Easy," Lars says. "And anyway, we can't erase her mind. She's going to know our secrets forever no matter what happens."

"Right. But if we allow her into the inner circle, she'll have power. And if she's smart, she will learn to grow that power. Then one day, Lars, one day we'll be somewhere enjoying ourselves, the memories of High Court long faded, and we'll turn around, and there she'll be. She'll make demands, or threats, or both. And whatever we hold dear when that happens will be up in the air. Why would you want to leave this loose end behind when we've spent the last three years doing everything in our power to avoid this very situation?"

"I get it. We should pay her off then. Pay her enough money that it's in her best interest to forget about us."

"Have you conveniently forgotten our fathers drained our bank accounts? And how fucking naïve are you, Lars? Do you really think they didn't plan this? They didn't put her here? I think they know something and they're just using us to get rid of her."

He folds his arms across his chest and looks me in the eyes. "And since when do you do your father's bidding?"

"Since I have no choice." It's my turn to sigh now. "Listen, if you're feeling guilty about this, we'll pay her off when we get our bank accounts back. We'll each chip in enough to keep her flush every month, as long as she stays quiet."

Lars looks at me. His expression is flat. We're not drawing the attention of anyone. Yet. "I get what you're saying. I understand it, I agree with it. But the only way to truly erase the threat that Cadee Hunter presents to us is to kill her."

"Jesus, Lars."

"That's what I mean. We're not going to kill her. This isn't going to work."

"We have to make it work. She's a nobody. All we have to do is scare her into submission and make her leave."

We both glance over at Ax, who is still circling Cadee. Spilling insults. Telling her she doesn't belong here. Describing what the rest of the summer will look like if she stays.

She looks like she's trying hard not to cry, but that's not what bothers me. The part that bothers me is that she's succeeding. She doesn't look ready to quit, that's for sure. She has a little gleam in her eye. Defiance.

"You see that, right there, Lars? That twinkle in her eye? She's planning something. She hates us. She wants revenge. All we have to do is break this girl.

Erase that twinkle. Put her in her place and send her on her way."

Lars takes a deep breath. "Fine." Then he looks at me. "Just like senior year at Prep?"

Ax is suddenly up next to us. "What's like senior year at Prep?"

"No," I say, looking back at Cadee. "What we did to her during senior year at Prep will look like child's play this summer."

"What are we talking about?" Ax says.

"Ruining Cadee Hunter."

"*Breaking* Cadee hunter," I correct Lars.

"Excellent." Ax chuckles, rubbing his hands together. "I could use a new target. When do we start?"

"Now," I say. "Right now."

CHAPTER TWELVE

The worst thing about my first day at my new job isn't the way Isabella and her stupid minions, Selina and Valentina, humiliate me over and over again. I mean, yes, when I first saw that costume, I was livid. And when I went outside wearing it, as everyone in the camp made fun of me, I was humiliated. And then when Cooper, Ax, and Lars made it very clear that this is how it will be all summer if I stay, I felt defeated.

But none of that compares to the feelings I have right now.

The day is over. I was forced to serve them all. On my knees, several times. Crawling over to Ax, and Lars, and Cooper as I desperately tried not to spill their drinks on the tray I was holding. I had to kiss Ax's feet a couple dozen times. Hell, at one point he had me massaging them.

Lars made me swim in the lake wearing the duck costume after Isabella spilled a bowl of maraschino cherries all over the front. That was how he wanted me to clean it.

I lost a duck foot and then they wouldn't let me come out of the water until I went under and looked around the brown lake water until I found it.

Then Cooper said I couldn't change. I had to wear the wet costume for the rest of the day until after dinner.

Valentina complained that I smelled and Selina dumped a box of powdered laundry detergent over my head. That was just a little while ago.

They've all gone home for the night. The pledges are staying in the student cottages across the lake and when I asked them if I could get a ride over there so I could sleep in my old garden cottage that the Chairman gifted me last night, they just laughed hysterically.

Victor and the other servers are cleaning up as I sit in the locker room, trying to peel the dirty, disgusting, soap-caked costume off my body.

I wish I was one of them. They weren't anyone's target today. They just did their jobs quietly and everyone left them alone.

"Knock, knock."

I look up to see Victor staring down at me with

sympathetic eyes.

"Do you have a boat, Victor?"

"No. Sorry, Cadee."

"You don't have a boat?" I sneer it. Because he's just lying. Everyone has a boat. "Then how the hell did you get here today?"

"There's a staff boat. I gotta go catch it right now."

"Oh." I brighten. "Awesome. Can you wait for me? I'll walk with you." I'm a little worried about getting turned around in the woods again. It's not dark yet, but it's pretty close. I don't like the idea of walking through the woods alone in the dusk. Not when I know that Cooper, Lars, Ax, Isabella, Selina, and Valentina are all staying the night on this side of the lake.

"Do you have a pass?"

"A what?"

"A boat pass, Cadee." He takes a laminated ID card out of his back pocket and flashes it at me. "They give these out in the employee packets. They won't let you on the boat without one."

"But surely—"

"Listen." He sighs. "I've been here at the camp for three years now. I know how it works. You're the Fugling." I wince at the word. "Sorry. I'm not trying to make this worse, but they're not going to let you on the boat. Usually the Fugling has to sleep here for at least a week. Then they…" He pauses.

"Then they what?"

"Then they make you sleep in the tomb. And torment you at night. I don't know why you're here. Maybe someone has promised you something nice if you stick it out?" He shrugs. "But no Fugling ever makes it to the end of the summer."

"No one?"

"I've only been here three years, so maybe they do? But no one has lasted more than three weeks. It's only going to get worse."

"What about Lacy Pendleton? And all that bullshit about the scholarship I stole from her?"

"Well." Victor looks uncomfortable. "Lacy's different. She's one of them. She wasn't going to be the Fugling. But you… you're not one of us. You never went to Prep. They don't like outsiders here."

"I grew up here. I have literally never lived anywhere else but the campus of High Court."

He just shrugs. "And I know what your next question will be. Can't we help you? Can't we do something? But if we help you, Cadee, then they'll make us a target too. No one will help you. All the staff who have been here before, we took bets last night on who would be the Fugling. Sometimes they don't target the staff. They choose one of the pledges. And we were all pretty sure it was going to be Mona Monroe once we saw her name on the list."

I huff. I would've picked her too. Then I remember the plan I made last night to get Mona on my side and turn her into the Cygnet. Wow. Was I ever dumb to think that would work. There's no way she would help me. She has to know she came very close to being the Fugling today. I sigh heavily. "So I just have to stay here? Or am I allowed to leave and go back to the Chairman's house?"

"I'm sorry?" Victor cocks his head at me in confusion.

"The Chairman. He's the one who gave me this job. He gave me a place to stay—the old garden cottage on the Prep campus. But I can't get across the lake."

"What's that have to do with his house?"

"He gave me a room to stay there, too."

"Huh. I don't know what to make of that. But hell, if I had a room at the Chairman's house, and I was you right now? That's where I'd go."

"Cooper," I whisper.

"Yeah." He takes his apron off, bunches it up, and tosses it in to the laundry. The other servers are calling him to hurry so they can catch the boat across the lake. "I know why they're doing this to you. You dated them. All of them. Cooper, Ax, and Lars."

"*Dated* them?" I scoff. "I didn't date them."

But wasn't I just trying to convince myself I did last night?

"I didn't know you when I went to Prep. But everyone *knows* you, Cadee. The prissy stuck-up girl who doesn't go to school here, but gets to take advantage of all the privileges like she does."

"I didn't *date* them. They bullied me relentlessly their entire senior year."

Sort of true. I mean, they did bully me fall semester. But then… it turned into something else. Something both bad and good at the same time.

"OK." Victor sighs, clearly tired of me. "If you say so."

He doesn't believe me, I can tell. And I can't say anything else, not without making everything worse. Because I can see how everyone would *think* I dated them. All at the same time. They made damn sure everyone knew I was their property that year. So I just… shrug and continue pulling off the duck uniform.

"I gotta go. You don't need to lock up. No one but the people who own this place has access to it. So… I guess I'll see you tomorrow?"

I nod, but don't say anything. Just drag one side

of the costume down my shoulder.

He turns and takes a few steps. But then he turns back. "There's a path, Cadee. Right behind the Glass House." He points in the general direction. "And that path takes to you to a gate. And outside that gate lives the real world. You could just slip out the gate and be done with it." He shrugs. "Up to you. But I'm serious when I say it's *not* going to get better."

I draw in a long breath. "Thank you, Victor." I smile at him and he returns it. "For taking the time to tell me all this. I appreciate it."

"No problem. I wish I could be the answer you're looking for. I think you're nice. And I never thought you were stuck up."

Then he turns and walks away.

Leaving me there in the locker room.

Utterly alone.

I don't go back to the Chairman's house. I know better.

I'm sure Cooper, Lars, and Ax are all just waiting for me to show up so they can torment me the way they used to. Make me do things. Say things. Be someone I'm not.

But that's not even true.

They didn't make me do anything but… *enjoy* them.

I enjoyed them. All of them.

That's the kind of power they wield.

There is no shower in the Glass House. So I strip off my costume, walk out to the lake naked, and wash myself off in the brown lake water.

When I return to the Glass House to find clothes, there is nothing to put on that is dry or clean except a too-big white t-shirt that belonged to one of the pledges.

I slip it over my head and curl up in one of the many chairs in the main room.

"Cadee Hunter."

I hear the words in my dream. Him. Cooper

Valcourt.

"Cadee!"

I open my eyes to the dim light of stars shining down from the glass wall. And then startle when Cooper is sitting in the chair across from me. "What? What did I do?" I scramble in my chair, realize I'm only wearing someone else's too-big t-shirt and no panties or shorts, and then quickly rearrange my legs to cover myself up.

"What the fuck are you wearing?"

"What?"

"Why are you dressed like that?"

I look down at the t-shirt. "I didn't have any clothes."

"What the hell are you doing here?"

"What do you mean? I thought I was supposed to sleep here?"

He gets to his feet and starts pacing. "My father is pissed off."

"Why?"

"Because you didn't show up for dinner. And when he sent someone to your cottage to get you—making us all wait at the fucking table as the food got cold—you weren't there."

"I couldn't get across the lake."

He glares at me. "Are you purposefully trying to

ruin my life?"

"Ha! That's a good one! You're the one trying to ruin *my* life."

"Get up. We're going home."

"Your house is not my home, Cooper."

"Well, my dad wants you there. To make sure you're OK. So get your fucking ass up and let's go." And then he's up, pulling me to my feet and yanking on my arm.

I wrench out of his grip and back away. "No. Fuck you."

His eyes trace down my legs. Then he narrows his eyes and they track back up to me. "Do you even have shorts on under that shirt?"

"Where would I get clean shorts? Huh, Cooper? You guys ruined my clothes."

"You were wearing them under that costume." He laughs like this is funny. Then he stops. "You don't have on underwear either. Jesus fucking Christ. Are you *trying* to get raped?"

I go instantly hot all over. Then I snarl at him. "I fucking hate you."

He shakes his head. "I don't care. But you'd better be careful what you say. I might take that admission as a threat. Are you threatening me, Cadee?"

"No." I fold my arms across my chest. Because

I'm not wearing a bra and the AC is still on and it's freezing in here. My nipples are all perky. And I do not want Cooper Valcourt to think he's affecting me like that. Because he's not. I will never fall for his lies again. Ever. Not after the way he used me that year.

Date them. Ha. That was funny. I never *dated* them.

He looks around for something, then walks away into the kitchen. Comes back a few minutes later. "Where do they keep the uniforms?"

"The what?"

"The fucking staff, Cadee. Don't play with me. Where do they keep the clean uniforms?"

"If I knew that, do you think I'd be naked under this shirt?"

His eyes track down my legs again. Then he licks his lips and meets my gaze. His fingers go to the buttons on his cargo shorts and the next thing I know, he's pulling them down his legs.

I back away, horrified. "What the hell are you doing?"

"Giving you my fucking boxers. I can't take you home like this."

I turn away as he starts pulling them off. A few seconds later they hit me on the head. "Put them on."

I grab them and tug them up over my hips before

turning back to him, catching him in the act of buttoning his shorts back up.

"Where are your shoes?"

"In the locker room."

He leaves and comes back a few minutes later with my shoes and throws them at my feet.

I just stand there and look at him. On the outside, Cooper Valcourt is the most gorgeous example of a man a mind could conjure up. He is the image that comes to mind when you think the word 'prince'. Or... male model. Or… Forbidden Nights dancer.

I almost laugh.

But seriously. Those blue eyes. That dark hair. The broad, muscular shoulders and the trim waist. His jaw is so cut and square, he looks like an artist's interpretation of a man. There's a bit of scruff on his face. Something he didn't have much of when we were… what were we? Not friends. Not enemies, though. Not boyfriend and girlfriend either. Hell, I would not even call us lovers, though we did have sex that year.

He was… I don't know. A… a *hope,* maybe. He was a hope.

I thought he was handsome back when we were together three years ago, but that was just a sneak peek of what he looks like today. He was too skinny then.

And now he's all filled out. I blow out a breath just thinking about how much he filled out while I picture him jerking on his cock last night in my doorway.

"Why are you just fucking standing there looking at me like an idiot? Put on the goddamned shoes!"

He yells it and I startle a little, then slip my feet into my sneakers, tugging on the backs a little as I hop on one foot to make them secure.

When I'm done, he grabs my hand and begins pulling me through the Glass House. We leave, not even bothering to close the door behind us, and then he's dragging me through the woods.

I trip over a root and almost fall. But he's still got my hand, so I don't. But he doesn't stop either. Just… drags me.

"Slow down!" I protest. "Your legs are way longer than mine."

"Just keep up," he growls.

The path he takes me on leads us right out on to the blacktop road across from his mansion. He pauses for a moment, looking around, then drags me towards the side yard in the direction of the French doors that lead to the room I'm staying in.

He's just pulling the door open when we hear, "Well, look who it is." And when we turn to look behind us, we find Mona sitting out on her patio smoking a cigarette. "The King and his Fugling!" She snickers, takes a drag on her cigarette, then blows the smoke out. "I can't wait to tell Isabella that you were sneaking around in the night. Did you have a good time?" She laughs.

"Thanks for reminding me, Mona."

"Of what?"

"That you were supposed to be the Fugling this year."

"Fuck you!" she yells.

Cooper shoots me a smile. And it's a real one. I know the difference. And when Cooper Valcourt smiles a real smile, and that smile is aimed at you—well, it's very hard to remember that he's an asshole.

Because he's not. Not really.

Cooper Valcourt was my prince during the last half of his senior year at Prep. And I thought we were real. I believed it.

But then… the pregnancy changed everything. And from that moment on, we were enemies again. Only worse.

And as sick as it is… in this moment, I realize… I have *missed* him.

CHAPTER THIRTEEN

I feel it when I smile at her.

I feel my whole past with Cadee Hunter.

Because it's a real smile. And it reminds me of what we had together once upon a time.

She was… what was she to me? To us? I don't think there's a word for it. But this girl is a witch. A very talented genius of a witch who can weave a spell over me like no other girl in the world ever could.

And that, Cooper, is why she's so dangerous.

Among other things, of course.

I drag her through the door, kick it closed with my foot, and then push her away from me. "Please put on a pair of real shorts."

"Just leave."

"I can't just leave, Cadee. My father sent me to find you. It took me *three* hours. He's waiting up. Don't you get it? You're fucking everything up for me right now."

"Me?" She laughs and points to her chest. "I'm the one fucking things up for *you*? You have some nerve, Cooper Valcourt."

"Put on. Some real shorts. Right. Now." I clench my jaw as these words come out, totally at the end of my patience with her.

She frowns at me, then walks to the closet. She's in there for a long time. Like several minutes go by.

"Hurry up!"

"There's nothing here. This is not my closet. It belonged to one of your stepmothers."

"What?" I walk into the closet and start pushing things on the rack. "Jesus Christ. What the fuck was my father thinking?" Then I spy the shelves of neatly stacked shorts. I grab a pair and throw them at her. "Just put these on."

She holds them up, crooked smile on her face. "These?"

I run my hand over my jaw. They are like… short. Very. Short. My third stepmother was a legit whore. A high-end call girl my father frequented for a while. I'm pretty sure she had dirt on him and that's why he had to marry her. But then one day—poof. She was gone.

I try not to think about that too much. Stella might've been a working girl, but she was nice to me.

A lot nicer than my father ever was. Not too smart though. You don't threaten a man like him. You don't want his secrets. Because no one, and I do mean *no one*, is safe from his wrath if you make him feel threatened.

"Cadee," I say, so tired of this day. "Can you please, *please* just help me out here?"

She huffs. "I can't magically conjure up a pair of shorts suitable to wear for a meeting with your father, Cooper." She turns back to the clothes, shuffles through them for what feels like a very long time, and then finds a pair of white leggings and drags them up her legs. "How's this?"

I look down her legs. They are long. And shapely. And these skin-tight leggings show every muscle of her calves and thighs.

Snap out of it, dickhead. Didn't you learn your lesson with this girl three years ago?

"They'll do. Come on."

I drag her out of the room and down the hallway, stopping at an intersection to listen. Making sure Dane and Jack aren't still here with their wives. That's the last thing I need right now.

Clear. So I drag her through a few more hallways and then pause when the door of my father's study comes in to view. "Listen to me," I say.

She looks up at me. She looks like a goddamned

princess. Her dirty blonde hair looks like Isabelle's when she comes back from getting expensive highlights. But Cadee's is natural. It's long and straight. She doesn't curl it, or style it, or do anything to it except tuck it behind her ear every once in a while, when she's trying to concentrate on something.

Her face is a perfect heart shape. Her eyes are wide and a very light brown color that sometimes looks green in the sun. Her lips are lush and plump. And right now, she's pressing them together as she waits for me to continue.

"I know you're probably thinking, 'Hey, if his father is so concerned about me that he sent Cooper out to find me in the middle of the night and produce me as proof that I am safe, he must certainly *care* about me.' But I'm going to tell you something right now, Cadee. He doesn't give a fuck about you."

She recoils a little.

"If you say one word about what happened today, he won't feel sorry for you. Understand me? He will learn—" Jesus Christ. Why am I telling her this? I *want* her to tell him what happened. I *want* her to spill all those details.

"He will learn what?"

"That you cannot be trusted. That's it, Cadee. That's what this is all about. I don't know why he's obsessed with you at the moment."

We stare at each other. Because we both have an idea.

"But," I continue, "it's just a test. Everything is just a test with him. If you tell him what we did to you at the Glass House, if you breathe a word of any of it, he will get rid of you so fast, your pretty little head will spin. So be nice, tell him thank you, and then go to bed."

"I thought you wanted me gone?"

"I do."

"Then why are you telling me this?"

I have no idea. But I don't want to think about it. So I don't answer. Just tug her over to the door and knock.

"Come," my father growls on the other side of the door.

I open it, push her forward, and say, "Found her. She was outside on the beach looking up at the stars."

My father stares at her, daring her to contradict me.

"I fell asleep. Sorry for worrying you, Chairman. And thank you"—she smiles at me—"for sending Cooper to be my white knight."

My father smiles at her from the massive wingback leather chair in front of his fireplace. He's not working.

He's wearing his smoking jacket. Waiting up for us, even though it is nearly midnight. Clearly infatuated with this girl for some reason.

But I can't blame him. Not really.

Because I am clearly infatuated with her as well.

I need to fix that. I need to get rid of this girl.

"I'm glad you're OK," my father says. "I thought you would come for dinner. But I understand. Are you sleeping here tonight?"

"Yes," I say.

My father glowers at me. "Don't answer for her, Cooper. Women don't like that."

"Yes," Cadee says.

"Cooper will help you move in to the cottage tomorrow night. Won't you, Cooper?"

"Sure," I sigh.

"I…" Cadee starts. "I don't think I can live there."

My father frowns. "Why not?"

"I don't have a boat. I can't get back and forth to the Glass House for work."

"Oh." My father frowns deeper. "Oh, I'm so sorry. I made an assumption. But of course, you don't have a boat. Cooper?" He barks my name loudly. Like I need those extra decibels to hear the order that's coming. "You will be Miss Hunter's chauffeur for the summer. Clear?"

"Yes, sir."

"That's not necessary," Cadee protests.

"Nonsense. I didn't give you a place to stay just so you couldn't stay there. Cooper doesn't mind, do you, Cooper?"

I grit my teeth and bite back the instinctual response that really wants to come out. Then I breathe. "It would be my pleasure."

"Perfect," my father says. "Well. Have a good night, you two."

We turn. But then my father says, "Cadee?"

"Yes?" She turns back.

"Did you have a nice first day?"

I do not move. I do not breathe.

Because part of me wants her to tell him everything. The sane part.

But another part wants her to just play along. Play the game with me. Just like we did three years ago.

"Yes," Cadee says.

And I breathe a sigh of relief. Even though I know she can't stay. And tomorrow we will do everything in our power to make her quit.

"Thank you for this opportunity," Cadee adds. "I really appreciate it. And I had fun today."

My father nods and smiles even wider. If that's even possible. "Good. That makes me very happy."

We back out of the room, close the door, and I take her quickly through the hallways and back to her room. She opens the door, and I'm just about to say something.

Thank her, maybe?

For being a… *good sport* about this day?

For sticking it out so I can use her again?

But she doesn't turn. Just shuts the door in my face.

My whole body gets hot with anger.

What the fuck is wrong with this girl? Is she playing me? Did my father send her to the Glass House as a setup to make me fail?

Or… does she just really hate my guts?

No. She didn't reject me. That's not what that was.

She *disrespected* me.

I lie in bed thinking about this. Thinking about how she is the cause of all my problems this summer. Realizing she thinks she's so much better than everyone, when it's all of us who are better than her.

She doesn't care that my father is paying her bills right now. She gives no fucks at all that she has been handed an opportunity that people would kill for.

Does she have any idea how many parents would fall all over the Chairman to get their kid a spot at High Court? They put their baby's name on the Prep preschool waitlist before the proverbial ink is even dry on their newborn's birth certificate.

There are only five hundred students in the college and lower school at any one time. That number has not changed in more than a hundred years. This is über-elite education. Hell, the school trips in Prep are insane. Students at Prep aren't taking buses to DC. They're flying in private corporate jets to Rome and Athens to study ancient ruins in person. And the guest lecturers are leaders in the field. Mostly super-successful alumni—and that list might be short, but it is mighty.

You need a summer internship? How about shadowing the billionaire who owns your favorite online retail store?

An apprenticeship, you ask? Learn to paint from modern masters.

Wanna be a writer? How about we let that number one *New York Times* bestseller read your manuscript and put you in touch with their agent?

These are the opportunities that come from sticking it out at High Court Prep and graduating from High Court College.

Interested in a PhD from Carnegie Mellon? Or an MBA from Wharton? Or an MD from Harvard? No problem. Here's your one-on-one meeting with the dean. You're having dinner with them. At their *house*.

And Cadee Hunter just *fell into this*. Her parents never paid a cent.

And I get it. She didn't go to school here. Ever. But that makes this scholarship offer even worse.

She didn't earn it.

I actually feel sorry for Lacy Pendleton. She did the work. She's been a High Court kid since pre-school. And one dead mother rips all that away in an instant because… why?

Why is my father bending over backwards for this average girl when all around him are exceptional kids who would die for this kind of personal attention?

She's sleeping in our fucking house. Right now. Probably wearing Stella's nightgown.

It pisses me off. It really does. And I have an almost uncontrollable urge to sneak down to her room and scream at her that she does not belong here.

But I control it. I'm breathing heavy with anger, but I control it.

I need to make her realize she's not welcome. My father isn't really interested in her. He's using her. And I want to disrespect her the way she just disrespected me.

I reach under the sheets and tug on my cock. It's swelling with blood, getting hard as the anger courses through me. And then I picture Cadee Hunter asleep on that chair. If I had known she was naked under that shirt while I was watching her sleep, I'd have looked a little harder. Maybe jerked one off right there.

And maybe she would've woken up. Her plump mouth opening up in a gasp when she saw my hand on my cock.

I close my eyes and picture her doing this as I slide my hand up and down my now-thick shaft.

She would untangle her legs and stretch them out in front of her as she leaned back in the chair. Then lift that white t-shirt up and play with her tits, slowly opening her knees to give me a peek at her pussy.

It would be wet. Glistening as her fingers played with her clit.

I breathe a little harder as I immerse myself in the fantasy.

Her eyes would be hooded and heavy. Her breasts rising and falling. Her heart pounding inside her chest.

Then I would beckon her with a finger. "Come here," I'd say. "On your knees."

And she would. She would not hesitate.

She would crawl across the marble floor, her eyes locked with mine, her tongue darting out to lick her lips. And then she would settle between my legs and take my hard cock in her hands. Smiling at me with her eyes as she lowered her mouth over the top of it, playfully flicking her tongue across the tip of my head. And then I would wrap both hands in her hair, gripping it so hard she would moan as she took my cock deep, sealing her lips around my shaft and gagging on me.

I come in my hand. Breathing hard and heavy from the fantasy.

But then I smile to myself in the dark as I grab a t-shirt and clean up my spilled mess.

It wasn't a fantasy.

This really happened.

And I've relived it in my head hundreds of times since I left her crying in her Alumni-Inn attic bedroom three years ago and told her I never wanted to see her face again.

I wake up the next morning before dawn breaks. Flush with a new punishment for Cadee Hunter. Excited.

I can't wait to make her pay for disrespecting me.

For showing back up in my life after I threw her away.

For forcing me to look at her every day for the rest of the summer.

I am the bully king.
I will make her pay for that.
And that price will be high.

CHAPTER FOURTEEN

I set my phone alarm for five AM and I do not dawdle in the shower. It does take me several minutes to find an appropriate outfit in the stepmother closet, but I get clever and decide to cut off a pair of jeans to make my own shorts.

The stepmother had lots of cut-offs too. But they were so short, not even Daisy Duke would wear them.

Mine are the appropriate length. I cut a little slit up the side of the thigh so they don't ride up. And even though I don't want to wear another woman's underwear, she left behind a whole drawer of brand-new lacy bras and matching panties that still had the tags on them.

The price too. Never in a million years would I pay what amounts to a car payment for a pair of panties.

I tug on a loose-fitting gauzy shirt in pink, with

three-quarter bell sleeves, and leave my hair down, but tuck it back with a pink headband.

In the bathroom I find a whole drawer of brand-new makeup samples that come with a free-gift zipper bag when you buy a bunch of expensive products at a department store. I'm not into makeup much, but I dab some pink gloss on my lips and when I look in the mirror I actually smile. I look pretty. Pink was always my color.

Then—because I learned my lesson yesterday—I pack another outfit in a small backpack. Just in case those bitches get any more ideas about sending me into the lake. Then I decide… maybe I'll take a couple other outfits. I don't have any clothes. The movers packed them all up. So I choose three more simple outfits and stuff those in the bag too.

Then I look down at Cooper's boxer shorts on my floor. I cannot believe I was wearing those last night. In fact, last night felt a little bit like a dream. And if I didn't wake up in this bedroom, I wouldn't have believed it happened.

Plus his father ordered him to drive me back and forth across the lake to my cottage.

Ha. I do not feel sorry for him. He deserves it. I don't even understand how I ended up in this life right now, but I do know one thing.

It's all his fault.

Everything is all his fault.

I look in the mirror again. Adjust my shirt a little. Smile. "OK, Cadee. Forget about yesterday. You got this. Because when you leave tonight, you have a home to go to. You have a few changes of clothes, you have a check to cash from the Chairman, and you are going to be just fine."

Better than fine. Because I don't care what Victor says. I'm going to make it the whole summer and come out the other end with a freaking scholarship to one of the most elite private colleges in the world.

Take that, Cooper.

Suck on this, Lars.

Kiss my ass, Ax.

I look for the path that Cooper took last night when we came home and find it easily now that I know what to look for.

"Wait up!"

I look to my right and find Mona Monroe jogging to catch up to me. I walk faster.

"Don't be a bitch!" she calls. "You know I can

outrun you any day."

I sneer at her, kinda pissed that she's cramping my good mood and positive attitude this morning. "Maybe. Before you started choking on cigarettes."

"Well." She laughs. "Someone has some pep this morning. So what are your revenge plans?"

"What?"

"Your revenge plans. The mean girls get you. Then you cry all night and come up with a plan. So what's your plan?"

"First of all"—I hold up a finger— "I didn't cry at all." This is true too. Which even surprises me. I should've cried last night. Hmm. Interesting. "Second, I am not going to waste one moment of my precious life thinking about *bitches*."

Mona laughs and lights up a smoke. She drags on it, then exhales in my face.

"Don't be a child, Mona."

"Well, that's all very mature of you, *Cadee*." She kinda sneers my name. "But they're going to be upping their game today. I know how this works. And trust me, I'm very glad you're the Fugling this summer. Because I was sure it would be me and I'm so *not* as evolved as you are. I would've fought back hard. But I have watched from the woods for about a dozen summers now. It's just going to get worse. And they never win. You won't win. You will not be here at the end of the summer."

"So I've been told."

"So why are you going? Hmm? What's the big prize?"

"A scholarship to High Court."

"Really? Damn. I thought everyone was kidding when they said you stole Lacy's scholarship. Well done, Cades. Well done."

"I didn't steal it. The Chairman offered it to me."

"Hmm. Also interesting. Since you're living at his house and I saw Cooper go into your bedroom last night."

I shake my head, so annoyed. "Mona, if you want to spread that rumor, I can't stop you. And I'm sure it will really piss Isabella off. But nothing happened."

"Oh, now come on. No one will believe that. You sucked his dick all year when he was a senior in Prep."

I go red with heat at these words.

"Not just him, either. Oh, hey. I have a question for you. Did you guys like… take turns or something? Or was it just one big sloppy orgy with their cocks stuck into every orifice of your body?"

"You're disgusting."

"Well, I'm disappointed. I had been picturing it as an orgy for three years and you just burst my bubble."

I walk faster when the Glass House comes in to view.

"Byeeeeee!" Mona calls. "Good luck today!"

I cannot believe I thought she would actually be on my side. She might be worse than Isabella.

I slip into the kitchen and find all the servers putting on their aprons and bustling around.

"You're back," Victor says.

"I'm back."

"Glutton for punishment, huh?"

"I'm just here to do my job."

"Good news. Your duck costume went missing. Did you burn it?"

"No. I took it off and left it in the laundry basket."

"Well, it's not there. And Isabella is *pissed*."

"She's already here? Why is she so early? Coffee doesn't even get served for another hour."

"She's checking up on you. If you did burn it—"

"I didn't."

"I'm just saying, if you did, you should just own up to it. She will at least just hand out your punishment and move on."

"She probably burned it. She's setting me up."

"Probably."

"Bitch. I hate them."

"Not all of them." Victor smirks as he fills the massive commercial coffeemaker with water using a stainless-steel pitcher. "Not Cooper."

"Especially Cooper."

"Whatever, Cadee."

"Whatever yourself." I stand there for a minute, my apron tied on. "Now what do I do?"

"Better go ask the queen. She's your boss, Fugling."

I turn on my heel and push through the kitchen doors, then mutter, "Asshole." Because I thought Victor was going to be my friend. And he's clearly not interested in getting involved. He only shows up to save his own ass. Just like all the rest.

"There she is," Isabella sneers as I walk out into the main room. "What did you do with it?"

"I don't know what you're talking about, Isabella." I say it sweetly. Like hurt-your-teeth sweetly. Which only makes her more suspicious.

"I'll get you another one. You will wear that costume all summer."

"Or," Selina chirps, "until she quits and runs away crying."

I just smile at Selina Reyes. I don't know her. Like at all. But I don't need to know her to understand what and who she is. She is one of Isabella's best friends. Enough said. That's all there is to it.

"She's not going to wear the costume anymore."

We all turn to find Cooper, Ax, and Lars walking towards us.

"What?" Isabella is pissed at being challenged about this.

Ax dances up to me shaking a white t-shirt at me like he's giddy. Or high. Probably high. "You have a new uniform, Fugling." He drops it over my head. "Put it on."

I yank the shirt off my head and force myself to smile. They will not win. I will not give them that satisfaction. Ever.

"Sure thing, my prince." I wink up at him and he stops his dancing to frown at me. Then I whip my shirt over my head and toss the pretty pink gauzy blouse on the ground.

I'm sad that I don't get to look cute all day. But my 'uniform' is just a white t-shirt. It could be a lot worse.

They all stare at me as I stand there in my pretty pink bra and start slipping the new shirt over my head.

"No." Cooper grabs the shirt from me. "Take off

the bra too."

"What?"

Those dangerous blue eyes are locked on mine. "You heard me. No bra."

I glance at Isabella and her friends. And now more people are here. Three more guys and two more girls. And they are all watching to see what I will do.

I reach behind my back, unclasp my bra, let it slide down my arms. And I stand there with my chest out and my nipples all peaked up and perky.

Cooper is staring at me. But he's not taking in the view. He's gritting his teeth in anger.

Oh, did I disappoint you, big strong man? Was I not properly embarrassed?

Like I care if these people see my body. I'm not ashamed of it.

Mona bursts out laughing on the far side of the room when she walks through the door. "Get 'em, Cadee!" she yells, kinda… cheering me on. Maybe. Probably not. Whatever.

Cooper throws the t-shirt at me. He's had his eyes locked on mine this whole time. But now he lets them slide down to my bare breasts. And they linger there until I pull the shirt over my head and straighten it out.

I look down at it, realize someone has written 'Call me Fugling' across the front in thick black marker, and just… let it go.

Play the game, Cadee. You're a winner.

I curtsey. Bow my head at Cooper Valcourt. "Thank you, Your Highness." Then I look at Isabella. "My queen, how can I serve you today?"

"Coffee," she barks. "Now."

I curtsey again. "It will be my pleasure."

Then I turn on my heel and walk back to the kitchen, passing Victor, who watches me with an open mouth, then follows me. "Oh, Cadee," he says when we're safely in the kitchen and they can't hear him.

"What?"

"You're just making it worse. Trust me. All you have to do is cry a little, be ashamed when they tell you, and hate every minute of this."

"That's giving up."

"No, Cadee. It's giving in. And that's what it takes to win the games they play."

I feel sorry for Victor. Because he's a quitter. He's willing to let these elite assholes run his life and determine his future and I'm not. We are two very different people. I look him straight in the eyes. "I'm not giving in."

He puts both hands up in the air like he's surrendering. "Fine. Do it your way. But they are gonna make it so much worse now."

I ignore him and start filling up a silver coffee pot.

You will not give in, Cadee. You will not.

You did that already. You let these boys run your life three years ago. You surrendered to them. Fell for them. Believed them.

And all they did was lie and abandon you when you really needed help.

You will fight back this time.

You will show them you don't need them, you don't want them, and you will win this time.

They will be the broken ones left behind.

Not me.

CHAPTER FIFTEEN

"Hear ye, hear ye!" Ax is strutting back and forth across the front of the Glass House great room wearing army-green cargo shorts, Doc Martens, and a white t-shirt with a black double-ended arrow pointing up at his face and down at his waist with the words 'TWO-SEATER' in the middle.

That t-shirt is so… Ax.

There's a chain wallet in his back pocket, his buzzed brown hair has a pentagram shaved on one side and an all-seeing eye on the other, and his colorful full-sleeve demon tattoos really pull the whole look together and give off an anarchist vibe that screams 'Chaos is mine, motherfuckers!'

I put a hand over my mouth to hide my smile.

"Welcome to the one hundred and forty-seventh Fang and Feather Summer Rush!" he growls, still pacing across the front of the room.

The pledges are seated in a sloppy semi-circle in the middle of the space. Boy, girl, boy, girl. All ten of them are staring at Ax like he's a freak show.

And he is. I know Ax Olson better than anyone but Lars and he's walking the edge of insanity on most days. How he ever graduated from Prep, I'll never understand.

Oh, wait. I know exactly how he graduated.

We made Cadee cheat for him. She did all his homework his entire senior year.

That's how this whole thing started. Ax and his inability to complete even the simplest of assignments.

Ax stops to hiss out some fake audience roaring noises in his cupped hand. Like he's a rock star playing a stadium and there are a hundred thousand people in the audience.

Sometimes I just can't with that guy. But I enjoy him anyway. He stayed up all night to pull together the opening day challenge, it's practically my job to be supportive.

He moves on to the rules.

It doesn't matter how unprepared everyone is for this camp and their lack of appreciation for Ax's theatrics will have no real bearing on the outcome. Because Fang and Feather Summer Rush is actually just a series of four challenges that last two weeks each.

They are not complicated tasks. They are really nothing but a way to figure out which of these kids can follow directions and which of them can't. It's that simple.

The ones who can will come out the other end with an invitation to the tomb. Then it's just… well. More of the same, only then we'll all be playing for real.

Fang and Feather isn't looking for out-of-the-box thinkers. We're not looking for people who want to change the world and we're not impressed by progressive ideas.

We're here to choose the next crop of minions and that's it.

"Listen up, you little pissant rank-and-file commoners!" Ax is clearly enjoying his role as MC this morning, because he's pacing back and forth across the room with a wild gleam in his eyes. "Your only purpose here is to prove your worth and you don't fool me!" He extends his arm with one finger pointed at the girl on his far left. Her blue eyes go wide and her too-fair skin turns blotchy before my eyes. Sophie Bettington. She points to herself, and starts to squirm in her chair. But Ax's finger moves to the right and points at all of them in turn. "I know you think you're somebody! And you're not! You. Are. Nobody!"

He's screaming now.

Lars and I are standing behind the ten pledges on opposite sides of the great room and when I look over at him, he's rolling his eyes at Ax's theatrics. I shrug at him. Hell, if Ax wants to play the part of carnival barker this summer, I'm fine with it. Someone has to be the asshole. And this act kinda fits him.

"Well." Ax lowers his voice. "Not all of you are nobodies. Six of you will get through. But only six."

"What?" a girl in the middle exclaims. I recognize her from the folder my father gave me. Maddie Lancaster. "What do you mean? There's a quota?" She looks around at her friends. "That's not fair! My father told me—"

"Your father is a nobody just like you, Maddie." Everyone turns in their chairs to look at me. "And if you don't want to get thrown out on your ass before the first challenge even starts, you will shut your fucking mouth and do what you're told."

Ax laughs. It's borderline maniacal and they all turn back around and start to get nervous. "You've all been lied to." Ax continues with the laugh. "Whatever your parents told you about summer rush, none of it was true."

"But don't feel too bad about it," Lars says. "In fact, you better get used to the lies. Because from this moment on, you'll never know what's true and what's not."

I cross my arms over my chest and nod my head at him. Because he's right. This whole club we have here is all based on perception, and loyalty, and secrets, and lies.

But mostly, it's about consequences.

That's what we're here to teach them this summer.

Consequences.

Valentina saunters up front and stands next to Ax. She's wearing a costume, just like Ax. But her attire doesn't have anything to do with anarchy and chaos.

She's dressed like a slutty little princess.

A very *rich*, slutty little princess. Because she's practically dripping with diamonds.

There are at least four carats hanging from her drop earrings. Another three on her wrist. The rings on her finger come in at a solid eight, at least. And who knows how much that choker of hers weighs.

She looks at each of the five Feather pledges—Mona Monroe, Maddie Lancaster, Natasha Waring, Sophie Bettington, and Elexa Simpson—and smiles at them. It's an evil smile. "Look at me," she coos. "Do you like?" She tilts her head. Angles her body to show off her bare shoulders. Bends one leg at the knee and puckers her lips. Her tank top is glittering with crystals, her silver skirt so short, I can practically see her white panties from here. And her long, black hair is piled up on her head in a way that almost looks messy. A very just-fucked look about this girl.

She wiggles her fingers at the girls. She's wearing dozens of rings. The sunlight beaming in from the windows catches hundreds of facets and a lightshow of sparkles dances across her face. "You want some? I have plenty!"

Two of the girls, Maddie and Elexa, actually sigh as they look at her. Their mouths drop open as they tally up just how much money Valentina's jewels are worth.

Then she places two fingers over her lips. "Ooops. Sorry. Getting ahead of myself. This is the *prize*," Valentina whispers. "For winners only."

Then she clicks her tongue and winks at Ax. She saunters up to him, wraps her hands around his waist and presses her lips into his as she gazes up into his eyes. He pulls a diamond-encrusted leash out of one of his many front pockets and clips it to Valentina's choker.

She looks at her initiates, her shoulders rising up as she smiles like she's the luckiest girl in the world. "He's my master," she coos. Then she looks back up at Ax and licks her lips.

The gleam in Ax's eyes brightens for a moment. Then he looks at the dudes as he pushes Valentina down on her knees in front of him and grabs her messy hair as he thrusts his hips forward. "You don't need diamonds. Your prize isn't money, it's the girl wearing it."

Valentina starts unbuckling Ax's belt and every single pledge gasps.

Will she?

Won't she?

Valentina winks at them, then rises to her feet and Ax lets go of her hair. "It's up to you." She says this in her normal voice. "You have to choose this life, ladies. And if you do, then you have to deal with the consequences." She paces back and forth, then stops at the girl on her far left. "You want the diamonds?" She continues to the next girl. "You want the mansion?" She moves on to the third girl who protested about the quota. "You want the lake, and boats, and the cars?" She moves on to the girls on my side of the room. "You want the security?" Then the final girl. "And the man?" She pauses then walks back and stands next to Ax. "Then you do what you're told." She shrugs. "If that's not what you want, then walk out any time. It's. Your. Choice."

"But let me just be clear here," Ax says, pushing

Valentina away and pointing at the boys. She stumbles across the room dramatically, gasping and whimpering. He points at each of the boys in turn—Michael Gottsworth, Dante Legosi, Roland Blanchard, Jamie Cruz, and Ivan Turgenev.

"Every one of you," Ax continues, "*will* cross the line. You do *not* get a choice. You're no good to us if you don't. Only the girls get to be pussies and walk out." He yanks Valentina's leash and forces her back to his side. She's still whimpering, letting these girls know—it's not gonna be easy. They will cry. They will be on their knees. And they will do it willingly. "And you will all be held responsible for your actions. So you had better play the game well."

He eyes them. One by one, as his gaze travels the semi-circle. Then he kisses Valentina. He grabs her hair, clenching his fists around it as they make out, moaning and writhing against each other.

Even I have to admit, it's a sexy fucking kiss.

I walk up to the front and push Ax and Valentina apart. "If this isn't what you signed up for, there's the fucking door." I point to the back of the room and find Cadee Hunter staring right back at me wearing her white t-shirt with no bra. Her t-shirt that begs us all to call her Fugling. Silver coffee pot in her hand. Superior look on her smug face.

We lock eyes. Neither of us daring to move.

Then I say it again. "There's. The fucking. Door."

She holds my gaze, then all the other servers are there, filing past her carrying trays of pastries and flutes of champagne.

Ax yells, "Let the Fang and Feather Summer Rush commence!"

Everyone is still for a moment. Then they repeat it, the boys yelling it with fists in the air, the girls looking at each other nervously, but with just as much excitement.

Expectations have been set. The rules of the game explained.

All ten of them are on board.

These girls want money and status.

These boys want sex.

And so does Cadee Hunter, I guess. Because she tilts her head up defiantly. Daring me to knock her down a peg.

Oh, I will, sweetie.

Trust me.

I will knock you down so far, you won't ever *get back up.*

CHAPTER SIXTEEN

I will say this about the stupid challenges. It keeps the royal court occupied. All the pledges are excited and happy and pay absolutely no attention to all us servers. Not even me. And I thought for sure that this t-shirt thing this morning was a sure sign that I was today's entertainment.

I serve their coffee, then help prepare and serve breakfast, and I play nice. Trying to stay in the background as much as possible. I struggle with this decision internally because it feels like I'm taking Victor's advice. In fact, he makes a point of nodding and smiling at me all through breakfast, letting me know that this is how you play the game.

To lose, maybe.

But I'm not playing to lose, just biding my time here. I'm not stupid. I don't want to make myself a target. I just want to be smart. Pick and choose my battles. And there is no point in challenging them without reason.

They linger at the long breakfast table for hours. No rush to do anything today. And for a little while, I figure this is all they'll do. Just drink and eat like stupid rich people all day because by the time Isabella claps her hands and directs us to clear the table, it's nearly noon.

But then everyone is in motion. Not just us, the servers, but all the pledges too. They are moving chairs and couches around, the white wooden folding chairs they were sitting in for Ax and Valentina's performance earlier long since removed.

Two loveseats are pushed into the center of the room and then two overstuffed chairs arranged on either side. The boys take their seats, clearly excited about what is to come. The girls disappear outside with Selina.

I glance over at Valentina. She's hanging off Ax like they're a couple.

Are they a couple?

Hmm. I really wouldn't know. I didn't spend any time at all over on the college side of campus the past three years. They could be dating, I guess.

Ax definitely kissed Valentina this morning like

they do it regularly. And his hands have been all over her body this morning. Fondling her like she's his property.

This realization makes me glance over at Cooper and Isabella. She's flirting with him. But that's very typical, from what I know about Isabella. She flirts with everyone.

But this… maybe goes a little beyond her normal tease routine. She plays with Cooper's dark hair, twisting those sexy waves up in her fingers as she looks him in the eyes and talks.

Cooper is smiling as she does this, listening attentively and gazing down on her with those electric-blue eyes like she's the center of his world. Laughing, even. Like they are very good friends.

Hmm. Maybe they are? Maybe they're dating? They're definitely doing something.

He glances around the room, checking progress of the new furniture arrangement, and then his eyes land on me and he instantly frowns.

I look away quickly and start removing the white tablecloth so I can take it in the back and start the laundry.

I'm just about to push my way through the kitchen doors when I hear "Cadee Hunter!" bellow through the room.

I stop, take a deep breath, and turn with a bright smile on my face. "How can I serve you, Your Highness?" I even curtsy.

Cooper is glaring at me. Then he beckons me with one curved finger, like I'm not worthy of speech, and leans in to Isabella's neck to whisper something. She laughs. Loudly. Smacks his shoulder playfully as I slowly cross the room towards them. Then he kisses her on the mouth, holding her face in his hands, and spanks her ass when she turns to go outside.

She squeals and skips a step, looking over her shoulder at him. He grins back at her, enjoying her playful reaction to his swat.

I roll my eyes.

But I shut that down quick when he turns to me and his gaze locks on. He folds his arms across his chest and I hold the tablecloth close to mine because his heated stare is no longer playful. It's mean and sends a chill up my spine, making my nipples bunch up in response.

"Yes, my king," I say, trying to sound… subservient.

I'm not sure I pull it off.

"Stand right here." Cooper points to the other side of him, next to the door that leads outside. "I'll be right back."

"O-*kay*," I mumble under my breath. He goes outside and I turn a little to watch.

"Hey, serving wench!"

I turn back around and look at the boys in the center of the room, then hate myself for looking. Because I just answered to the name 'serving wench'.

They laugh at this. Like I am the butt of their joke.

"Did Cooper Valcourt say anything about turning around and watching him?"

"Uhhh…" I'm not sure I answer to these boys. So I'm not sure if I should be rude or not.

But I don't have to answer, because Lars is suddenly in the center of the room, in front of the boy speaking. I recognize him as Ivan Turgenev. The Bully King of Prep. I've heard some stories about that boy over the years. He's far worse than Cooper ever was.

"Did I give you permission to talk, *cockling*?"

Cockling? I snort out a laugh. Haven't heard them called that before.

Ivan doesn't back down. "She's a fucking servant. I can talk to her any way I want."

Well, I guess we all know how he treats his family's house staff. I feel sorry for them.

Lars—not a guy known for using his fists the way Ax is—reaches down, grabs Ivan by the collar, and pulls him right out of that cushy loveseat and on his feet. "Did you just talk back to me, *boy*?"

Ut-oh. Lars is mad. He won't hit him. That's not Lars' style. But it is Ax's style. And everyone knows, if you fuck with one of them, you fuck with all three.

Even I know that.

I stifle a laugh. Because that can be interpreted in more than one way.

"Are you having fun here, *Cadee?*"

Cooper's words make me tingle all over, because his lips are right up to my ear and his deep voice enters my body as a low vibration.

I take a deep breath. "No, sir. I'm not."

He slides his body around mine and grabs my hips, tugging me close to his body. His hands slide down my ass and stay there, the heat from his touch so intense, I flush. "Well, that's too bad," he whispers. He licks his lips and my eyes dart down before I can stop them. I look up quickly. "But I think I can rectify the situation."

I gaze up at him, recalling another time we were this close to each other, so close I can see the swirls of green that outline his blue irises. He uttered those exact same words to me.

I think I can rectify the situation.

As if my *problem* at the time was a *situation* to be *rectified.*

I stiffen, tilt my chin up, and glare at him. "Don't do me any favors, *Christopher*."

He laughs and backs off, turning away from me.

Whatever was happening with Lars and Ivan, it's over now. Ivan is back in his seat and Lars is all the way across the room.

Every single set of male eyes is now one hundred percent on me.

Cooper throws something at Ivan, who catches it one-handed. It's a water balloon. And it breaks, spilling all over Ivan's lap. "What the fuck?" he says, standing up, his shirt and pants drenched. He looks down at himself, then back up at Cooper, glaring at him.

"Do not," Cooper says in a low growl, "talk to my servants without permission, you *fucking pleb*." Ivan opens his mouth to say something but Cooper beats him to it. "Do not look at my fucking servants without permission. Do not think about my fucking servants without permission. And if I ever"—he pauses—"*ever* catch you *touching* one of my fucking servants without permission, I will *ruin* you, Ivan."

Ivan's scowl disappears. "I didn't fucking touch her. I was joking."

Cooper looks back at me. "Did you think it was funny, *Fugling*?"

Fuck. I catch Victor's eye from across the room.

He's shaking his head at me. And I can practically hear the words in his mind. *Do not engage.*

"No," I say, straightening my back and lifting my chin. "I didn't find him funny at all."

Cooper's heated glare lingers on me and for a moment I think I catch the beginning of a smile. But it never really materializes. Then he's looking back at Ivan. "She doesn't think you're funny, Ivan. Do you want to try again?"

"What?" Ivan is confused.

And so am I.

"I said do you want to try again?"

"Am I supposed to make her laugh?"

"Do you *want* to make her laugh, Ivan?"

Jesus Christ. He's not trying to save me. Cooper Valcourt is *setting me up.*

"Uh…" Ivan chuckles. "Sure. I'll give it another try."

Cooper looks at Lars and growls, "Find me some rope."

CHAPTER SEVENTEEN

Lars snickers as he disappears into the kitchen. He knows what I'm going to do. And it is pretty funny. Cadee Hunter will laugh, no doubt about it.

I look over my shoulder at her. But she's not laughing yet.

She looks scared.

What could he possibly do to me with rope? I can read her mind.

Oh, Cadee. I can think of lots of fun things to do with rope.

This wasn't my original plan for her on opening day, but fuck it. That other one will hold until later. When she thinks the day is done and she made it through. That's when I'll spring my original plan on her.

If she makes it that far.

Lars returns with the rope and hands it to me.

"Thank you, Lars."

He grins. "Any time, Coop."

I turn back to Cadee. Hold up the rope. "You can walk out, you know. You have all the power here, Cadee. All you have to do is say, 'No, thank you' and get the fuck out of my face. *Forever.*"

She thinks about it. But I'm not surprised when she shakes her head no and whispers, "I'm not quitting."

I shrug. "Fine with me. But when you leave here today, leave here knowing that this was your choice. Your decision." I glare at her. "This is *you*. Giving *me* permission."

She frowns. Shakes her head again. "I can take it."

"Can you?" I laugh and turn to my pledges. "She can take it! So let's get the first show on the road. Ivan." I point at him. "Come stand right here." I beckon Cadee with a single finger. "You. Come stand right here." I point to the space between Ivan and me.

She barely hesitates. This is what I've always liked about Cadee Hunter. She's dumb. She knows what's coming and she obeys my commands anyway. Her eyes are even locked on mine the whole time she walks over to me. Still defiant.

I place my hands on her shoulders and turn her around so she has to face Ivan.

Ivan looks like he's about to bust his nut before this party even gets started. Fucking boys.

I lean down and press my lips up to Cadee's neck and whisper, "Put your hands behind your back."

She sucks in a deep breath, but complies.

I take her wrists and start tying the rope around them. Tight. She doesn't move. No one moves.

But then the door opens and Ax says, "OK, we're ready for you." We all look at him and he laughs. "Fuck them, this looks way more interesting." He leans against the door and folds his tatted-up arms across his chest.

I finish tying her wrists together and then lean down again to whisper, "Last chance, Cadee."

"Permission granted, my king."

Everyone laughs and starts talking.

"God, you're dumb." My whisper is lower now. Private. "You're not going to win."

She turns her head so I can look her in the eyes. They are a very light brown color. Almost amber. When she's angry, those eyes make her look like a demon. When she's sad, they make her look like a child. And when I've got my fingers between her legs and she's screaming out her climax, they make her look like a goddess. "I've already won," she whispers back. "All I have to do is limp across the finish line."

I slide my hands to her hips and kiss her neck. She sucks in a breath of air, not expecting this. I pull up her t-shirt just enough to show off her belly to Ivan and the others while I play with her nipples. I bite her earlobe and whisper, "Tell me to stop and it's over."

She shakes her head.

I slide the tips of my fingers up and down her ribs. It's a light, fluttery touch that sends chills through her body and the skin on her arms pricks up. The next time I touch her nipples, they are hard, tight bunched peaks.

She likes it, I realize. And why shouldn't she? I know how to turn this girl on. She told me exactly how she likes it. She spelled it all out for me back when she was just fifteen years old.

But when she actually moans a little, I pause for a moment, my eyes going to each of the other boys in the room. Lars looks concerned. He knows what I'm going to do. Ax looks excited. He knows too. Ivan looks like he's having a hard time keeping his hands to himself.

He meets my gaze and I caution him with a fierce look. "Follow my lead," I say loud enough for everyone to hear. "Understand me?"

Ivan nods. "Sure. Fine. Whatever."

"You may touch her, Ivan."

Cadee gasps a little.

"Is that a stop, I hear, Cadee? Ready to walk away now?"

She holds her breath and shakes her head. "No. I'm staying."

Ivan grins. They've all heard about what they do during summer rush. They have probably spent the last several years jerking off to the fantasy.

But they *don't* know. They don't have any idea. And not just because it's different every summer. The King makes the rules and plans the games. No two summer rushes are exactly alike. But because they think this is about sex the same way the girls think it's about money.

And summer rush isn't about either of those things.

It's about *power.*

And how they don't have any until it's bestowed upon them.

And if I have to be stuck here running this shit, I'm gonna make damn fucking sure I have fun.

I peek over Cadee's shoulder and watch Ivan's fingertips caress her stomach. I wish I could see her face. Lars has moved closer to get a better look, his hesitance nothing but fascination now.

I kiss Cadee's neck and massage one of her breasts. This makes her knees buckle a little. Like I make her *weak*.

Ivan takes a step forward, pressing his hips up to hers. He wants to kiss her. Even makes a move to try, but I turn Cadee's head and claim her lips for myself.

She kisses me back immediately and my cock grows in my pants.

That wasn't in the plan, but oh, well. I grind it against her ass as I play with her tongue, then slip my hand down her ribs, right past the waistband of her shorts, and find the wetness between her legs.

Ivan's hand follows mine and I pause, holding my breath for a moment. Because I want to stop him, but I want to leave it there too. And when I look at Lars, he's shaking his head at me.

I crossed a line there with Lars, so I pull Ivan's hand out and he doesn't protest, but his fingers are already wet.

The room is totally silent. Like… I'm pretty sure *everyone* is holding their breath.

"Are you laughing yet, Cadee?" I whisper these words past her lips as I kiss her.

She huffs. But she smiles too.

I stop kissing her and look at Ivan. He's… transfixed. I'm pretty sure this kid has never, *ever,* even in his wildest fucking fantasies, thought about sharing a girl like this in front of a whole room filled with men.

But after today, it will be all he thinks about.

All of them will jerk off tonight picturing themselves as me and Ivan with Cadee between us. I mean… isn't that why Ax, Lars, and I started the whole Cadee Hunter experiment back when we were seniors in Prep?

Because we heard about it?

And then we couldn't stop the fantasy?

I hate to break it to poor Ivan here. Hate to burst his little bubble, but this is just day one. He's not getting off that easy.

And neither is Cadee.

I pull my hands away from Cadee and step back. She looks over her shoulder at me, her eyes heavy for a moment. Then she squints them. Questioning what I'm doing. Wondering why I'm no longer touching her.

I point to my pledges one at a time. Michael, Dante, Roland, and Jamie. Then I say, "You also have my permission to touch her."

Cadee gasps, squirming a little in Ivan's embrace. Both Lars and Ax are on either side of her as the other boys step forward, grinning and laughing with excitement. All of them are hard beneath their shorts. Dante is even grabbing himself.

I slip back up behind Cadee and start tracing the back of my fingers up and down her ribs. Her shirt is up to her neck, her breasts round and firm and her nipples hard from all the hands on her. But they're gentle hands. Because I am gentle. And I set the standard. The King always sets the standard.

I lean into her ear one more time. "Last chance to walk away, Cades." Fuck. That nickname just slipped out. "*Cadee.*" I correct myself. "Say stop and we stop. Say nothing and this goes on until it's over."

She says nothing.

"You're so *stupid*," I whisper as I slip my fingers into her hair and wind it up in my fist. I tug on it. Not hard, or the boys might get the wrong idea. "Why are you doing this?"

She stretches her long, slender neck, her soft cheek right up next to my scruffy one. She looks me in the eye and says, "Why are *you* doing this?"

I'm instantly angry. "Because I belong here," I growl. "And you *don't*."

She lets her cheek move away, releasing me. And instead, she presses it up to Dante's neck, urging him to pick up where I left off.

They kiss.

And I *rage* inside.

Calm down, Cooper. She's playing you.

And she's not allowed to play. She's just a pawn.

Remind her of that fact.

Oh, I plan on it. The fun is just getting started.

We've made her feel good—that's for sure.

But we haven't made her *laugh* yet.

I poke her pit with one stiff fingertip and she squirms and giggles. I do it again, and this time she tries to get away. "Hold her, Ivan."

He looks confused for a moment, but then nods and holds her still.

I poke her again and again. In the ribs, in the pits. Dante starts making grabs at her knees. She buckles, laughing hysterically, squirming, and writhing, and wriggling as poky fingers come at her from all directions and make her jerk and squeal until she finally just collapses on the ground.

They don't stop. They keep going. Grabbing at her ribs now, her armpits, her knees, over, and over, and over again.

She's not laughing anymore. She's screaming. Her legs kicking. Her back twisting. Her hands tied behind her back. Helpless.

And then she's crying. Sobbing.

Ax is sitting on one of the loveseats with his hand in his pants, jerking off. Lars is leaning up against the wall, arms folded across his chest, wearing a frown.

I bend down and grab Cadee's hair, make her look at me as they tickle her. "Say stop, Cadee. Say stop and walk away and that's exactly what will happen."

She manages to spit at me. "Fuck you." It hits me on the lips and I wipe it away and just watch her cry as they torture her with tickling.

I just. *Watch.*

It only takes another minute before she loses control and pisses herself, the dark stain spreading between her legs.

"What the actual motherfucking *fuck* is going on in here?"

Everything stops—the poking, the wriggling, the laughing, the jerking, the frowning, the watching... and then the only noise left in the Glass House as we all turn to look at Mona Monroe standing in the doorway is the sound of Cadee Hunter's jerky *sobs.*

"Fuck you," Dante says to Mona. "This is none of your business." He leans down and puts his mouth on Cadee's nipple, greedily grabbing at her breasts.

Cadee doesn't move. She just cries on the floor, tears streaming down her already stained cheeks, great heaving, blubbering moans coming out of her mouth.

But Ax does move. He's up from the loveseat, his foot pulling back—and then he's kicking the living fuck out of Dante Legosi. He pulls him up off the floor, screaming at him. "Did we tell you to suck her fucking tits? Did we give you permission to put your mouth on our Fugling?"

Ax throws Dante down on the floor, sits on his chest, and starts pummeling his face with both fists.

"You," Mona roars, "are a bunch of sick fucks!"

Ax is still screaming at Dante. Dante has his hands up to his face.

"Shut up, Mona. Go back outside and wait for us. You're next." Then I pull Ax off of Dante and point a finger in his face as he backs up. "Calm down, Ax. Right now."

Then I turn to look at Mona. Wait for her to tell me to fuck off.

She wants to. Oh, hell, yeah, she wants to.

But she knows what that means. She will be the next target.

We all know Mona doesn't want to be here. Would do just about anything *not* to be here. But Mona *is* here.

And that means she *has* to be here.

She was *put* here.

She can't quit.

I don't know what will happen to her if she doesn't cooperate, but it must be something pretty bad if she showed up to play the game in the first place.

She turns her head away and leaves.

Slamming the door behind her so hard, the whole Glass House *trembles*.

CHAPTER EIGHTEEN

I just lie on the floor while the boys file out of the Glass House. I do not move. Not one inch.

I pissed myself. But it's OK. That's why I packed extra clothes. I was ready for them.

Regardless, the tears don't stop streaming down my face even though I'm not actually crying anymore.

The door slams and the room goes quiet.

"Cadee?" Victor appears. "Are you OK?"

I take a deep breath, let it out slowly, and nod. "I will be. It was tickling. That's all."

"That's not all it was and you know it. They were touching you. Dante—" He grits his teeth and stares out the window.

"Well, I gave them permission. Several times. And Ax made Dante pay for breaking the rules."

"So?" Victor is pissed. I just look away and stare

out at the forest beyond the glass walls, embarrassed. "That doesn't mean anything. He wasn't mad because Dante was violating you, Cadee. He was angry because—" But he stops. I look back at Victor and find him staring at the door.

My head turns to see what he's looking at.

Or not what. Who.

"Because why, Victor?" Ax sneers Victor's name like he just bit into a rotten piece of fruit.

Then he crosses the room and stands just inches from my head. "Tell me why, Victor." And now he's snarling.

"Because you're jealous," I say.

Ax's guffaw bounces off the ceiling, that's how loud it is. "Jealous? Go back to work, Victor. Or you're gonna find yourself owing a whole lot of back tuition money when you lose your scholarship."

Victor takes a deep breath. But he doesn't look at me. And he doesn't talk back. He just turns on his heel and walks back to the kitchen.

It makes me sick the way these Kings think they own the world.

But Victor makes me sick too. Because he's too weak to fight back and he's a six-foot-tall man, for fuck's sake. He has shoulders just as wide as Ax's. He could at least… *try*.

Ax bends down, rolls me onto my side, cuts the rope tying my hands together, and then steps back. "Get up, Cadee. Cooper wants you outside."

"Why?"

Ax steps around to where Victor was standing and offers me his hand. I stare at it for a moment, then look up and meet his eyes.

He's breathing heavy. And I'm not sure if that's because he's still riled up over the fight with Dante or because I'm the focus of his anger now. "Take my fucking hand, Cadee."

I take it. And he pulls me to my feet in one swift motion.

Then he looks outside real quick as he absently straightens my shirt. "Don't worry about Dante. I'm going to take care of it."

"Don't do me any favors, Ax. I'm a big girl. I know what I'm doing."

His eyes track down my body and then rest on the dark wet spot between my legs. "Yeah." He laughs. "I can tell." He looks back up and I meet his gaze. "Just… leave, Cadee." He says it softly, almost pleading with me. "You don't belong here."

"Why don't I belong here, Ax? Because you say I don't? Because you, and Cooper, and Lars are the Kings? You're not kings, Ax. You're just a bunch of bullies. And I am not a victim, OK? I'm *not.* A victim."

He grabs my shoulders and shakes me. "Listen to me. You don't *want* to belong here. There is nothing at High Court for you."

"Says you."

He closes his eyes and grinds his teeth, making the muscles in his jaw tighten and relax. "You're not listening to me."

"I don't need your advice, OK? Just fuck off." I bring my hands up between his arms and crash my wrists against his, breaking his hold on me.

Then I walk away and go outside to see what fresh hell is waiting for me out at the pool.

I step into the hot sunshine and shield my eyes, looking for Cooper or Lars. I find Cooper first, and he points to the outdoor kitchen under a thatched-roof hut. I walk that way and for a minute I figure they're going to have me cook them something. Which sounds tolerable. I can handle myself in a kitchen. It'll keep me busy and—

"*Cadee,*" Cooper says, grabbing my arms as he enters the kitchen space. He drags me over to the sink and points to a pile of plastic bags filled with balloons. "Fill these up."

"Yes, Your Highness."

"Shut the fuck up."

"What?" I look at him and see the rage on his face.

"It's only gonna get worse."

"Yep. Pretty much everyone has made that very clear."

"I won't be able to protect you every time."

"Protect me?" Now I guffaw. Just like Ax did inside. "Is that what you think you're doing?"

He breathes hard and heavy for a few moments. Just *glaring* at me with *hate*. Then he whispers, "It was the best solution at the time."

"Is that right? The very best one, huh?"

"Did you want to have that baby?"

I point my finger up at his face and my words come out through clenched teeth. "Don't you dare talk about that baby. Ever."

"I did what I had to."

"You're a fucking coward."

"You're a fucking bitch. All you want to do is blame someone and I'm convenient. And that makes you a bitch. Because you refuse to see that I *helped* you."

"Helped me?" I literally snort. "Did you just say you helped me?"

"What are we talking about?" Cooper and I both turn at the same time and find Isabella standing behind us. "Hmm? Looks like a pretty heated argument from over here."

"Isabella, go back to the pool. This is private."

Isabella does not go back to the pool. She hooks her arm in mine and says, "The Fugling belongs to me. So either you fill me in on what this little argument is about, or I'll just take her off your hands so you can cool down and relax."

"She disobeyed me," Cooper says.

Isabella tsks her tongue. "Fugling, you should apologize to your King." Then she pats my hand. "You're not allowed to disobey, sweetie. So get down on your knees and kiss his feet—every single one of those sexy toes." She giggles and waggles her eyebrows at Cooper. "Remember that time we—"

"Shut up, Isabella." Cooper looks at me. "Kiss my feet, Cadee. And then get to work."

"Fug. Ling. How many times do I have to remind you, Christopher?"

I wince. I know I called him Christopher earlier, but he hates that name. And I was doing it to pick a fight.

So Isabella is also trying to pick a fight.

I lower myself to my knees in front of Cooper and

settle on the hard, slate floor. Then I lean my head down and kiss his toes. One at a time.

And when I'm done, I look up at him. He says nothing. Just stares at me.

"Good job, Fugling," Isabella says. "Get up now. Up. Up."

I stand up and direct my gaze to her instead of him. Because Cooper Valcourt was just looking at me the way he used to.

And Isabella saw it.

I don't know what they are to each other, but it's definitely more than nothing. And I don't need her getting the wrong idea. Or hell, the right idea, either.

She can't know my secret.

No one can know my secret. It's bad enough that Cooper knows. I wish I had never told him. Life would've been so much easier.

"Fill up the water balloons, Fugling," Cooper sneers. And then he walks away.

Isabella gaze follows him and so does mine. He whips his t-shirt up over his head and then dives into the pool.

"Mona told me what happened inside, Fugling."

I look at her and wait.

"It's only going to get worse."

I nod.

"You should leave while you still have a chance."

"I'm not leaving."

She sighs, but it's a bored one. "Suit yourself, Fugling. But just in case you haven't figured it out yet, Cadee"—she slides her mirrored sunglasses down her face and I get a little lost in my own pathetic reflection during her dramatic pause—"no matter how hard you wish, or pray, or hope… things *never* get better."

Then she turns and walks away.

"What?" I whisper.

She doesn't turn back. Just walks over to the pool where Cooper is and sits down on the edge to dangle her feet.

Cooper's gaze immediately tracks to me. Then he grins, places his hands on either side of Isabella's hips, pulls himself up from the water, and kisses her on the lips.

Like I care, Cooper

I'm not jealous of Isabella.

Oh, sure. She's beautiful. She's got the long blonde hair and green eyes. Her body is perfect, she has good taste in shoes, and she lives in one of the lake mansions.

On the outside, Isabella's life looks pretty sweet.

But there's something wrong with her.

Sometimes she doesn't make any sense. And that

last sentence is one example. Because I get it. She just warned me that things were going to get worse.

But I don't think she was talking about me. No. She was the one wishing, and praying, and hoping for things to get better. Not me.

"Get back to work, Fugling!"

Cooper's yell snaps me out of my introspection and I realize I was staring at them while I was thinking about Isabella.

I flip him off, then turn my back and do as I'm told.

I spend the next several hours filling up water balloons and by the time anyone comes over to check on my progress, it's late afternoon, I didn't get a lunch, and I have amassed a small arsenal of water balloon grenades in two giant plastic tubs.

The person who comes to check on me is Mona. She lingers at the small concrete table to my left, silent.

"What?" I snap.

"Wonder what these are for? Oh, I know. The wet t-shirt contest."

I glance at her and roll my eyes. "Figures."

“Right?” She pulls a smoke out of her wild hair and a lighter from her bra and lights it, taking a long, deep draw before blowing out. She’s the only one who isn’t wearing a bikini. She’s wearing coveralls cut into shorts with a white t-shirt over it—all the girls are wearing white t-shirts now.

Just like me.

And all of them have something derogatory written across the front in black marker. Ax’s handiwork. I can tell by the sloppy writing.

While mine says ‘Call me Fugling,’ Mona’s says ‘Call me Bitch Face.’ But the ‘Bitch Face’ part has been scratched out in red marker and an arrow has been added pointing to new words so it reads, ‘Call me anything other than Mona, and I will rip your balls off and stuff them down your throat.’

I laugh unexpectedly when I read that.

Mona chuckles too. Even though the cigarette is hanging between her lips. She takes another drag and blows it out. “I feel for ya, Fugling. You should just leave.”

“Jesus Christ,” I mutter. “I’m tired of hearing that. I’m not leaving.”

“Well.” Mona sighs, watching the other pledges as they sit around under thatched-roof cabañas playing Crimes Against Humanity or whatever it’s called. “If I could leave, I'd be gone." Then she directs her gaze to me and lifts up her sunglasses so I can see her very bloodshot eyes. "And when you get to the end of the summer—and you will, Cadee. You will get there. Because you're one of those determined go-getters, I can tell—you're gonna wish you could go back and walk away when you had the chance. Because it really won't get better."

"Do you need something, Mona?"

"Nope. Just… visiting."

"Well, I'm busy here. So…"

"Right. Water balloons. I can't *wait* to see how this ends." Then she laughs, gets up, and walks away.

"Line up!" Selina is clapping her hands at the girls. "Come on! It's time to get down to business!"

It's four thirty in the afternoon. They've been doing nothing all day except playing at the pool like spoiled rich assholes, and now it's time to get down to business?

I watch Valentina approach Mona and they have an argument. I can't hear the exact words, because they are doing the whole whisper-fight thing. But after a few minutes Mona whips her t-shirt over her head, unfastens her coverall clasps, and drops them to the ground. She's wearing a black bikini underneath. But that's when things really get interesting. Because all the girls start taking off their shirts. They have their backs turned to me, and the boys, since they are off to my left, so no one gets a peek at anything. But instead of staying that way, they each remove their bikini tops and pull their white t-shirts back on.

Ah. Mona was right. Wet t-shirt contest.

Have fun, pledges.

I glance at the boys and find them leering at the show across the pool, eager to see what comes next.

Part of me is happy that the girls are going to get their due. I got mine. They should get theirs.

But the girls didn't do anything to me this morning. The boys did. And it doesn't appear that they have to do anything to win this game.

How's that fair?

"Cadee!" Cooper calls. Then he winces. "Fugling!" he corrects himself before Isabella can yell at him. "Bring the water balloons over here."

I dry my hands on my shorts and go to pick up one of the tubs and then fall backwards right on my ass, because that fucking thing is heavy!

Everyone laughs at me. But I don't care. I get up

and try again. But I literally cannot lift this stupid tub.

"I'll get it," Lars says. He jogs over to me. "Step back, Cadee. You're never going to be able to carry them."

I always did like Lars. He's definitely the nicest of the three. "Thanks," I mumble.

But he doesn't look at me. Just walks off and sets the tub down in front of the girls. Then he comes back and takes the other tub. "Come with me."

I follow him, even when he veers off to the right to set the tub down in front of the boys. But Cooper's strong hand darts out to grab my shoulder.

"Ow," I say, turning on him. "What do you want?"

He narrows his eyes at me. Points to the ground at the top of the deep end. "Stand right here and do not move."

"Whatever," I mumble.

"Hear ye, hear ye!" Ax says, his town crier act back for the grand finale. He didn't swim today. Didn't even take off his shirt. He's still wearing his Docs, his stupid wallet chain, and his army-colored cargo shorts. "We have a sinner amongst us! A sinner who needs to be taught a lesson in the town square!" And he looks over his shoulder at me with a twinkle in his eyes.

"Shit," I mumble.

Cooper is standing next to me. His arms crossed across his bare, muscular chest. And when I glance up at him, he's grinning.

Ax points to me. "Sin-*ner*! Sin-*ner*! Sin-*ner*!" he chants. And then they are all yelling. He works them up into a frenzy, until their chant is the only thing I hear. Then he suddenly bellows, "*Punish her*!"

That's when I realize there's only one girl in this wet t-shirt contest. And it's me.

They start throwing the water balloons at me, yelling and screaming like this is the best game ever.

The girls mostly miss. I'm silently thanking my lucky stars that Valentina isn't taking part in the battle. Because she *can* throw. She played baseball with the boys as a teenager.

Mona gets a thigh shot in—and yeah, that hurts. But the rest can't throw far enough to cover the distance. They splat at my feet or in the pool in front of me.

But the boys.

Those boys *can* throw.

And they hit me. Every. Single. Time.

CHAPTER NINETEEN

Lars, Ax, and I stand to the side and just watch them pelt Cadee Hunter with the water balloons. Some of the guys—Dante in particular—are taking this hazing incident very seriously.

"It's just water," Ax says.

"Yeah, right," Lars says.

My eyes slide over to Lars. "We're only on day two, dude. Better fucking suck it up if you want to make it to the end of summer."

Ax sighs. "I want to beat the fuck out of Dante."

"You kinda already did," I say.

"He's got more coming."

"Ooooooh." Lars winces and looks away. "That one hurt."

"All she has to do is cry," I say. "She cries, they'll stop. I gave them the orders before they started."

Besides. I like the way I can see Cadee Hunter's

nipples through her soaked white t-shirt. And I'm gonna enjoy that for a moment. It's the first almost pleasant thing about this day. Even if she is getting pelted with water balloons.

Lars sighs. "OK. I think I see a tear." He puts two fingers in his mouth and a sharp whistle makes all the pledges stop and look at us.

Ax jumps into action and paces up and down the side of the pool deck in his boots, his wallet chain banging against his leg. "Thank you, pledges! Congrats on a great opening day! Your King has some words for you, so listen the fuck up!"

"Girls," I say. "Goodbye. You are dismissed."

"Hold on, hold on!" Isabella steps out from under her thatched-roof cabaña. "Mandatory meeting tonight, ladies. Meet me at the dock immediately."

"What?" they all complain. "Why?"

Isabella lifts up her chin. "I do not repeat myself. Grab your shit and meet me at the dock immediately."

They grumble, but get busy picking up their crap and then wander down the path in the woods towards the lake.

Then I turn to the boys. I cross my arms over my chest and stare them up and down as I walk towards their side of the deck. "We had two incidents today that require consequences." I lock eyes with Dante.

He shakes his head at me. "It's no big deal."

"Maybe it is. Maybe it isn't. It doesn't matter. You have a mean side, Dante."

He shuffles his feet.

"And that's why I'm promoting you to lead. You're in charge."

All the boys look stunned.

Dante is a little dick about his new status. Because he immediately starts yelling, "Yeah! Fuck, yeah!" And I make a note of that.

Lars comes up behind me. He shuts up and doesn't say anything because I'm not done talking yet. But I can already tell he's gonna have a lot to say about this decision.

"And tomorrow," I continue, "you all understand what you need to bring with you to participate in the first challenge?"

They nod.

"Cash," Ax growls. "I don't give a fuck how you get it, you bring it in cash. We do not accept credit cards, money orders, cashier's checks, gold, or gemstones." He shoots them his trademark evil grin. "I hope you know the combination to your daddy's safe."

They grin at each other like idiots. Of course they do.

We'll see.

"That's it then. See you tomorrow." Then I look over toward Cadee. "Where the hell did Cadee go?"

"I dunno," Lars says. "But what the fuck, Coop? Why would you make Dante the lead?"

"Because what he did so far isn't enough, Lars. We need to get rid of him. He's dangerous." I look Lars in the eyes. "Give that kid a little power and he'll hang himself. That way we can cut him and his family won't have shit to say about it. Now where the fuck did Cadee go? I have to take her across the lake to her cottage."

"Why?" Ax laughs.

"Because my father gave it to her to live in this summer and she doesn't have a fucking boat. So he made me her new… driver." Isabella was pissed about that when I told her earlier.

"Oh, that's funny," Ax says.

"You guys want to come with me?"

Ax looks at the woods in the direction of his house. "Sure. I'll go."

"Lars?"

Lars shrugs. "I guess."

"Lars," I say. "It's not my fault she wants to stick around. How many more ways can we say it? She's being a total fucking bitch about this. I'm starting to think we should tell her we *want* her to stay, because then she'd leave just to spite us."

"That's kind of a good idea." Ax points to the Glass House. "There she is."

We all follow his finger and find Cadee in the glass house. I nod. "OK. You guys go ahead. I'll meet you at the boat. I'm gonna make sure she knows I'm waiting for her. Meet you there in ten."

They turn and start walking towards the woods. Lars grabs his t-shirt off a chair as he passes and tugs it over his head. Ax kicks rocks like a kid.

I wait until they're out of sight, then go inside the Glass House and interrupt a conversation between Victor and Cadee. I glare at him with narrowed eyes. "Good night, Victor."

He locks eyes with me for a moment, like maybe he's thinking about talking back. But he's a pussy. And in the end, he just mumbles, "Goodbye," to Cadee and walks out the door carrying his pack.

Cadee doesn't look at me. She's sitting at the dining table, lacing up her red sneaker. She's changed her clothes. But she was sitting in those soiled shorts all damn day. She never said a word. Not one complaint.

"What do you want?" And she doesn't look at me when she asks her question.

"I'm taking you across the lake, remember?"

Now she does look up. "Oh. I forgot about that." Then she brightens.

"Cadee—"

"No." She puts up a hand. "I'll take your ride because I want to sleep in my own place tonight and forget about you, and these people you call friends, and this fucked-up summer rush. But you do not get to talk to me."

I sigh and clench my jaw. That's fair, I guess.

"Let's go then."

I head towards the door and hold it open for her. She walks through, sneering at me, huffing out a little air of contempt for good measure. But my eyes track down to her nipples poking against her t-shirt.

She didn't put her bra back on.

Did she do that on purpose? To tease me? Because her nipples are clearly still very hard. And her tits are nice and round. Big enough to bounce a little with each step.

Jesus Christ. I need to get laid or something. Stop thinking about her. Cadee Hunter was the worst thing to ever happen to me and right now, I wish we had just left her alone that year. Just kept on pretending she didn't exist.

But that was never going to happen. We were

obsessed with her during senior year of Prep. We stalked her. Relentlessly. We made her do Ax's homework. We made her into our little bitch. We yelled at her, and humiliated her, and pushed her.

We were always pushing her.

It was touching at first. Then kissing. Then… more. A lot more.

And she never said no.

By the end of first semester we had even settled in. It was a routine by Christmas. And New Year's Eve was downright fun.

Until it wasn't.

I sigh. But if Cadee notices, she doesn't say anything.

It's just a long silent walk.

But then I spy my father. A few moments later my brothers and their wives come out of the mansion. They laugh and linger in the driveway as Cadee and I come out of the woods.

I pull her aside. "Stay here." I point my finger at her. "You understand me?"

She swats it away, scowling.

"Don't move."

I walk out of the woods and greet my brothers and father in the driveway. "What's going on?"

Dane is shoving shit in the back of the limo as the

wives get inside. Tennis racket, duffle bag, backpack. "Vacay, man."

"What? All of you?"

My oldest brother, Jack, comes up to me and claps me on the shoulder. "I heard you drew the short stick." He shoots me a lopsided grin. Jack and I have always been close. "Sorry, man."

"Where are you guys going?"

My father walks up. "Bali."

"Bali. And I have to stay here? What the hell, Dad?"

"You're in charge of rush, *Christopher*."

Shit. I should've called him Father. Now he thinks I just did that on purpose.

"Better luck next summer," Dane says. Then pulls the limo door closed.

He's such a dick.

But my father is already climbing in the other side. Only Jack pauses. He leans his hands on the roof of the car and sighs. "Sorry, man. But you know there'll be a next time. Plus side—you have the entire house to yourself for six weeks."

"Six weeks! Are you fucking—"

"Have fun!" Jack disappears inside and then the limo pulls forward through our circular driveway. And five seconds later, they're gone.

Didn't even look back.

Cadee comes out of the woods. I expect her to say something, but she just walks right past me and heads towards the boat. And I'm kinda grateful for her shunning right now.

I follow. What choice do I have? She's already climbing in when I arrive at the boat slip. Lars is kicking back on the bench seat and Ax has claimed his chair on the port side.

Which means Cadee will have to sit in front with me.

Or… not. She walks straight over to Lars and he smiles at her and pulls his legs up.

She sits down on the opposite end and they tangle their legs together just like the old days. Like three years haven't passed. Like nothing happened.

Lars always did like Cadee the most. And in his mind, nothing did happen. He doesn't know about the abortion. He wasn't the one who made all the arrangements and drove her to the clinic. He wasn't the one who had to lie about all of it.

So of course, he still likes her. At least a little. Enough for me to know he's not on board with the whole Fugling thing. Maybe she's counting on that? Or maybe he's planning something else? Maybe he's thinking about a little reunion?

I catch them laughing as we head out. Like they're sharing a fantastic joke.

"Hey," I call back to them over my shoulder. "I figured you'd had enough laughing for one day, Cadee. But if you need more, I can arrange for it to happen again tomorrow."

"Cooper, shut the fuck up," Lars yells back. "Her day is over. She's allowed to fucking relax."

"Fuck you both," I mutter as I step aboard and take the driver's seat.

And then I slide my sunglasses down my face and head across the lake.

By the time I ease the boat into my personal slip at the college marina and turn off the engine, the sun is behind the tall trees, casting this part of campus in dark shadows, even though it won't set for another hour or two.

Cadee is already hopping off the boat, eager to be away from us. Lars hops out too and catches up with her.

Ax walks over to me. "What do you think that's about?"

I stare at Cadee and Lars. They are talking. I can tell because they glance over at each other every few seconds as they walk. "I dunno. But he needs to rein it in. We're not getting involved with her. We're getting rid of her."

Ax and I follow behind Lars and Cadee. It's kind of a long walk over to the little cottage she used to live in years ago. And it's in the woods, a good way off from the school buildings. So they flash in and out of sight as they walk the narrow dirt path that ends at a small pond.

We can hear the music from a pretty good distance away, but it's still a shock to see the cottage lit up and dozens of summer students standing near a line of kegs.

"Hell, yeah," Ax says, jogging ahead. He passes by Lars and Cadee, both of whom have stopped on the edge of the clearing to gape at the scene before us.

"What the fuck?" I whisper.

There has to be more than a hundred people here. The little swimming hole is packed. There's a volleyball net set up and a game going on in the fading sunlight. A loud clinking sound makes me turn my head to find a game of drunken horseshoes in progress. And—

"Is that a croquet setup?" Lars laughs.

"What the hell is going on here?" Cadee whirls on

me. "You did this, didn't you? Just so I wouldn't have a place to call home! You are such an asshole, Cooper Valcourt. I hate your ugly guts!"

She stomps off and neither Lars nor I make a move to go after her.

He stands next to me. "Did you do this, Cooper?"

"No, I didn't do this. When would I have time to plan a party today?"

Lars sighs. "It looks like it's been going on all day."

He's right. Someone didn't just throw this together. There's a catering table, for fuck's sake.

Then I see *Isabella*. Lars sees her at the same time and points. "She did this."

I can't say I don't agree. Her and her pledges are all sitting in a circle of Adirondack chairs in front of a small campfire, chatting and laughing, their faces bright from the fire and glowing from the sun today. They're still wearing their derogatory white t-shirts that Ax made. Like a badge or something. Clearly not fazed by his attempts to shame and humiliate them.

And why should they be? It's a joke to them. They don't take it seriously. It's just part of the game.

"Fuck it," Lars says. "I'm staying with Ax. You coming, Cooper?"

I look over my shoulder to see if Cadee's around. She's not. So I'm just about to say yes when I sigh.

"Nah. I'm going home. You guys can find a way across the lake when you're done, right?"

"If we don't show up for rush tomorrow, you know where to find us." Then he walks off, calling for Ax to grab him a beer.

I turn back to the woods and head towards the boat. Surely, Cadee will be there. Where else could she go?

But when I get there, she's not.

Fuck it. I jump in, take a seat, and I'm just about to turn the key and take off without her when I stop and just lean back in my chair to pause for a moment. And think.

I don't know how long I sit like that, but it's very dark and the stars are out when I hear a voice behind me say, "Why didn't you stay at the party?"

Cadee. I don't turn to look at her. Just keep my eyes trained on the sky. "I'm tired, Cadee."

She rocks the boat a little when she steps in. And then she slips into the passenger seat to my left. "Me too, Cooper."

"I get it," I say, still not looking at her. "I do. I understand that you've been dealt a shit hand and you're pretty far in the hole right now. But my life isn't fun. It isn't…"

I stop. It's stupid to even try to explain. No one

gets it. I am Christopher Valcourt. What could possibly be wrong with my life?

Cadee doesn't say anything. But from the corner of my eye I watch her bring one leg up and prop her head on her knee. She's got her body angled towards the center of the boat. Like she wants to have a conversation or something. Or maybe she's just… listening.

I turn my head without picking it up from the back of my seat and stare at her. "You know I didn't mean any of that shit today."

"Do I know that?"

I stare at her for a little bit, even smile. Because I *like* Cadee Hunter. I have always liked Cadee Hunter. I have known this girl my whole life. And that's not just a throwaway expression. It's the God's honest truth. We never ran in the same circles—hell, she never had a circle other than her parents. But all growing up she was always there. On the edge of things. Like a sweet mystery. Or a promise of something better beyond the tall walls of High Court and past the dark forest of trees surrounding us.

But she's bad luck or something. Terrible things happen when we're together. We fight. We get angry. We upset the normal fabric of society here at High Court and change the world when we're together. And change here is never a good idea. People hate it. Because if things change, then we'd all have to admit that we're not safe.

And doesn't everyone want to feel safe?

"I didn't plan that party, Cadee."

"I know."

"Then why did you blame me?"

"Because whenever something bad happens to me, you're always there. You're always the reason."

"I could say the same for you. I could put it all on you too. And I don't."

"Yes, you do."

"I don't say it to your face."

"Yeah, that's your problem. You just say it behind my back."

I sigh and look back up at the stars. "Well, where are you going to sleep tonight?"

She doesn't say anything for a few moments. Like she's considering her options. Which is stupid. She doesn't have any options. "I think I'll stay at Ax's boathouse."

"What?" I actually laugh.

"Yeah. He stays there, I think."

"What?" This time I don't laugh. I sit up in my seat and turn to her. "What do you mean?"

"I caught him in there the other night. There was

a sleeping bag. And a little lantern and some junk food. That's where I slept that first night when you were fucking Isabella in the hallway outside my room—"

"I didn't fuck her. We were just—"

"I have zero feelings about what you do with Isabella."

"It's not what you think."

"I don't think anything."

"Well, obviously you do. Because you ran out of your room and didn't come back."

"Why do you care?"

"Because regardless of what you think, I don't hate you."

"You've told me you hate me so many times, Cooper, it's become cliché."

I let out a long breath of frustration. "I like you. You know I like you."

"Well, you have a very… *interesting* way of showing it."

"It's just a game."

"Well, I don't want to play."

"Neither do I."

It's her turn to exhale loudly. "You go along though, don't you?"

"What choice do I have?"

She shrugs. "Walk out. That's what I'm gonna

do."

"You could've walked out plenty of times today and you didn't."

She snorts. "Well, I'm not gonna walk out *now*."

"Why? Because we're all telling you to and you don't want to do what you're told? That's stupid."

"It's not stupid. It's smart. For some reason, your father has taken an interest in my wellbeing—"

I laugh so loud she pulls back in surprise. "Don't fool yourself. He doesn't care about you. He's using you!"

"For what?"

"How the fuck should I know? If I knew what my father's plan in life was, I'd do something about all this shit."

"Just like you did something about it three years ago?"

"That's not fair and you know it. It was the only option we had."

"The only one?" She sits up straight now too, her voice louder. "That was the only option you could think of?"

"Fuck you. I did my best."

"Yeah, fuck you too."

We sit in silence for a while after that, thinking about what happened three years ago. She starts to sniffle. Like she's crying. And I want to say all the right things and make her stop, but I don't have any clue what those right things might be.

"Do you want me to drop you off at Ax's boathouse then?"

She turns her back to me and pulls both legs up to her chest, hugging herself.

There's a long stretch of silence after that. So long, I hear some of the partygoers coming towards the marina so they can head home for the night.

"Everyone's gone at my house. They went to Bali."

"Good for them," she whispers. "Must be nice."

"Yeah," I agree, then sigh. "So I'm gonna take you home, and you're gonna sleep in your room. And then tomorrow, Cadee? You're going to stay there. All day. You're gonna eat junk food, and watch TV, and play video games—"

She laughs. Loudly. "Video games?"

"I don't know. Whatever the fuck you like to do. Read books or something. But you are not gonna go out to the Glass House. Do you understand me?"

She doesn't say anything. And I take that as a good sign.

"If you need money, I'll have some tomorrow—"

"I don't need money." She turns to look at me.

"Your father gave me a check for two hundred and seventy-five thousand dollars."

"What?" I just blink at her. "When?"

"That first night."

I can't process this. I'm dumbfounded picturing all that shit she went through for the past two days. All that humiliation. All that… meanness. From all of us. "Then why didn't you just… leave? Why are you doing this? You don't need the scholarship. Hell, you don't need this school, Cadee. If I wasn't forced to go here, do you think I would?"

"You say that because you have choices."

"I don't have choices!" I laugh. And it's a real one too. Because this is so funny. "I have zero choices, Cades."

She looks at me when the nickname I gave her all those years ago slips out. "Don't do that, Cooper. Please. Just… don't."

I stare at her. And then, without thinking, I say, "You make me sad."

She huffs. "Right back at ya, Cooper."

"Will you go home with me tonight? And stay home tomorrow?"

She doesn't answer me.

"Cadee, it only gets worse."

"So I've been told."

"And regardless of what you think, I'm not in charge of anything. It's just a job I was ordered to do. And even though I don't want to do it, I have to. Because if the wrong people get through into Fang and Feather, bad things will happen."

"Well, that's not cryptic. You're very dramatic tonight, Coop."

I shake my head at her. "You don't get to call me Coop if I don't get to call you Cades."

"Fine with me."

I throw up my hands. "I give up. You win. Do whatever you want. It's none of my business. But if you show up tomorrow, expect the worst, Cadee. Because that's exactly what's going to happen."

And then I start the boat, ease out of the slip, and take us back across the lake.

CHAPTER TWENTY

Cooper and I don't talk as he drives us back across the lake. I don't even look at him, so I'm not sure if he looks at me. But I get the feeling he's done.

Done with me. Done with rush. Done with Fang and Feather. Maybe even done with this life at High Court.

Right.

None of them ever walk away. Plenty of them bitch about their stupid, worthless, pointless lives. Lots of them, actually. But they don't walk away.

Cooper's question was legit though. I have money. I can leave. I could start a whole new life in a whole new place. Forget all the bad things ever happened. Be an entirely different person.

But why should I have to leave my home?

If his father is using me—and let's be real here for

a moment, I know what that check really was. Hush money—what does he want me to be quiet about? Why does he feel the need to pay me off?

There's only one thing I can think of. The pregnancy and subsequent abortion.

And this just pisses me off.

Because they all get to pretend it never happened. And it didn't. Not really. Because it didn't happen to them. It happened to me.

I didn't walk away today because my truth matters.

I'm not sure I really understand how this all relates back to the Glass House, or the secret society thing they have going in that tomb in the woods, or the scholarship. Especially the scholarship, because if the Chairman wants me to walk away and never come back, why bother offering me this opportunity?

Why offer me a brighter future if he's just planning on ripping it away from me in the end? Is he just cruel?

From the way Cooper talks about him, he is. But how would I know? And don't most of these rich kids have complicated relationships with their parents? I mean, Ax is sleeping in the boathouse, for fuck's sake.

Cooper eases the boat into the slip and cuts the engine.

We look at each other for a second. Then he says,

"Just say you'll think about it, Cadee."

"Think about what? Quitting?" I scoff. "I'm not quitting."

"Why?" He's pleading with me now. "Tell me what you need, Cades. And I'll get it for you. Anything you want, it's yours."

"*If* I walk away."

"Why would you want to stay here? We're going to ruin your life, Cadee. And I'm not being dramatic. I'm being real."

I stand up and walk over to the steps, then look over my shoulder. "Well, you can try, I guess. We'll see how far you get."

Then I step out of the boat and walk down the deck. He follows, catching up with me. But when we get to the path that leads to the main door of the mansion, I veer to the right, heading for the side entrance to my room.

"Really?" Cooper calls. "You're really just gonna walk away from me?"

I don't answer and I don't look back. I just slip around the side of the house and head towards the little patio that leads to my room.

I'm just reaching for the door when I hear Mona call out from next door. "Lovers' quarrel?"

I look over my shoulder and study her. She's

kicking back on her patio couch underneath a light that must also act as a bug zapper because it's zap-zap-zapping away. Her legs are crossed and her feet are up in the air. She's wearing some kind of feathery, high-heel red slipper shoes and a short, purple satin robe open in the front to reveal a scarlet lace nightie.

Her dark hair is piled up on top of her head and I know this looks like she spent hours making it messy, but cute, the way people like Isabella do. But I know for a fact that Mona Monroe doesn't give one fuck about her looks. She wore cut-off coveralls to the Glass House today.

And, of course, she is smoking.

"No," I say, finally answering her question.

"Come over here," she says. "I have a joint. Wanna smoke it?"

I hesitate.

"Don't tell me ya don't smoke. Come on. It's legal now so what's the problem?"

I don't smoke. Anything. Not cigarettes or joints.

But… I don't know. It's not like I have a better offer waiting for me inside.

She laughs and sits up when I start crossing the grass between us. Her patio is a little bigger than mine. Both of them have a concrete floor and an awning overhead. But hers is surrounded by a short brick wall that matches her dark brick house. And there's a little gate to pass through before you can enter.

I like the gate. If that patio was actually mine, and I actually had money to own a house, then I would consider half-walling in my patio and putting up a little decorative gate too.

But of course, that's not my patio or my house so I don't know why the hell I'm having renovation fantasies about it.

I push through the gate and plop down onto a huge overstuffed, circular patio chair. "How come you're not at the party?"

"Do I look like the kind of girl who parties with Isabella Huntington?"

"They come to your parties."

She pulls a joint out of her mess of hair, the same way she pulled a cigarette out of it down at the pool earlier, then smiles at my reaction. "Yeah. Because they want to use me."

"Does that bother you?"

"Why should it? It's not my money paying for anything around here. Besides, I like to trash the house at least twice a year so it can get redecorated."

Wow. "Don't your parents get mad about that?"

"Parents?" She laughs. "Have you seen any parents around here?"

I think about this for a moment. "No. But… I've never been on this side of the lake until a few days ago."

"I don't have parents."

"Hmm. Me either."

"Yeah. I like that about you." She lights the joint and takes a draw on it, blowing out a sweet, but skunky-smelling puff of smoke. She hands it to me.

"I've never smoked before."

"That's not a secret." Then she wiggles her fingers for me to take the joint.

I do and look at it for a moment.

"Just put it up to your lips and suck." She giggles. "Pretend it's Cooper's cock."

I shoot her a look.

"Or Ax's. Or Lars'. Bully king of choice. They're all the same, I suppose." She pauses and looks at me, her cigarette still between her fingers. "Aren't they?"

"Aren't they what?"

"All the same."

"No," I say, putting the joint up to my lips and slowly sucking on the tip. I blow out the smoke, coughing.

"Easy there, Killer Cades. Just breathe in naturally. Enjoy it for a second. And then let it out. You'll see. This is good shit. You'll probably only need two hits to catch a buzz."

"Catch a buzz?" I laugh. "I never thought I'd be having a conversation about catching a buzz with the infamous Mona Monroe."

"Quit stalling. Take a real hit."

I do. And this time I don't cough because I just take a little teeny bit. I take a moment to taste it—gross—then blow it out.

Mona claps for me, smiling, truly looking delighted that I'm partaking with her. "OK. Don't bogart."

"What?" And oh, my God. I think I feel it. "I think I feel it," I say. Then I take another quick sip of it.

"What did I just say? You're bogartin'."

I giggle the smoke out of my lungs. "I don't even know what that word means."

She giggles too. Then we laugh. Long, loud laughs. And I suddenly wonder why I have never smoked joints with Mona Monroe before tonight. "Just one more," I say. "I've had a *day*."

She laughs again. And so do I. And suddenly I completely understand why people smoke pot.

"Girl, that wasn't a day. That was a whole year's worth of shit you went through."

"Yeah. Tell me about it." I take another sip of smoke, then stop my bogarting—whatever that is—

and pass it back.

She takes a long draw, gets a little dreamy look in her eyes as they cross to look at the joint between her lips, then holds it in and falls back into a mound of cushions. Her words come out with her smoke. "You should just walk away from it." She holds the joint out for me.

"Yup," I say. "I should." Then I get up and walk over to her couch and sit down next to her to make sharing easier. I take another draw, then a few more when Mona doesn't protest, enjoying this little moment of comradery, and then pass it back. Pretty sure I'm good now. I can feel the buzz and it is nice. I lie back in the pillows too, then take a deep breath and close my eyes.

"So how are they different?"

"Who?" I mumble.

"The Kings."

"Mmm. I dunno. Lars is nice."

"Yeah, I've always thought so too."

"And Ax is protective."

"He sure was today when that Dante fuck tried to suck your tits. And Cooper?"

I push the memory of Dante and Ax away and just think about Cooper for a moment. It's a dangerous thing to do, thinking about him and all the things he admitted to me tonight. "Cooper is sad."

She says nothing to that. But when I open my eyes, she's staring intently at me.

I want to set her straight about Cooper and I. Tell her all my secrets. But I can't. Because Cooper would get very mad at me. So I just sigh. "He's just… I don't know."

"You like him."

"I like all three of them, actually. But yes. I like Cooper more. He's… both."

"Both what?"

"Nice and protective."

"Hmm. You know him far better than I do. So I'll take your word for it. But I kinda like you, Cadee. I've always thought you were interesting. Schooling at home. Wandering around the woods. That painting you like to do. And you always had a book. I have often dreamed about being you."

"What? Why the hell would you want to be me when you can be you?"

"Why the hell wouldn't I? You don't belong here and I do."

I tsk my tongue. "Yep. Everyone's been telling me that today too."

"My point is—I like you. So I'm going to tell you something now. And I really want you to hear me.

OK?"

I take a deep breath and nod.

"He's dangerous, Cadee. We're all dangerous. And no matter what you think, the reason everyone is telling you that you don't belong, it's not because we think we think we're better than you. It's because we want one of us to get away."

"What?"

"And if it can't be them, or me"—she continues without explaining—"then it should be you."

I just stare at her for a moment.

"I know what everyone thinks of Isabella and her little minions. But she's not what she appears to be. Trust me. Ask Cooper. He knows. It's an act, Cadee. We're all just… acting here. Nothing is what it seems. And if you keep going to the Glass House this summer, and God fucking forbid you actually make it to the end and get that scholarship, you're going to be trapped here with us. We don't want to see that happen. We really don't. And if Isabella is mean to you, it's because you have everything she wants, but won't ever get. Half the time she's jealous of you and the other half she just thinks you're too stupid to live because you refuse to see what's right in front of your face."

I'm… silent for a moment. And I can't think straight. My head is all fuzzy and dizzy.

"What the fuck?"

We both jolt up and see Cooper walking across the lawn with a mean scowl on his face. "Cadee, what the—Mona! What are you doing?"

Mona leans back into her pillow and then realizes she's got a joint in one hand and a cigarette in the other, and starts to laugh as she smokes them both at once.

"We're just smoking," I say.

"You don't smoke!" And boy, is he mad. "Let's go, Cadee." He side-eyes Mona, then drags his heated stare back to me. "I said let's go. *Now*."

CHAPTER TWENTY-ONE

I hold her hand tight as I take her across the lawn, biting my tongue until I open the door, shove her inside her room, then shoot Mona Monroe one last angry look before I slam the door closed.

I whirl on Cadee, but she's already collapsing onto her bed. "What the fuck were you doing over there, Cadee?"

"Just… relaxing. Jesus." Her voice is muffled because she's got her face stuffed into a pillow. "Leave me alone. You had your fun today." She turns her head a little and I catch the glare in one bloodshot eye.

"I cannot fucking believe—after all these years of your pious purity act—that you let Mona Monroe talk you into smoking a joint."

"Me either." Then she giggles. "I'm gonna do it again tomorrow."

"You are not going to do it again tomorrow. And trust me, neither is Mona. For fuck's sake. Why is that girl so stupid?"

"I think she's pretty smart. She's the only one who plays the game right."

"You're high."

She laughs and turns over, smiling up at me. "I think I am. I like it, Cooper. It's all…" She sighs. "I feel all…" She sighs again.

I try not to laugh. Because this is not funny. Mona just fucked up bad. And she did it on purpose. But Cadee's smile makes me want to pause and enjoy it.

So I do. Because she's pretty much the only nice thing about this place. And she's definitely the best thing about this summer.

Maybe that first day I was able to tell myself the lie. That I'm over her. She's over me. We're just… over.

But nothing is over between us. Because I walked out after the abortion. I turned my back on her and washed my hands of the whole sad situation.

She's silent for a few moments, her eyes closed now, her face a mixture of serene and stupid. "I feel… numb." She opens one eye. "And I like it. Numb is nice."

I turn away from her and open the door to her

patio, fully intending on going next door and shoving Mona's head up her ass for putting me in this situation. But her bodyguards have beat me to it, because they are fighting with her, trying to pull her inside. One of them spots me, points at me, then shakes his head.

"Fuck." I slam the door.

"What's wrong?" Cadee asks sleepily.

"Mona, that's what's wrong."

"It was a joint, Cooper. Who cares? It's legal. Don't be a bogart."

I laugh. "What?"

"Don't be a bogart. You're such a fucking bogart."

I laugh again and shake my head. "Do you even know what that word means?"

She giggles. And even though I should be very angry with her right now, I'm not. I like her happy. I haven't had a lot of chances to see her this way.

"Mona was calling me a bogart. So I just figure it's something bad. Like a bitch." She sits up and opens her eyes wide to stare at me. "You're a pussy, bitch bogart, Christopher Valcourt. That's what you are."

I place two fingers on her forehead and push, making her fall back into the pillows again. "Go to sleep."

"No. I don't want to go to sleep." She swings her legs over the side of the bed like she's going to go somewhere.

But I grab her ankles and slide her legs back on the bed. She doesn't put up much of a fight. "How much did you smoke?"

"Only a few sips."

"Sips?"

"Sips."

"Define a few. Two?"

"Mmmm…*ore*."

"Three?" She thinks a little too long about this. "Four?"

She lifts up her arm slowly and holds her thumb and forefinger close together. Her eyes cross as she looks at them. Then she laughs and lets her arm fall back on the bed.

"More than five?"

She shrugs. "I forget."

"Jesus Christ. You were only over there for like ten minutes."

"Mona had it all ready." She hums the words out. "Did you know she keeps that stuff in her hair?"

"Her hair." I sigh and take a seat on the bed. Why the fuck weren't her bodyguards checking her hair? "Tomorrow is going to be a disaster."

"Why?" Cadee turns over so she's on her side, facing me. But her eyes are closed. She's still smiling.

"Why, Cooper?"

"Because there's a drug test, Cadee. And she just made sure she failed."

"Is that bad?"

"Very bad. Because the instructions my father gave me explicitly stated that Mona Monroe must get through to the end."

"Oops. I guess I'll fail too."

"You're fine. You don't need a drug test. You're not one of them, Cadee. You're just a stand-in."

"Oh, that's right. I don't count. I'm just the Fugling."

I roll my eyes. "Trust me on this, you do not want to count in this situation. The Fugling has it easy compared to the pledge girls."

"That's funny. They didn't piss their pants today. They didn't get pelted with water balloons by the boys. They got to lounge by the pool all day and work on their tans."

"It's not real. Tomorrow they'll be crying before breakfast and you'll be thanking your lucky stars that you don't count."

She reaches out and touches my waist. Then she slips her finger underneath my t-shirt and hooks it around the belt loop of my shorts.

I look down at it and hold my breath as she tugs

on it. Like she wants to pull me closer. "What are you doing?"

"Come down here with me."

"Why?" My heart is beating fast.

"Because…" She pauses and lets out a long breath. "Because I'm sad too, Cooper." Then she frowns so deep, I can't help but follow her lead. "And that good feeling has suddenly turned into something very dark and scary."

I briefly wonder if Mona's joint was laced with anything. But Cadee tugs again. Harder. With more insistence. And wasn't this what I really wanted in my senior year of Prep when Cadee and I got close?

Something slow, and easy, and *real*?

My defenses down. Her able to admit she likes me.

She does like me. But admitting it out loud? That was always a step too far for Cadee. That was always a line she refused to cross.

I would've killed for a moment like this with Cadee Hunter that year.

"Don't do that," she mumbles. "Don't reject me right now, Cooper. Not after the day I had. Just be nice to me for a little bit. Even if you don't mean it."

"I don't want you to go back tomorrow, Cadee."

"I'm going back."

"Why?"

"Because I'm not going to be a victim ever again."

"You're not gonna win anything in the end. Not anything good. I promise. I will give you anything you want—"

"Then lie down next to me."

I consider using emotional blackmail. Make her promise to stay home tomorrow if I comfort her.

But I'm tired. And sad. And I just don't have it in me.

So I give in and lie down next to her. She snuggles her body up against mine and I have an uncontrollable urge to put my arms around her the same way I did that one night three years ago.

"I forgive you," she says, her words just a low whisper.

"I'm sorry, you know. I am. I'm sorry for all of it."

"Never mind, Cooper. I don't want to talk about it. I just want someone to hold me until I fall asleep. I promise it won't take long."

I hug her a little tighter. It's not her fault. None of it was her fault. It was *my* fault. I should've made better choices. At the very least, I shouldn't have… *blamed* her. I should've stayed friends with her. And checked up on her. Or… done the right thing.

I should've done the right thing.

"I know you did your best, Coop. I really do know

that."

And then I hold my breath for so long, my head starts to spin. And when I let it out, I say, "Thanks, Cades."

But she's already asleep.

So I just lie there in her bed. Holding her. Thinking about what Mona did and how I might fix it.

But there is only one way. Only one answer.

Sometime around five AM I pull myself away from Cadee and get up from her bed. Then I lean down and kiss her head. "You're not one of them. Just please remember that tomorrow. You're just a stand-in."

A part of me wishes she would wake up and ask me what that means.

So I could tell her the truth.

So I could prepare her for what's coming.

So she could have one last chance to bow out and not make me go through with this.

But the part of me in control knows I said the words too softly for a reason.

I need her now.

I need her so I can save Mona.

CHAPTER TWENTY-TWO

I wake up because my head is pounding. And Cooper is knocking on it.

"Stop that!" I push his hand away. "It hurts."

"Time to get up. We gotta go. It's not my fault you got high last night."

"Oh." I groan and cup my hand over my eyes. "Why did I do that?"

"Because you're dumb."

I squint my eyes, then stop. Because that makes my head pound worse.

"I have to go. I'm late. Are you staying?"

I open one eye and peel part of my hand away from my eyeball to see him. "Staying home? No. I'm going."

"Then get your ass up. Take a fucking shower. And…" He pauses. "Look pretty for me today, huh?

And bring a bikini." He pulls me to my feet and kisses me on the cheek as he turns to the door.

My hand comes up to touch the place where his lips just were. "Look pretty for you?" Then I have a brief panic attack. "Did we… *do something* last night?"

He opens the door to my patio and looks over his shoulder. "No. What the fuck? I wouldn't take advantage of you when you're wasted. Give me some fucking credit." Then he points behind me. "I left some aspirin on the nightstand. Take it. It'll help. And there's a travel cup of orange juice and a croissant in that bag. Eat on your way. There's no breakfast this morning. Today is all business."

Well. OK, then. I feel like a jerk. "Sorry."

"Just… put on something nice, OK?" He grins at me. And suddenly those electric-blue eyes that normally broadcast the full depths of his despair are bright and… twinkling. "I know my stepmom's clothes are kinda slutty, but… I saw your tits yesterday, Cades. Several times. Thanks for that. Kinda got me through the day. And they're pretty nice. If you've got it, might as well flaunt it."

Then he winks at me.

My mouth drops open. But he doesn't hang around to explain these comments. Just leaves and closes the door behind him.

I don't really know what to think about that. Does he… like me? I mean I know he likes me. As a friend. Or 'frenemy' might be the more accurate word. But I am living in his house and he was nice to me last night.

I think.

I remember some of it. I remember him holding me. That was nice.

But does he *like*-like me? Or is this just some new way to get something he needs?

I don't know. I don't understand anything right now.

I reach for the aspirin, swallow them, and take a swig of OJ. Then consider the idea that Cooper Valcourt and I might be starting something.

Jesus, Cadee. The effects from the pot must be lingering. I must be high to imagine myself with Cooper. He's the King. You're the Fugling.

Never the two shall meet.

And yet… here I am. And he wants me to wear something pretty today.

No. He said, "Look pretty for me today."

That's quite a bit different than just 'Wear something pretty today.'

"Uggh." I feel like such a dumbass right now.

The shower feels way too good and even though I know I'm in a hurry, I linger in there, letting the hot water pound on the back of my neck until most of the tension and throbbing subsides. I finish washing, then wrap a towel around myself and go back out to find something to wear.

I'm pretty familiar with the closet. I have sorted through most of it already. So there's not much here that isn't meant to make a sexy statement.

But then… that's what Cooper wanted, right?

Shouldn't a good Fugling please her King?

Yeah. I am never smoking pot again. It's really fucking with my head.

But I do decide to wear something cute and sexy.

I choose a flashy beaded bikini. Cooper did say this was going to be a bad day for the pledges and an easier day for me, so I see a pool in my future. Then I cover it up with a flirty yellow flare skirt made of several layers of sheer chiffon and a loose gauzy button-down that I leave buttoned down.

When I study myself in the mirror, I do look both sexy and cute.

I put my hair up, trying my best to make it look professionally messy the way Mona does, and then hurriedly slip on my sneakers. They don't match. They're red, but oh, well. I did my best. Then I grab my croissant and slip out the door, hoping Mona might be smoking on her patio and we can walk to the Glass

House together.

But she's not.

Bummer. I feel like my original plan with Mona might not be so stupid. We could be friends. And if I make it through the summer and go to High Court next year, I'll need a friend. I could do a lot worse than Mona Monroe. She gives off a certain kind of vibe that none of the other girls have. Like she knows things.

Yeah. Wasn't she telling me something about that last night?

I can't remember.

The walk over to the Glass House is familiar now and it only takes a few minutes. But when I get there the place looks totally different.

First, there is a large canvas tent. The sides have been drawn back and tied up, so it's open all the way around. That's where all the servers are. But they are not fussing with coffee or breakfast. They are setting up white wooden folding chairs in front of a stage.

Hmm.

The next thing I notice is that all the boys—including Cooper, Ax, and Lars—are wearing suits. I'm talking full-on wedding day attire.

Jesus. What's going on here? Are people getting married?

And then I notice the Glass House is no longer

glass. Well, it is. But inside the curtains are drawn. Did it have curtains yesterday? And all the girls are missing.

"Cadee," Lars says, walking towards me.

"Hey. You look nice."

He smiles, then stops and gets serious. "Cooper needs you inside." He juts his chin at the Glass House. "Isabella has been drinking since five AM and Valentina and Selina aren't being very helpful."

"Well, that's not very professional."

Lars doesn't smile. He grabs my arm. Tight. "Just go inside and fucking help. We've already got a huge problem. Mona is missing."

Oh. I suddenly remember Cooper saying something about a drug test. "OK," I say, jerking my arm out of his grip. "I'll see what I can do."

Lars walks off and I look around to find Cooper. I swear he sees me, but when I wave, he pretends he doesn't. Jerk.

So I just go inside the Glass House and find all the pledges crying. Just like Cooper said they would be. Elexa Simpson is almost hysterical. "Why?" she cries. "Why do we have to do this?"

Isabella is lounging on a loveseat with a sleep mask over her eyes that says 'I need my bitch sleep', ignoring her.

"Because," Natasha Waring says. "It's the fucking

rules, Elexa. How many times do we have say it?"

"I don't want to do it."

"Then walk the fuck out!" Selina screams. And that's a real scream. I'm talking high-pitched and shrill. "We don't have time for this baby bullshit, OK? We're behind schedule, Mona is missing, and the nurse will be here in twenty minutes for the blood draw! Now say the fucking script word for word, and get your fucking ass in the room, Elexa! *Now*!"

That's when I realize that Valentina is holding up her phone, shooting a video. Natasha is holding a white index card. She thrusts it at Elexa. "Pull yourself together, Elexa. It's not that bad! Just *read* the card and—"

"I'm not a virgin!" Elexa shouts. "OK? I'm not a virgin."

"Oh. My. God-*daaaaahhhh*." We all turn in time to see Isabella throw her face mask across the room and get to her feet. She struts over to Elexa, slaps her face, grabs her shoulders, and shakes her. "None of us were fucking virgins, you dipshit!"

"What?" Elexa looks like she wants to laugh, but can't quite work up the nerve.

"Wait!" Natasha Waring says, raising her hand. "I'm *soooo* virginal, it's not funny."

"Me too," Sophie Bettington says meekly.

"Well, you two are stupid," Isabella says. "Our fathers pay the doctor off, dumbasses!"

"So we don't have to do this?" Elexa says, hopeful.

"You *do* have to do this!" Isabella shakes her again. "It's protocol." She takes a deep breath and the next time she speaks, her voice is low and calm. "Just let him examine you and he will check all the right boxes."

Oh, fuck.

I suddenly feel very sorry for them. But especially Elexa. Because she says, "Oh."

And she says this one, small word with hope. Like… when she gets up on that table, that's *all* that will happen.

Stop it, Cadee. You don't know.

"That's it?" Elexa says. And all the pledges are looking at Isabella now. Begging her with their eyes to lie to them and say, *Yes, girls. That's all that will happen.*

But Isabella is drunk. And I'm getting the feeling she's reliving her 'exam' from three years ago in this very moment. "Just close your eyes, Elexa. And think of something else. Because your only other choice is to walk out."

"I can't walk out. My father—"

"I know," Isabella says, somber now. "Trust me. *I know.*"

"Where's Mona?" Sophie says. "Why isn't Mona here?"

"She will be. Soon." But Isabella doesn't sound convinced, so none of us believe it.

"Elexa," Valentina says. "We've all been you. We all made a choice to stay. And if that's your choice, we need the certification before we get this day started."

"Started?" I mumble. Jesus Christ, what comes after the rigged virginity check and drug test? I don't even want to imagine.

"Choose," Selina says. "Either read the card or walk out. It's up to you. But if you read that card, you better really be on board. Because it only gets worse from here, Elexa."

The words they've been telling me for days suddenly feel heavy with threats now that they're in context.

Elexa nods and takes a deep breath. And then she stands there while Natasha pats her face down with a hot cloth and cleans away the tears.

Then Elexa looks at Valentina and begins to read the card for the camera, giving her explicit permission for the doctor to examine her.

Isabella turns to look for her facemask, then catches my eye as she heads back to her couch. She shakes her head. "You should've stayed home today,

Cadee. Don't say we didn't warn you."

"Me? What do I have to do with this?"

But then a door opens in the back of the room and a nurse calls Elexa Simpson's name.

Elexa tips her head up and walks to the door with her back straight and her chin high, disappearing inside the room.

I just stare at that door, horrified, while Natasha, Sophie, and Maddie—who has not uttered a single word this whole time—recite the words on the little card for Valentina's camera.

I know Cooper sent me in here to help them, but I can't help them. I sit on a chair in the corner and just… am *one of them.*

I pretend it's not happening.

Soon enough though, all the girls have read the card and gotten their checks. The doctor comes out and not one of these girls looks at him.

They leave, but he's not out the door but a few seconds before another nurse comes in with a medical bag. She sets up at the dining table and one by one draws blood from the girls and neatly tucks the vials away in a black bag.

When she leaves we all look at each other, wondering why the fuck any of us are doing this.

I want to judge them. Find fault with their

decisions. Maybe even sneer at them for being greedy. After all, these girls have everything. They don't need to be in this secret society.

But if I did that, then I'd have to take a good long look at myself and admit I'm greedy too.

Because I don't need that scholarship. Chairman Valcourt gave me all that money. He was probably counting on me skipping out on the first day.

That's what a smart girl would've done.

And yet here I am.

The door opens and Cooper peeks his head in. "Isabella?"

She doesn't even remove her eye mask. "What?"

"Mona's a no-show. I have people looking for her—"

"She's out then," Elexa says. "Fuck Mona. She didn't show? Fuck her! She's out!"

Cooper sighs. "Isabella?"

"What?" She throws her facemask again. "What do you want me to do? Go find her? She's got bodyguards for that!"

"The bodyguards are on it. I'm sure she'll be back tomorrow. But we're still short a girl."

"No!" Elexa is screaming now. "No! She didn't show, she's out! She can't just waltz in here tomorrow like—"

"Shut up, Elexa!" Isabella is really losing it today. She stands up, takes a deep breath as she smooths down her skirt. "So what do you propose, Cooper? Hmm? What should I do? Pull another girl out of my ass?"

And then his gaze migrates my way. And those electric-blue eyes turn dark and disturbing. "Use Cadee. Get her ready."

"No!" I say, jumping up to my feet. "No fucking way!"

"Ha!" Elexa points at me. "Ha! You get the same choice as the rest of us, Fugling! Now you'll know how it feels to be—"

Isabella slaps her. "Go to the bathroom and calm your ass down! Do you hear me?" She points her finger right in her face and it is trembling bad.

Elexa stomps off and slams the door behind her.

"No. I'm not doing it," I say. "I'm not doing it."

"You don't need an exam, Cadee," Cooper says. "You're not one of us. I keep telling you that. You're just a stand-in. Mona will have her exam when we find her."

"Why don't you just kick her out?" Sophie says. She's not hysterical like Elexa was. She sounds… defeated.

"Same reason I'm not gonna kick you out, either,

Sophie."

Then he leaves without another word.

He knows. He knows what just happened in here. And he did *nothing.*

Elexa comes back out of the bathroom just as Isabella walks over to a side table where I now notice there are several champagne buckets. She picks up a bottle, pops the cork, and then starts sloppily pouring the light golden liquid into eight glasses.

She picks one up and looks at us. "Well, what the hell are you all waiting for? Pick up a fucking glass!" The girls start moving towards the tray. "You too, Cadee!"

Right. *But you're not one of them, Cades. You're just a stand-in.*

Cooper was right. When he said that last night.

For the first time ever, I'm glad I'm not one of them.

We all lift our glasses in the air and Isabella says, "Welcome to the real Fang and Feather Summer Rush, ladies. There's really no going back from here, even if you try to walk out."

Then she downs her drink, pours herself another one, and sinks into a nearby plush chair. Spilling the champagne all over the front of her shirt.

"But… what happens now?" a frightened Natasha

asks.

Isabella won't look at her. Or any of us, actually. "Now… you will be *sold*."

CHAPTER TWENTY-THREE

Lars and Ax are standing on either side of me at the front of the tent. All three of us have our arms folded across our chests and scowls on our faces. It's like ninety degrees outside and we're dressed up in coattails.

Could this summer get any worse?

I shouldn't say that. It's just tempting fate.

Lars turns to me. "This is a very bad idea. You better know what you're doing."

I have no idea what I'm doing. But telling him that will only make him doubt me, and I don't need that right now. "What else am I supposed to do, Lars? Mona was smoking pot last night with Cadee. She knew." I'm so angry about that. Not only that she got Cadee to smoke with her. Cadee—the girl has never even tried a cigarette and she hit that joint so many times, she lost count? Just what the fuck? "She fucking knew there would be a drug test today."

"Obviously," Ax says. "Where is she? Do you know?"

"No. But as soon as this auction is over, you can bet I'll go looking."

"The bodyguards should have her."

I side-eye Lars. "Then why isn't she here?"

"She probably told them," Ax says. "And they know the only person who gets the drug test results is your father. The whole virginity check thing comes with a wink and a nod. Everyone knows, and expects, to pay that old pervert off. But the drug test doesn't work that way. Trust me, I know." He scoffs. "The Judge had me locked up for two months before our rush. Remember? They're keeping her at home so they can talk to you first."

He's probably right. And he would know. He was sent to rehab the day before Cadee had her abortion, so he never saw her afterward. Which makes me think back to what Lars was doing during that time.

Oh, yeah. His father wanted him working at city hall after classes.

Funny. Back then I didn't really notice that both Lars and Ax were essentially out of the picture during the Cadee crisis.

At first, I thought Ax really had a problem with

drugs, but in the years since I have figured out that he was just trying to get the judge to cut him loose. Didn't work for him, and it won't work for Mona, either. "We're lucky we can substitute Cadee for a day."

"A day?" Lars laughs. "Gonna take weeks for that pot to get out of her system. She's gonna go home with one of these assholes tonight, Cooper. That's what's gonna happen."

No. That's not going to happen. "I'll just have to call my dad. Explain it to him. If he wants Mona to get through so bad that he ordered me to make it happen, then he'll have to make an exception for the drug test. I will find Mona and she will take Cadee's place."

"Have fun with that," Ax mumbles. "I'm not talking to the Judge for Mona Monroe. Not a fucking chance."

"You're gonna have to," I say firmly. "It's not for her anyway. It's for Cadee. And you'll have to talk to your father, too, Lars. We all know my father won't lie to them."

"I don't have a problem with it," Lars says, shrugging.

"You wouldn't," Ax sneers.

I shoot Lars a look that says, *Do not engage*. And he just sighs and shuts his mouth.

Michael, Dante, Roland, Jamie, and Ivan are

grouped together in the back near the bar, talking excitedly about who they will be bidding on.

That's why they had to bring cash. Large sums of cash. Because the first challenge of the Fang and Feather Summer Rush is an auction to buy yourself a girl.

Not to marry. Just to take for a spin. See how this might shake out at the end.

And it makes me sick that Cadee will be up on that stage in a little bit, being bid on.

If I didn't know that my father had written her a check for two hundred and seventy-five thousand dollars, I might be able to console myself with the idea that the girls get to keep the money. Even if they walk out later, getting through this one challenge will bring its own reward.

But Cadee doesn't need the fucking money.

She doesn't *need* to be here.

She *shouldn't* be here.

I should've tied her up this morning. Left her in the closet.

Who am I kidding? I couldn't do that. *Wouldn't* do that. Because I came up with this plan last night right after she fell asleep.

I am using Cadee Hunter to save my own ass. Because Mona Monroe *must* get through. The packet made it very clear. All the reasons were spelled out in terms a baby could understand. *She knows too much to get away.*

That fact is my only consolation right now. I know my father will agree to give her a pass about the drug test. If he were home, I'd have sorted it last night. He would call his buddies, the Mayor and the Judge, and by now I'd know one way or the other what they decided.

But he's in Bali. Actually, still on his way to Bali. And even though I tried to get through to the jet, no one picked up the sat phone.

"Here they come," Lars says.

We all look at the Glass House as the girls file out.

And the saddest thing? I told her to dress cute today. Because I knew. And she does look damn cute. Not as fancy as the other girls, who brought designer gowns with them this morning to change into, but still, very fucking cute.

"About fucking time," Ax grumbles. He pulls on his starched collar. "I'm dying here. I'm about to strip naked."

"That's funny," Lars deadpans. "Like you'd ever take your shirt off."

"Lars," I snap.

"You're an asshole, Lars," Ax snarls.

"That was uncalled for. Ax isn't the enemy. We need to stick together."

Lars sighs. But says nothing.

Isabella is drunk. And I knew she would be. Valentina is leading the girls up to the stage while Selina holds Isabella up and takes her over to the loveseat in the back so she can slump down into it.

But I don't have time to worry about Isabella right now. Cadee is glaring at me like I am the biggest piece of shit in the whole entire world.

And I am, aren't I?

All three of us sigh. Like Lars and Ax are both thinking the same thing.

We had a good plan to get away. And it almost worked. If I had known that the winners of the summer rush had to run the camp entering senior year, I wouldn't have gone to that party after the Prep graduation last Friday. I wouldn't have listened to that girl when she asked me to take her to the wrong side of the lake where a car was waiting. I wouldn't have gotten drunk or arrested. I would've gotten all of us out of here weeks ago and said fuck it to all the family responsibilities.

But then Cadee might still be here. And someone else—someone worse than me, that's for sure—would be running this shit show right now.

Dane, probably.

I shudder just thinking about it. Then force myself to look Cadee in the eye.

She's breathing hard, I can tell from here. But she's not crying or anything. In fact, she's taking this better than all the other girls in the tent right now. Probably consoling herself that she is just a stand-in.

If I can't get Mona back before it's time to go home…

Who will buy Cadee?

I don't even need to wonder. It will be Dante.

And then, like he can read my mind, he's next to me. "Why is Cadee up there?"

I look over at him. Find all the boys asking the same question with their eyes. "Mona is sick today. So Cadee is standing in."

"That's not fair," Ivan says. "I mean, how is that going to work? Do I get to take her home?"

"You're not taking her home," Dante says. "I'm buying that little slut."

I reach for Dante's throat, but suddenly Lars is between us and Ax is pulling me backwards.

"Let's go over here, boys," Lars says "We have a few ground rules to go over before we start."

"Easy," Ax says, blocking my view of Dante.

"He's gonna buy her, Ax. And he will take her

home. Because I know I won't be able to find Mona, or if I do, she'll be wasted. And Cadee will have to—"

"Relax," Ax says. "I'll just follow them home if that happens and threaten him. I know for a fact my father might hate Dante Legosi more than he hates me. So if Dante does anything"—Ax pauses to smile that evil smile of his—"I'll take care of it."

Everything happens fast after that.

The rules are explained, and they are very simple.

Highest bidder wins. Girls keep the money. Girls can walk out at any time, so these boys better treat them well.

Sounds simple. But it's not. I know.

Because when it was my turn to buy a girl three years ago, I bought Isabella.

And she tried to kill herself that very first night.

Lars is the auctioneer and he barely puts in an effort, wanting to put this day behind us as quick as possible.

Sophie is bought first by Michael. There is a very competitive bidding war over Sophie. She's sweet, but that's the problem. Way too meek for my tastes. Then Natasha is bought by Roland. I guess that pervy doctor must've tipped the boys off about their virginal status. Natasha is also sweet, but at least she stands up for herself if you push too hard. Sophie just breaks out in tears.

Maddie is bought by Jamie. No one else even bids, so it's over in like thirty seconds.

Elexa goes next and she starts to cry when Ivan and Dante both refuse to bid on her.

"Fucking hell," I mutter, rubbing my temple because I have a thundering headache. "Step back, Elexa," I call from the side of the stage. "We'll do Cadee first."

And when I meet Cadee's eyes this time, she shoots me… *hate*. Complete loathing. Utter disgust.

But she doesn't complain.

And there are no tears welling up in her eyes.

She simply lifts her chin and steps forward on the stage.

Dante wins in the end.

We all knew he would.

And he pays a hundred and twenty-nine thousand dollars for the pleasure of torturing Cadee for an afternoon.

Or a night.

Or hell, what do I know? Maybe Mona won't come back and he'll really get to keep her for two whole weeks?

CHAPTER TWENTY-FOUR

All of us girls walk back into the Glass House without saying a single word when it's over. Valentina and Selina have to hold Isabella up to get her inside, because she is *wasted*.

They help her over to the loveseat in the back and she slumps back into the cushions. "Fugling!" she yells. "Drink! Now!"

I'm confused for a moment. For a couple reasons. Are we playing a drinking game and it's my turn? Or is she seriously asking me to serve her a drink? "Uh… I don't think so, Isabella. You don't need any more drinks. And I'm not in the mood to serve anyone right now, least of all you."

"Ignore her," Valentina calls. "She's cut off."

"Fuck you! Fuck everyone! Fuck—"

Selina cups her hand over Isabella's mouth. "Shut

up." Her words come out like a hiss. "Just shut the fuck up." Then she reaches for the champagne and pours her a new glass.

"Selina!" Valentina protests.

"What? I'm not going to listen to her whine and cry all day. This is happening to everyone, not just her." She hands the drink to Isabella, who is placated. But when Isabelle goes to take a sip, she spills most of it right down the front of her dress.

She doesn't even notice.

"Oh, my God," Sophie says.

We all turn and find her pointing to the dining table. There are five silver trays with stacks and stacks of cash on them.

"Holy shit!" Natalie breathes. Then she smiles. "Which one is mine?"

"This one," Sophie says, pointing to the tray with a large stack and a little white card off to the side with Natalie's name written in flowing, curvy calligraphy. "And this one's mine." Sophie actually smiles. And why not? She fetched the highest price today. A hundred and forty-three thousand dollars. "This one is yours, Cadee." She points to another tray with a healthy stack of cash.

"This is so fucked up," Elexa complains. Then she sighs dramatically and takes a seat in the chair in front of her tray of money. It's a pretty small stack, since she only got the minimum bid of twenty thousand.

"That's not your money, Cadee," Isabella snaps. "It's Mona's."

"Fine with me," I say. "I wouldn't take it anyway. I'm worth way more than this."

Everyone giggles. And so do I.

Natalie even snorts. "I hear you, Fugling." I shoot her a dirty look. She doesn't notice. "But if we have to do this, we might as well get paid."

But that's the thing. Right? *Do* we have to do this?

Maybe they do. I don't know what kind of fucked-up arrangement these lake-mansion families have going on out here in the woods, but I'm definitely not part of it. And as far as I can tell, they're allowed to walk out any time they want.

Well, not Isabella, Valentina, and Selina. Obviously, they signed their deal with the Devil three years ago when they went through rush. But all the pledges are here by choice.

"So…" Sophie says. But then she gets distracted and doesn't finish her sentence. Because she's shoving the cash into the front of her dress. And there's no way it's all going to fit in there, but then I realize she's got hidden pockets in the side of her gown. Still, there are only so many places to stash stacks of money on your person.

"What are you doing?" I ask.

"I'm out."

"What?" Maddie says. She's been very quiet through all this.

"Yeah." Sophie laughs. "Michael and I had an agreement."

"You're not *out*, Sophie."

All of us turn to see Cooper standing in the doorway.

"Like hell," Sophie says. "It's my decision and I say I am."

"No, Sophie." Cooper is calm. Like he officiates the selling of virgins all the time and this day is not turning into a crazy waking nightmare. "You're here, whether you want to be or not."

"That's not true!"

But Cooper's words come back to me. And I'm sure they come back to Sophie too. He won't kick Mona out. Or her.

"We're allowed to leave!" Maddie says. "My dad said so."

"Yeah, you are, Maddie." Cooper looks her in the eyes. "Because you're only here to make things… interesting."

"What does that mean?" Natalie says.

"Look." Cooper sighs. He closes his eyes for a moment, then opens them and looks straight at me. "I don't make these rules. I have nothing to do with this, other than I was ordered to be here with you all summer. And I was told to make sure that Mona and Sophie got through. That's all I know."

"No," Sophie says. "No. Michael and I have a plan! We're leaving! We're—"

Cooper interrupts. "Michael can go wherever he wants. But you can't. So he's stuck here for two more weeks, whether he wants to be or not. Because he's the one who just bought you."

Sophie is shaking her head. "I'm not coming back tomorrow. We're leaving tonight."

"You can try to leave," Isabella says from the back of the room.

We all turn to look at her. She's standing up. Not even weaving. Like she sobered up in an instant.

"You can try," she repeats. "I did. And look where I am now." Isabella shakes her head and her eyes get all glassy. Like she's about to cry. "They come get you. Just ask Cooper."

We all look at Cooper. He's already crossing the room to Isabella. He takes her arm and then leans down and whispers something into her ear. She shakes her head no. And the tears fall out of her eyes. But when he tugs on her arm, she lets him lead her across the room and right out the door of the Glass House.

We're all quiet. Staring at the door. Wondering what happens next.

We stay in the Glass House, just looking at our money. Sophie cries softly. She manages to stuff even more stacks on her person. She has garters on underneath her pink gown. So she clearly has not given up on the idea that she's leaving tonight with Michael.

But it's a stupid, pointless act, because about thirty minutes later, Ax appears in the doorway and says we need to change into our bikinis.

That's it. That's all he says. And he doesn't look any of us in the eyes. Just spits the command out and leaves.

The boys are waiting.

It's only ten in the morning and this day is far from over.

I guess I know why Cooper told me to bring a bathing suit.

He wasn't interested in seeing me in a bikini. We were never going to hang out at the pool together.

Nope. He just wanted to make sure Dante got his money's worth.

Victor approaches me while I'm waiting on the other girls to change into their bathing suits. "You OK?" His words are soft and filled with the right amount of concern.

And I want to like him. I don't think Victor is a bad guy. But he's been a part of the summer rush for three years. Four, actually. This is the fourth time for him. So four times he has shown up here for money.

I get it. It's one hundred percent total bullshit. I am living at the height of hypocrisy right now. In fact, I'm worse. Because I wasn't actually paid to come here. I was paid *before* I came here.

It feels like an out right now.

And I also get that Cooper's father runs this shit show. So his offer of concern was dirty. I can't quite fit all the pieces together yet, but I am starting to understand. Behind that clean-shaven face and well-coiffed silver hair, underneath that expensive suit and hidden behind that massive executive desk up in his high tower of an office—lives the worst kind of monster.

It's one thing to come face to face with the Devil and know what you're dealing with. It's quite another to realize the beast is stalking you from the shadows.

And right now, Victor feels very much like one of the beasts stalking me from the shadows.

So I smile at him. "Fine. Why? Something wrong?"

"Cadee." He kinda laughs my name. "Come on. Nothing is fine."

"Hey." I shrug. "I got my pile of money. I'm good."

"It's not yours. It's Mona's. They're not going to let you keep it. They're not gonna let you keep anything. Not until you're all the way in. That's how this works. Valentina can show off her diamonds all she wants, but they're not really hers. It all belongs to them until she commits."

Commits. Hmm. What does that mean, exactly? She's already in Fang and Feather. How much more commitment do they need?

I wish I could ask Victor, but I just don't trust him. I don't trust anyone right now. "So? I can wait it out. You have, right?" I try to keep my tone neutral. But I don't really succeed. And Victor isn't a dumb guy. I don't know what his real story is, but he's not a nobody.

Everyone at High Court is somebody.

There's just a very tall scale that measures them up. And he's down at the bottom, for sure. But compared to me? Yeah. I'm somewhere down in the negatives.

And he's in, Cadee.

He's in 'till the end.

Or he wouldn't still be here.

He's so close to that sweet prize, he can practically taste it.

Victor's eyes flash dark for a moment. Anger? Is that anger? Or shame? I can't tell, but I'm gonna go with anger, because that's the typical reaction to shame anyway, isn't it?

He doesn't get the chance to answer because Valentina comes out of the dressing room. "Get back to work, Victor. Now."

He sucks in a deep breath and mutters, "Be careful, Cadee," on the exhale. Then he turns around and goes back in the kitchen.

I'm not sure if that was a warning or a threat.

I guess I'll go with both to be safe.

"Don't talk to him, Cadee."

I turn to Valentina. She's wearing a bright yellow

bikini with crystal patterns sewn into the bra. And her skin is brown to begin with, so she doesn't need a tan to make that suit look great. Her long, black hair is piled on her head like Mona wears. Her makeup is perfect—her lips glossy and pink, eyelashes long and lush and cheekbones glowing. Her body is well-toned with curves in all the right places. She's an athlete. Played baseball on the boys' team when she was younger. And she's smart too. I do remember that much about Valentina. Valedictorian her senior year at Prep. I was in the central gardens helping my father the day of the ceremony so I heard her speech.

She is gorgeous in every measurable way.

Before this moment I might've made myself feel better by imagining her as ugly on the inside. And three days ago, I'd have believed it.

But she's not. She's just playing a game like everyone else. She's… acting, I realize. It's just a role she needs to master.

"Why shouldn't I talk to him?"

"Because he's dangerous. Just a spy. All the servers and cooks here, they're all just spies. That's how they earn their place. That's how they earn their money. One wrong move, one misspoken word, and he will rat you out to anyone who asks. Don't trust anyone."

"Not even you?"

She doesn't even blink. "Not even me."

"Thanks," I say.

"For what?"

"The truth."

She smiles and slides her sunglasses down over her round, brown eyes. "We're in this together now, Fugling. We're all gonna swim or sink together."

I should be offended at the name. But she doesn't say it unkindly.

She says it… inclusively.

I'm one of them now.

Like it or not, I'm in.

"So now what?"

Valentina and I both turn to find all the girls waiting for instructions. Even Selina.

Valentina lets out a long exhale. "Now… we do whatever they tell us."

"What?" Sophie is panicked. Her face is all blotchy from crying. And her skin is so fair, her hair so red, this is not a good look for her.

"Don't worry," Valentina says. "They're not gonna make you perform sexual favors."

"How do you know?" Elexa asks.

"Because you have to consent to everything, Elexa. So if you suck Ivan's cock, it's because you said yes."

Elexa crosses her arms over her chest. She's the only one wearing a one-piece. "I'm not going to say yes."

Valentina shrugs. "Then don't. But everything has consequences. Ivan will get his say if you don't make him happy. Trust me."

"What's that mean?" Maddie asks. Like Sophie, she's also on the verge of panic.

"You'll see. Can't give away too many spoilers. Might ruin your summer. For two weeks you will do what they tell you or you will say no. And if you say no, they're gonna remember it for the next challenge. So pick and choose your battles, ladies. Try to make friends with them. If you can do that, it will make this whole thing a lot easier."

They don't believe her.

Hell, I don't believe her.

"Listen," Valentina says. "I get it. I was you three years ago. And do you know who bought me? Ax Olsen."

Everyone looks at the door that leads outside, even though none of us have x-ray vision and can see him on the other side.

"Ax Olsen," Valentina repeats. "Not quite a catch, is he?"

Everyone but me and Selina agrees.

"But he and I are on the same side now. I have his back, he's got mine. And let me tell you something right now, Elexa. Ivan Turgenev is not a bad guy to have on your side. Take my word on that. Ax will fuck people up if they touch me. And if you play Ivan right, he'll do that for you too. Try to make him happy. Smile today. Let him know you're not gonna hold things against him. He's playing his game just like you're playing yours. Be on Team Ivan and he'll take care of you, Elexa." Then Valentina looks at me. "But I'm not going to give you the same advice."

"What?"

"Dante?" She shakes her head. "He's just bad. But Mona can handle him. She's the only one who *can* handle him. So if you're asking yourself why Cooper would throw you to the wolf like that? That's why. Mona can take care of herself and you're just her stand-in."

I swallow hard. The reality of what is happening suddenly sinking in. "How do you know she'll be back?"

Valentina frowns. "She just will."

Selina steps forward and smiles at them, folding her hands in front of herself. "Now. Let's go out there and have some fun." She waves her hand at the door, inviting us to go first.

But we don't move.

"Come on, children," Valentina says, clapping her hands to bring us to attention. "I'll play babysitter for the day. And remember, Ax is here. They won't cross him and he won't abandon me."

Still, no one moves.

So fuck it. I go first.

If you're going to meet the Devil, you might as well meet him head on.

CHAPTER TWENTY-FIVE

Isabella stumbles most of the way through the woods as I lead her back to my house.

"I don't want to go." She's been whining this, over and over again, since we left the rush.

"I don't care. You're drunk. There's no point in staying out there. You'll just... get sun stroke." *Sun stroke, Cooper? Really?* I roll my eyes at myself. "I'll make you breakfast and you can sleep it off in my room."

But when we get to my house, there's no way I can get her up the stairs. And when I lead her over to the couch in the great room, she falls into the cushions sideways and kinda passes out.

I step back and look at her. She is a fucking mess.

But passed out I can deal with. Stumbling around drunk, shooting off her mouth?

Nope. We're not going there today.

I still need to figure out what happened to Mona.

When I go outside, I'm not sure if I should go to the front door or just hit up her patio. But in the end, it's not my decision to make because the next thing I know one of her bodyguards is approaching me.

"Can I help you, Mr. Valcourt?"

Hmm. I don't know any of them. Can say with one hundred percent certainty that I have never talked to one of Mona's bodyguards. So I'm not sure how to approach this giant dude in a black suit. I finally decide on ignorance. "Have you seen Mona? She didn't show up for rush this morning."

"Miss Monroe is inside. Follow me."

That was easier than expected. Never a good sign from my experience. But I follow him around to the front of the house and we enter together.

Mona is right in front of me. Well. She's in my line of sight, but sitting on a couch in the back of the house. In profile, she doesn't look my way, busy clicking a remote.

"Are you fucking kidding me, Mona?" I cover the distance of the hallway in twenty strides and then walk around the large, overstuffed brown leather couch to block her view of the TV.

She doesn't even acknowledge me.

"Mona?"

"I can hear you. You don't have to yell at me."

"Where the fuck were you?"

She pauses her Netflix surfing to gaze up at me. "What's the point? I can't do the drug test today anyway."

"We could've paid her off."

Mona scoffs.

"We could've tried."

"I already talked to your father."

"You did?" Hm. "I tried to call him. He didn't pick up."

"Yes. He mentioned that. Told me to tell you that he doesn't want to be, quote, 'bothered with any more summer rush bullshit while he's on vacation,' end quote." Mona finally looks at me. And smiles.

"All right." I mean, he's a dick and I hate my father a little more every day. But fuck it. I'm not gonna let Mona in on my daddy issues. "So. What did he say?"

"He said I can take the drug test in two weeks. I'm under house arrest. Those meathead assholes you see behind me"—holy shit. There are a lot of meathead assholes lounging on couches and chairs on the far side of the room—"will make sure I behave. And he won't be responsible for what happens to me if I don't. I am a worthless piece of shit who thinks that this good life I've been provided is a right instead of a privilege. I'm also greedy, stupid, lazy, and will never amount to anything."

I nearly guffaw.

"I'm glad you find that funny."

"Sorry. It's just… I get the same speech all the time."

She huffs.

"What the hell were you thinking?"

She shrugs, then whispers. "I don't want to do it."

"None of us want to do it."

"That's not true. Dante wants to do it. Ivan wants to do it. I'm pretty sure Elexa wants to do it too. Natasha is a maybe." She looks up at me. And maybe for the first time ever, I take a good hard look at my next-door neighbor. "Why can't the Chairman just be happy with *them*?"

"I dunno, Mona." I say it quietly. Sympathetically. Because I get it. I don't want to be here either. "Isabella is next door at my house."

"Why?"

"She started drinking some time around five AM this morning. She's passed out in the great room."

Mona laughs. "Oh."

"But I could carry her over here and—"

"No. Thank you."

I just stand there. Unsure what to do next.

"Have a seat if you're staying."

I do sit. I probably shouldn't stay. But I'm not ready to go back yet.

"How did the auction shake out?"

"Cadee stood in for you."

Mona sits up straighter and covers her mouth. "Shit. Cooper, I'm sorry."

"Whatever. Ax and Lars are there to make sure Dante doesn't do anything."

"Dante! Are you kidding me? Why would Dante buy *me*?"

"He didn't buy you, he bought her."

"Right. So how much did I go for?"

Fucking Mona. "You didn't go for anything. Cadee sold for one twenty-nine, I think."

"What the… *what*?"

"Yeah. He really wants her, I guess." I get a sick feeling in my stomach and then my head is pounding again. "So… I get that I'm just your asshole neighbor, and I've barely noticed you for basically your entire life. But it really sucks that you're out for the whole two weeks because I was kinda counting on you, Mona."

"I'm sorry. I just… lost control last night. And it was nice to talk to Cadee. I like her."

I nod my head in agreement. Because I like her too. I walked away three years ago—chased her away, actually—and then didn't think of her again until she bumped into me in front of the admin building. And now I feel like she's constantly on my mind. And not only that, I feel somehow responsible for her involvement. Which means… now I have to fix it.

"Mona. I need to make her leave."

"She doesn't want to leave."

I sigh. "I understand that. And I understand that it's not really my place to make that decision for her. But you of all people know how destructive this path she's on is."

Mona looks at me like… like she feels sorry for me. And for a moment I start to get angry. Who is this girl—this troubled, angry girl who is the actual cause of this problem I'm trying to fix in this very moment? Who does she think she is?

"Cooper, you can't blame me for wanting to save myself and then in the same breath, you're trying to help someone else. That's not fair."

And didn't I just say that to Cadee last night? Putting all the blame on me for what happened three years ago wasn't fair.

And she didn't care. She was gonna blame me anyway. Just like I'm gonna blame Mona.

"It's a vicious cycle," I say.

"Yup. And it's easy to be the victim. So much

easier to just show up for summer rush and go along. Because fighting back is hard. If I really wanted to leave, Cooper, I'd have done it a long time ago. But then I'd lose everything, wouldn't I? So I make excuses. I tell myself this is all I have left of my family. This stupid fucking house and these stupid fucking bodyguards." Then she stands up and looks at them. "And I know I give you guys all kinds of shit. I probably drive you crazy on a daily basis. And hell, you all probably hate me by now. I don't make it easy. But you—" She points at them. Looks at them. No. *Reveres* them.

All six, seven, eight… *ten* of them.

"You guys? You're all I have besides this house. You're the last thing left from my old life." Then she looks at me. "And I'm not gonna give them up. I'm not gonna walk out on them because they haven't walked out on me. And I'm not leaving this house. Ever. It's mine. The only home I have. So fuck it. I'm staying. Maybe I never get away from here. Maybe they do own me. But as long as I have *them* watching my ass, I'm gonna fight back every chance I get."

I look over my shoulder at her bodyguards and smile. "Maybe there *is* something you can do?"

I leave with five of Mona's bodyguards and as we walk through the woods towards the Glass House, I feel a little bit less like a piece of total fucking shit than I did an hour ago.

But when I get there and see Dante trying to put his arm around Cadee as she skirts out of reach, it all fades.

I turn to the bodyguards. Mona told me their names. There was a Chad, and a Bing, and a Rock. The others, I lost track after that. "OK. Here's what I need you to do. You see those girls out there? The ones with the guys hanging all over them?"

Each meaty head turns to look at the girls. Then they turn back to me. Don't say anything, just nod.

"OK. You each get one. You treat her like she is Mona. You do not leave her side. Ever. When she goes to sleep, if she's alone? You go stand guard at the door. If she doesn't go alone, you refuse to give them privacy. One night. You do not let these girls out of your sight unless they're sleeping alone. You understand me?"

They nod again.

"Tomorrow, the other five will take your place and we'll trade off like that until I can figure out what the next step is. Today, you do not let those boys even think about touching those girls. There are five weeks left of this rush. Plenty of time for that later if they choose to stay. Now go. And remember—they are Mona as far as you're concerned."

I sigh as the meatheads turn away and walk over to the girls. And even though I didn't assign them to anyone in particular, they all seem to know which girl they are protecting. There is no hesitation.

Cadee ends up with a huge white dude with a round, shaved head, a neck so thick I'm pretty sure his starched white shirt under his suit coat is custom-made, and a look of utter evil pasted on his face.

I cross my arms and hold my breath as he approaches Dante, who is still trying to get all hands-y with Cadee. He doesn't even look at Dante. Simply talks softly to Cadee. Her eyes dart around until she finds me.

And then… she smiles at me, mouthing the words, *Thank you.*

I nod at her, then watch Dante for a moment. He's angry. Trying to argue with big white dude who I am just going to call Meat for now, since I don't know his name. But Meat simply crosses his arms and slides into an at-ease position, daring Dante to make a move.

Dante doesn't. His gaze swings over to me and

then he's heading my way.

Ax and Lars slip in next to me and we wait for Dante's outburst.

"What the fuck, Cooper? This is not how it's supposed to be! A babysitter? What the fuck did I just pay for?"

"You got what you paid for," I say calmly.

"She's mine," he growls.

"She is," I agree. "But I'm running this rush. And I say these girls need a moment. They need to take a breath, Dante. So I'm giving them time to come to terms with things. None of the other guys seem to have a problem with it. So if you do, that just makes you an asshole."

He looks around, wishing my words to be a lie. But I'm right. The other guys are kind of enjoying their new additions. Jamie and Michael both look a little relieved, from what I can tell. Hell, Ivan is pouring his guard a fucking shot of vodka as we watch and Roland is high-fiving his.

Dante looks back at me. Pokes me in the chest with his finger.

Ax makes a move, but I put my arm out and stop him. "Let Dante have his say, Ax."

"This isn't over. You might think my father is a nobody, but he has more power than you know."

"That's interesting," I say. "Because I was given a list of people who must make it through this summer, Dante. And your name wasn't on it. But Mona's was. So…" I shrug. "Play your game well and maybe she'll bring you along for the ride. But if you fuck with Cadee, I will cut your ass from this rush so fast, your father's head will spin."

Dante glares at me, then at Lars and Ax. "Fuck you guys. We'll see who's running things next year."

Lars laughs. "Well, even if it isn't us, it sure as hell won't be you."

"Walk away, Dante," Ax says, shooing him with a flip of his hand. "We're the ruling class whether you like it or not. Better just swallow that fact whole right now so you can digest it over the summer."

I nod and smile at him. "We're the bully kings. Accept it. Or don't. I don't really give a fuck. But this is your only warning, Dante. I won't bother with another one."

And I'm dead fucking serious about this.

I will not be responsible for another Isabella. Ever.

My first night of challenge one was a bloody disaster. And that isn't a figure of speech.

It will never happen again. *Ever.*

Dante storms off, clearly unhappy. But I don't

care. I turn to Lars. Because I just got a very bad feeling about Isabella. "Go to my house. Isabella is passed out on the couch. Make sure she doesn't do anything stupid."

Lars looks at the woods. "Fuck." Then he looks back at me. "No problem, Coop. I'll take care of her."

And he will too.

Ax and I watch Lars disappear into the woods. Then I turn to him. "You watch that Dante fuck. Hear me? I don't care that she's got a bodyguard. You stay with Cadee until Mona comes back."

"And then what?"

I think about what Cadee told me. How Ax is sleeping in his boathouse because he doesn't want to go home. "Then you stay with Mona too."

He lets out a long breath. And I recognize relief when I see it. Then he claps me on the back and says, "You got it." And walks off, calling out, "Cades, my sweet little sparkly tart. You wanna play strip poker with me? I like that suit. Fucking flashy, babe. But I like what's underneath better."

Dante almost loses his shit as he starts walking towards Ax with both hands out, looking like a total asshole and spewing threats to back him up.

I laugh. I can't help it.

Because Ax—that dude lives by his own set of

rules.

It's why he's on my team.

He's an out-of-the-box thinker if ever there was one.

And between him and Meat, Dante hasn't got a chance in hell of getting a moment alone with Cadee.

CHAPTER TWENTY-SIX

I want to hate Cooper Valcourt. I really do.

I want to rail against him. And blame him. And hold him responsible for every bad thing that's happening during the two-week period I spend wearing Mona's surrogate shoes.

But I can't rail, or blame, or hold him any more responsible than anyone else involved in this rush. Including myself.

Because we are just doing our best.

And while the bodyguards don't erase anything that's happening, they do make it tolerable.

Dante, however, is a resourceful little fuck. And he takes advantage of every free moment when I'm not being watched. He uses every opportunity during our two weeks together to torment me and put me in my place.

And he does it well. I will give him that. He is an opportunist to the nth degree.

So here's how challenge one shakes out for me.

During the day we spend our time at the pool. Or inside the Glass House. Sometimes we go other places in the woods—he took me to the tomb once. Thought he was going to take me inside, but the bodyguard had other ideas, and then Cooper appeared and shoved Dante back to the Glass House while I tagged along behind them.

But for the most part we just sit out at the pool.

Most of the boys are enjoying their partners. They get a game of chicken going and they play in the water. They swing mallets at croquet balls. Eat long, leisurely lunches. It's actually not a bad time.

If you're one of them.

Because Valentina was right. Maybe Ax gave the boys the same speech about making us partners, because those boys seem pretty happy. Even Sophie and Michael have a pretty good time. He holds her hand and serves her drinks and little finger snacks. He tells her she looks nice and they take long walks together. She still shows up every morning with a too-red blotchy face. But she settles. And eventually, sometime around noon, she even laughs at Michael's dumb jokes.

Even Ivan and Elexa seem to be enjoying themselves. They don't hold hands or take long walks—and Ivan is a little crude for my tastes—but Elexa didn't sic her bodyguard on him when he slapped her ass as he asked for a beer on day three. She seemed fine with it. At the very least, she made her peace. And even though Ivan's words aren't pretty, I can tell he has respect for Elexa. He's not going to push her to suck his dick at night—even though Elexa sent her bodyguard back to Mona on day five and I'm pretty sure she *is* sucking his dick at night now. Ivan and Elexa have come to an agreement that they are in this together.

Maddie and Natasha seem to tolerate Jamie and Roland. They don't commit quite so much, but there is no drama.

Dante and I, however… yeah.

That's drama.

He just has it out for me. Bad.

Every day there is an incident. Every day I'm thankful for that bodyguard. And every day Dante reminds me that I don't belong and that when he gets to the end of the summer and finishes the first rite, he will show me—and Cooper, by extension—how much power he really wields.

I try not to roll my eyes at him, but most of the

time I can't hold it in.

However, I am a little worried about the words 'first rite.'

Not for me. I'm not going to the final ceremony at the tomb with the other girls. That will be Mona's job.

But Ax is always somewhere close by when we're at the Glass House. So he and I have gotten close again. He mostly lives to make Dante's life miserable and I don't interfere. But every now and then he'll take a break and sit next to me under one of the thatched-roof huts and start telling me things.

Things like how the boys have no idea what's coming. And how Dante won't make it to the end because Cooper hates him and will make sure of it, but even if he does, he's in for a big surprise.

Little hints like that.

It makes me worry about the girls. Mostly Sophie. Because even though I thought I knew these High Court Prep girls, and didn't think a single one of them possessed a gentle soul, I was wrong.

Sophie is gentle. She is sweet, and good, and just wants out.

And she is one of two who can't leave.

I'm actually surprised that Maddie and Natasha don't walk out before the end of the two weeks.

They're not invested. They do not care. I think they are happy with the booty they collected from the auction. I think the only reason they're still here is because Jamie and Roland asked them to stay.

But if challenge two gets intense, I have a feeling they will bail.

Anyway. Dante tries hard, every day, to make me pay for whatever crime he thinks I committed against him.

His parents, as well as his brothers and sisters, are all home when we go there every night. They don't seem to think that Dante bringing home a strange girl from an auction in the woods is a big deal. Or the bodyguard who comes with her.

The first night we had dinner with them and they asked me a lot of questions that ran the gauntlet between *Who the hell are you again*? and *Why isn't Mona here*? None of which I answer because—wait for it—Dante has forbidden me to talk to his family. Told me I'm just a stand-in and no one cares what I think.

His parents don't find that weird either. His mother doesn't stop sipping her apple martini and his father—a slightly better-looking, but shorter and older version of his son—actually winks at him when Dante reveals my no-talking rule.

I can practically hear Mr. Legosi's words of

wisdom to Dante the night before the first auction when he had to beg for all that cash. *You lay those rules down hard, son. Put them in their place right from the start.*

Such a catch. I wish I could spend all my time with the Legosis.

Gag.

Of course, the bodyguard can't be watching all the time. The one Cooper calls Meat—and Meat doesn't mind, because he starts identifying himself to the Legosi security as Meat on day two—he is on top of shit. I'm talking spectacular.

But my other guard—the one Cooper calls Chatter because he doesn't talk, the one who watches me from seven AM to seven PM—is not quite as invested as Meat. So Dante did actually corner me in the butler's pantry on day seven while Chatter was taking a bathroom break.

I let him kiss me. Because Dante was counting on a fight. He's so predictable. He wanted to catch me off guard and steal that kiss against my will. And I'm not going to give him that kind of satisfaction.

So I kissed him back. It was a long, slow, sloppy kiss that grossed me out and made me want to hurl. Luckily Chatter opened the pocket door with a bang and Dante backed away.

But he was smiling. Like he won.

He didn't win. I threw the fight.

I'm not dumb. I had one week left and to be honest, that week went fine. He didn't try to kiss me again. Though he did walk around naked in his bedroom apartment the entire last four nights.

I pretended to be impressed with his cock. But come on. I got a good long look at Cooper Valcourt's big, fat cock that first night I stayed at his house.

Dante's prick didn't even come close to living up.

I expect Dante to make one more attempt to get to me the last day of the first challenge, so when he doesn't, I'm surprised.

Did he learn his lesson?

Maybe.

Or maybe he just figured I'm not worth the trouble?

I'm really not, if you think about it. Mona is the girl he needs to worry about. I'm just the stand-in.

Cooper has been watching me all day out at the pool. He's kept a wide distance from me the past two weeks.

I guess he figured Ax and Meat had the problem of Cadee Hunter covered. And Mona wouldn't need all this coddling. Mona will have bodyguards on her all the time. I wonder if Dante's parents will be able to ignore all ten of them?

This makes me laugh.

"What's funny?"

I look up and shield my eyes to see Lars. He steps in front of the sun glare and creates a shadow. "Just thinking about Mona's bodyguards at Dante's house tomorrow night."

"What makes you think she'll be at Dante's house?" He sits down next to me and slips his feet into the water.

"Won't she?"

Lars shoots me a sideways grin. "No spoilers."

"Hmm. Now I'm curious."

"You don't need to be, Cadee. You're out."

"Right. I'm out."

"But you're OK, right?" He pauses. Squints his eyes a little as he looks at me. "He didn't bother you, right?"

"No."

"And you'd tell me if he did?"

"Yeah. Why?"

"I've heard a rumor, Cadee."

My stomach sinks. "What kind of rumor?"

"That someone…" He pauses, sucks in a deep breath. "Never mind." Then looks away without asking.

There is a part of me that wants him to ask. A part

of me that wants him to know what happened that year. If that's the rumor he's talking about. And what other rumor is there?

But that part of me isn't brave enough to push the issue.

"I'm sure it's just a stupid rumor," Lars says. Then he smiles and looks at me again. "Forget I mentioned it. And anyway, you're free now. Are you excited to go home?"

"Home? Hmm. You mean Cooper's house?"

"It's not a bad place to belong."

I sigh, then flick water with my toes. "Yeah. I guess. I'm looking forward to it. At least I'll get to see Mona again."

"Do not smoke with her again."

I laugh.

"Not because of you, Cades. It's her. She can't. So… if she asks you again, discourage her."

"You act like we're friends or something."

"I think you are."

I don't reply, but yeah. I think we are too. Even though we haven't seen each other since that night two weeks ago, I have been thinking about her a lot. Maybe even missing her.

"You wanna hear something funny?" I ask.

"Sure."

"My original plan when I figured out I was going to be working at the Swan Camp—"

"Swan Camp?"

I laugh. "That's what I called it in my head all these years. But when I first realized that's where I was going I made up this big, grand plan to make Mona my best friend and together we were going to oust Isabella and take her Cygnus crown."

"You? The queen?"

"Not me." I punch him in the arm. "Mona was gonna be queen. I was just gonna—"

But I stop. Because I suddenly remember what my part of that deal was.

The truth. I wanted everyone to know the truth about what Cooper did at the end of his senior year at Prep.

"You were gonna what?" Lars pushes.

"Nothing." I sigh, then lie. "Just… be one of her minions."

"Is that what you want?"

I look over at Lars and find him to be… way too serious for this conversation. "No. Not really."

He puts his arm around my shoulder and pulls me into him. "Good. I don't want you to be a minion either."

I pull away a little and look at him. "What's going

on with you, Lars? You're acting weird."

He just smiles, shakes his head a little, then gets up and extends his hand. "You ready to go home?"

I take it and let him pull me up. Because I don't want Lars to think too hard about any rumors he might've heard about me. "Sure. Ready as I'll ever be."

"Go change and I'll walk you. Cooper and Isabella already left. And Ax is—" Lars scans the pool. That's when I notice only Elexa and Ivan are still here, having a private conversation over in one of the huts. I guess everyone was eager to go home for a night of freedom. "Gone, I guess."

I go inside and slip my shorts and t-shirt on over the bathing suit that Sophie let me borrow. And then I stop to smile about that. Because they've all been pretty cool to me these past few weeks. We've been hanging out every day. We didn't spend all our time with the boys. And I got away from Dante every chance I could. And every morning when I go into the server's locker room, there has been a bag of clothes for me. Each of them went through their closets and found things they didn't want and gave them to me. And OK, they're not really my style, but when you literally have nothing, who cares. It's truly the thought that counts. And they have all been thoughtful. Even Isabella has brought me clothes from her closet. And lots of them still had tags and everything.

It's almost like they care about me. Almost like I really am one of them.

Which is ironic. Because now that I'm in… I'm thinking maybe I don't want to be. Maybe they were all right when they told me to leave. And even if I do make it all the way to the end of the summer, maybe I should say 'no, thank you' to that scholarship?

I push those thoughts away for another day. We still have six weeks left. And tomorrow I won't be Mona's stand-in. She'll be back and I'll be the Fugling again. So we'll see.

When I go outside Lars is leaning up against a tree near the path through the woods. He pushes off it when I approach and steps in line with me.

"You're my bodyguard now, Lars?"

He shoots me a sideways smile as we walk. "You know… I'm on your side, Cadee."

"Thanks."

"No, I mean it. Regardless of what it is. I'm on your side."

"Right. I get it. And… thanks. I appreciate it."

"None of this was my idea. It was Cooper's."

I don't know where he's going with this, so I stay quiet.

"Those first days, he was wrong to do that to

you."

Jesus. What is he getting at? "He apologized, Lars. The night Isabella threw that party at my cottage. We talked it through a little."

Lars draws in a long breath, then lets it out slowly, like he's trying to think of what to say next. "Did he apologize for everything?"

"I don't know what you mean."

"I think you do, Cadee."

"If you're referring to these rumors—"

"I am."

"Look," I say, stopping on the path. "It's all in the past now." He opens his mouth to say something, but I put up a hand. "I mean it, Lars. Whatever you heard, it's not about you. It's about me. And I'm telling you to let it go."

"Cadee—"

"No. This is my life. I'm making my own decisions. And if I want to try again with Cooper—"

"Try again with Cooper? So that's what it was, huh? Just Cooper? That's all you were after that year?"

"No. Of course not. It was all pretty equal, don't you think?"

"I did. But then I heard—"

"Stop. Just please stop. I don't know what we're doing. But my feelings for you, and Ax, for that matter?

They haven't changed. I'm on your side too, Lars. And you know damn well that Cooper would never choose a girl over you guys."

He doesn't look convinced. But then he nods. "OK. It's your life. Come on. I think I smell dinner."

We're just across the blacktop road from Cooper's house when Lars makes a big production of smelling the air. And he's right. I smell food. "I thought the house staff was on vacation?"

"They are." Then Lars smiles, takes my hand, and leads me across the road.

The first person I see when I enter is Meat. "Hey!" I say. And then I realize what that means. "Mona!" I start walking towards the kitchen.

"Surprise!" She pops out from a side hallway. "Are you ready to party, Cadee?"

She hooks her arm around mine, forcing Lars to let go of me, and leads me towards the kitchen. The back wall of windows has been opened up so that the patio facing the lake is now an extension of the great room and outside there's smoke blowing in the breeze, the smell of barbecue in the air, and everyone from rush is in Cooper's back yard.

"What's this?" I ask.

"Cooper wanted to throw you a welcome home party."

"Shut up."

"I'm completely serious. He's been hanging out at my house almost every night since you got sentenced to Dante duty. He made Meat check in with him every two hours."

"Stop it."

She laughs. "I'm serious, Cades." She shoots me a crooked grin. "He likes you. He wanted to throw you a party but didn't want it to come off weird. So I told him I'd come. We have a lot of catching up to do. Now go talk to your man." She pauses, cocks her head a little. "Men? Man? I'm not sure. I think you have all three of them, sweets."

"I don't know about that. Ax has been pretty busy with Valentina these past two weeks. And it appears that Lars and Selina have a thing going too."

"Right. They do. But that's work, honey. You?" She points her finger up and down my body. "You're just pleasure. It's gonna be tricky, but not impossible. Can I give you a piece of advice?"

"Sure." I laugh, unable to stop smiling.

"Just don't break their hearts. Be careful with their hearts, Cadee. They're only tough as nails on the outside."

I nod. And agree. "I know that."

"Then…" She pans her hand towards the

backyard and I see Cooper waiting just outside the fold-away doors. Hands in pockets instead of crossed over his chest. Grin on his face and his eyes… not dark with the depths of despair.

For the first time in a long time, I see the electric blue of a peacock feather instead of the poison of a gas flame.

He extends his hand. Inviting me to join him in the back yard.

To join his world.

And I feel, maybe for the first time in years, that maybe… everything will be OK.

CHAPTER TWENTY-SEVEN

I see her the moment she walks through the door and I hold my breath, waiting for her to see me too.

Mona finds her first. But I'm not focused on Mona.

All I see is Cadee.

I've seen her every day. I saw her just a few hours ago. So this shouldn't feel any different. But it does.

For two weeks I have kept my distance. I might not know Dante Legosi all that well, but I know his type. He's been coming to my house for parties like this—thrown by my father instead of me—for as long as I can remember.

But he's not invited tonight.

I didn't invite any of the pledges, except Mona, of course. This isn't about them, this is about us.

My little team.

Cadee sees me and I smile just a little. Just enough to let her know she's the reason this is happening and I'm glad she's home. Then I shove my hands in the pockets of my shorts, a nervous gesture. Because I don't know what to do with them.

Do I hug her? Take her face in my hands and kiss her?

Because that's what I want to do. Have an overwhelming urge to do, in fact.

She stops in the great room and stares at me. Waiting, I think. For me to make a decision.

And then I do know what to do.

I extend one hand and invite her to join me.

She walks forward smiling, then laughing. And by the time she places her fingertips in my open palm, she's breathless.

I don't think I've ever smiled this wide in my entire life. "Welcome home."

She giggles, then sucks in a deep breath of air and says, "Thanks."

"Go on, go on," Mona prods, pushing Cadee forward a step so we're so close she has to tip her chin up to keep her eyes locked with mine. "Have fun, kids. Life is short, gotta enjoy it. You only get one, and… all those other cliché sayings." Mona winks at me and turns away, walking past us, calling out for Lars.

Cadee and I just stand there for a second. And maybe it's a little awkward, but isn't that how it's supposed to be?

"So," I say.

"So."

We laugh.

"I heard you did this for me," Cadee says. She breaks eye contact, but just barely. She finds her nerve quick enough and then holds the moment, like she's enjoying it.

"I did." I let out a quick breath and turn a little, looking at the celebration I planned. It's got all the makings of a summer barbeque on the lakeshore. White lights strung around the dock and boathouse. The fire pit roaring, casting shadows on the faces of Ax and Valentina. Selina flipping burgers and dogs in the outdoor kitchen. Isabella sitting on the granite countertop nearby, nursing a beer.

Mona and Lars walk past us, arm in arm. And even though I have noticed that Lars has been distant with me over the past week—and I know this is about Cadee—he seems at ease tonight, letting Mona guide him over to the beer.

"I did," I say again. "This is for you, I mean. I'm fucking sorry, Cades. It was a shit move to stick you with Dante and I'm sorry."

She looks around for a moment, takes it all in, then looks back at me. "The bodyguards were a stroke of genius. I really do appreciate that."

"So you didn't have any problems with Dante?"

"No." She shakes her head a little to emphasize her answer. "He caught me in the pantry once."

"What?" My whole body stiffens.

"Relax," she says, tugging me towards the backyard. "He kissed me, that's it. And before you ask, I let him. He wasn't going to steal that from me, so I gave it away. I think I kinda stunned him. He was expecting a fight."

"Yeah." I let out the breath I was holding. "He's the kind of guy who likes the fight."

"Exactly. So he got his stupid kiss, but he didn't get the fight."

I think way too hard about those words and feel a little bit sad. "Cadee—"

"Nope." She places her hand on my chest, shakes her head a little. "We're not going backwards tonight. It's over. All of that stuff is over now."

And then, like he's listening in on our conversation, Ax stands up on the patio table, holding up a beer. "Listen up my diabolical partners in crime!" He paces back and forth along the length of it in typical

Ax fashion, his boots scuffing along the wood and his shoelaces dragging behind him. "Here's to the end of challenge fucking one of the Fang and Feather Summer Rush!" Then he goes sober for a moment, stops his pacing, and looks straight at Isabella. "And we're all. Still. Here. Fuck all those evil people who live for our demise. Fuck all those lies they tell. Fuck all those expectations they have. We beat you this time, assholes! And we're gonna do it again tomorrow!"

Isabella manages a smile. And in my expert opinion, it looks real. She lifts up her beer. "Cheers to that, you maniac."

We laugh and cheers back. Even though Cadee and I don't even have a drink yet.

"He certainly has a way with words, doesn't he?" Cadee says.

"Yeah," I say. "Yeah, he does. But he's right. We are going to win. Come on, let's relax. No one can hurt you here, Cades." I keep her hand in mine and lead her over to the kitchen.

"I'm seriously not worried about it, Cooper. I'm fine. I swear. Dante was actually… not that bad. I think maybe he gets it."

"Gets what?" Mona asks.

"You know. That we're—well, you guys—you're all in this together." She looks at Valentina, who has dragged Ax into the kitchen area with her. "Right? It's either swim or sink." She looks at Mona. "And swimming is something we all know how to do."

Mona's face goes serious. She's probably thinking about how she almost became an Olympic swimmer. Then she says, "We are a bunch of damn good swimmers."

Valentina holds up her beer. "I'll cheers to that, sister."

"All right, all right," Lars says. "Enough about the day job. Quitting time happened an hour ago and I'm hungry." Everyone agrees and starts making plates for burgers and dogs.

Quitting time. It's a weird way to put it, but he's right.

It's just a job.

We all eat together at the outdoor dining table. Laughing and joking. Talking about things that have nothing to do with the day job. And the sun sets while all this is happening and suddenly the backyard is lit up with white lights and the flicker of fire.

Ax goes to the fire and starts poking it with a long branch. Everyone else kinda settles in to smaller conversations. But then I glance over at the side yard and see Michael and Ivan coming towards us with Sophie and Elexa.

"Interlopers!" Ax yells, his poking stick on fire now. "Halt! Who goes there?"

"It's just us," Michael says.

"It's a private party, kids," Lars yells. "You'll see us tomorrow."

Michael looks at me. "I came to talk to Cooper real fast."

Ax stalks up to the crashing pledges, circling them as he holds the flaming stick in front of his face so he looks like the demons tatted up on his arms. He leans into Michael's face. "So why did you bring them?" He nods his head to Ivan, Elexa, and Sophie.

Michael looks at me nervously. I don't think any of the pledges are afraid of me or Lars, but pretty much everyone is still afraid of Ax. He's just weird and unpredictable. He hides the violence and anger inside him pretty well, but no matter what, it always leaks out through his eyes. He can't quite plug those two dark pits that lead straight to his black soul.

I step forward. "What's on your mind, Michael?"

Michael's still not sure that Ax isn't about to set him on fire, so he talks while maintaining eye contact with him. "I just need a few minutes. In private."

"Fuck," I moan. "Can't this wait?"

"No, Cooper. It can't. You're in charge, so I need to talk to you."

I look down at Cadee. "Give me a sec, OK?"

"Sure." She smiles at me and then walks off to join Mona and Isabella.

Michael walks towards me, while Ivan and Elexa start making themselves at home near the beer fridge. Sophie just kind of stands there until Selina takes her hand and pulls her over into the crowd.

"OK, what is it, Michael?"

"Can we go inside?"

I sigh. "Jesus Christ. This is starting to sound like a whole lot of drama that I'm not really interested in dealing with tonight."

"Five minutes, Cooper. I don't think that's asking too much."

I scowl at him. "This better be important."

"Well, you can tell me once we're done talking."

"Whatever."

I lead him through the fold-out patio doors and into the great room, then keep going until we're on the other side of the house in a small library. He follows me in and closes the door while I find a light and flick it on. "OK. Spill."

"Do you know what Dante's up to?"

"In reference to what, Michael?"

"Anything."

I cock my head at him and try to control my

building anger. "Either you have something to tell me, or you don't."

"I've heard rumors about him. And about Cadee too."

"Cadee? What rumors?"

"About you and her. And that something went down a few years back."

I control every physical reaction with precision. But inside, I'm starting to feel sick. "What did you hear?"

"Bits and pieces about an abortion. And… other things."

I clench my jaw. "And how does Dante fit into this?"

"He's the one spreading them. He said Cadee told him things. About you."

"Bullshit."

"Why is it bullshit? Because it's not true? Or because it didn't happen?"

Oh, I don't know if I'll be able to let this boy get away with that one. I might have to make an example of him. "Why do you care?"

"Because I think Dante's dangerous. And the only reason I'm here in rush this summer is to get Sophie away safely."

"Listen to me, Michael. And listen very fucking

closely. Sophie isn't getting away. Not this year, at least. She has four more years to figure out a real plan, just like the rest of us. But she will get through the rush. And she will be in Fang and Feather before fall semester starts. So if you really do love that girl, you will make her understand these facts. Do not lie and fill her head up with fantasies of running away. It's not going to happen. As far as this Dante stuff goes, let me handle it. Whatever rumors he's spreading about Cadee, they didn't come from her and they didn't come from me. And if the rumors are about us, then we're the only ones who matter."

Michael stares at me for a moment, then nods. He's just about to turn away and I'm just about to let out a long breath of relief when he looks me in the eyes. "You should know… Lars knows too. He's been asking around about it."

"About *what*?" I snarl these words out.

"An abortion, I guess. You tell me. And maybe I don't know what really happened between the four of you a few years back, but I do know that it involved the *four* of you, Cooper. So, you know, maybe it's *not* just about you and Cadee. Maybe Lars should've had a say in things too."

And then he turns and walks out.

The next thing I know I'm over at the bar cart

pouring myself a drink of whatever my father keeps in the crystal decanter. I gulp it down, then pour another and take it over to the large, wingback chair near the window and sit, rolling Michael's words around in my head. Trying to make sense of them.

Did he just threaten me?

If so, I will give mad props to Michael for not only having balls, but also wording that entire conversation so carefully.

He wants Sophie out.

I have a secret I'm hiding from everyone, including my two best friends, who probably should've been included in this little plan of mine three fucking years ago.

"What are you doing?"

I look up and see Cadee in the doorway. "Come here."

"What?"

"Come here."

She smirks at me. But she comes. I pull her into my lap and put my arms around her.

"What's going on, Cooper? What did Michael say?"

"Did he leave?"

"No, he's still here. Elexa and Ivan are playing a drinking game with Ax and Isabella."

"Fuck."

"Don't worry. Lars is looking after Isabella."

I glance up at her. "He is?"

"Yeah. It seems like Lars is always looking after somebody."

"Yeah."

"So… why are you sitting in here all by yourself?"

I sigh. "Michael came to…" I squint for a moment, choosing my words. "He came to threaten me, I think."

"About what?"

"Sophie. He wants her out. I don't have that kind of power. I mean, I could kick her out, but someone would drag her back in. So what's the point?"

"How is that a threat?"

I hold her a little closer. And then decide I'm not going to tell her the rest. She has put up with so much shit these past two weeks, this news needs to wait. "Oh, hell! You know what?"

She sits up in my lap a little. "What?"

"I almost forgot. I put you in a new bedroom."

"What? What's wrong with my old one?"

And here, this moment right here, this is the time to be honest tonight. This is what she needs to hear. "It was too far away from mine."

She giggles. "Hmm. I don't know what to make of

new Cooper. I don't see you for three years, then suddenly I'm living in your house."

"I didn't do that."

"Agreed. But then I have to move out of your house for two weeks to stand in for Mona at Dante's, and you're suddenly… what? In love with me again?"

"Again? Did I love you?"

"You tell me."

I look up at her. I want to kiss those plump, sexy lips so bad. And then I want to kiss so many other places on her body. But I need her to hear me first. "Cadee Hunter, I have been dreaming about you since I first saw you running through the woods when I was ten."

"Ten, huh? It took you seven years to notice me?" She laughs.

"I was a pretty dumb kid, wasn't I?"

"Sooo stupid."

"I'm smart now."

"Is that so?"

"Mmm. And I did love you." Both our smiles drop and she stares into my eyes. "I did love you, Cadee. It took me a while to figure that out that year. In fact, I'm just gonna be honest here and say I just figured it out like a week ago."

She smiles again.

"I was wrong."

"No, Cooper. You weren't. You were right. Because if you didn't take me to the clinic that day, I would be living a lie right now. Or something much, much worse."

I know I should tell her that Lars might be on to us. At least some of it. But I've been waiting my whole life to feel this way about someone, and I'm tired of sharing.

I stand up, still holding onto her. And then I set her down, take her hand, and lead her out of the library.

She doesn't ask where we're going. I hope she doesn't need to.

I pull her down the long hallway until we get to the foyer, then I take her up the stairs to my apartment. I debate stopping at the door. Ask her lots of things. Make her admit things too. But there's another part of me that just wants to step up and take control. Be the hero.

And if this were Isabella, I'd do that. Because Isabella is the kind of girl who needs a hero.

But Cadee Hunter is no Isabella.

"Cadee," I whisper, my hand on the door knob, ready to open it. "You can always say no." I glance over my shoulder to check her expression for any hidden clues about what she's thinking.

"I know that, Cooper. I have always known that."

There is a lot more to be said, but if we go there, we won't come back any time soon. So maybe taking control and being her hero is a selfish act, but I can't seem to stop myself.

And she doesn't protest.

I kick the door closed with my foot, then we just stand there in the dark, barely able to see each other. And then, before I can question my own motives any further, she takes the first step, pressing her body up against mine, gripping my shoulders as she leans up on her tiptoes and kisses me on the mouth.

I try to keep it slow, but my desire for her—the passion between us that we've been denying for so long—overtakes everything else. And I kiss her back hard. And forcefully. And unapologetically.

Her fingertips find the edge of my shirt and she starts pushing it up my chest. I whip it over my head and toss it aside, looking down as she studies my tattoo, the tip of her nail slowly tracing the K in the center of the High Court coat of arms.

"King," she whispers.

"So they tell me."

She lifts her eyes up to mine and we're suddenly on pause. "Why?"

If she were any other girl, I'd push play so fast.

Get on with what's about to happen next.

But Cadee Hunter has never been just any other girl.

"Why what?"

"Why do people want to be king? I don't understand. Why do they want to control everyone? Why can't they just be happy controlling themselves?"

"Ha," I huff. "I think you just answered your own question. They don't know how to control themselves, Cadee. We both know that."

"Yeah."

"Do you want to stop?"

"No." She smiles. "No. Not at all. Sorry to break the mood. I just have always wondered that. Because you're right. Just being responsible for me is hard enough. There's no room left over to even think about being anyone's king."

I place my hands on her cheeks and stare into her eyes, letting her know I see her. "That's because you're good, Cades. And most of the people around you aren't."

"You're good."

"Right."

"And Ax is good."

"I think everyone would disagree with that."

"And Lars too."

"Hmm. Now that one, I do agree with. You and Lars are a lot alike. Always patient. Never letting the anger and resentment steal too much of your souls."

She leans up and kisses me again. Only this time I don't hurry it up or try to turn it into something else. I just accept what she gives me.

"It's a nice balance, isn't it?"

She's still kissing me, so I whisper, "What's that?" past her lips.

"You and Ax. Me and Lars. Us."

I stop kissing her, suddenly confused. "Are you sure you want to do this?"

"Why do you keep asking me that?"

"Because… Ax and Lars."

She shrugs. "I guess if they wanted in on this, they'd be here. Wouldn't they?"

I laugh. I can't help it. "You did not just say that."

"Oh, I did." She winks at me. Then she takes my hand and starts leading me across the room. She stops in the middle, looking around. I didn't turn any lights on when we came in, but the moon is bright outside and I have a huge window that looks out across the lake, so we can see well enough.

"Where's the bed?"

I chuckle. "This is the living room, Cadee."

"You have a living room in your bedroom? Jesus.

Maybe there's something to that King thing after all?"

Then I remember the real reason I was bringing her up here. Not that I wasn't bringing her up to mess around with her, because I was. I lead her over to one of the other rooms and flick the light on.

"Oh, so this is your bedroom. Hmm. It's nice. Kinda sparse."

It is kinda sparse. It's not a place for girls. Just a queen-size bed, and a couple of nightstands. Ax and Isabella are really the only people who ever use this room.

"It's not my bedroom, Cades. It's yours."

"What?" She turns to look at me and I swear to God, I barely recognize the girl before me. She is golden from all the sun these past two weeks. Her eyes are bright with possibilities instead of dull with defeat. And her surprise is innocent and real.

This change in her causes a litany of questions to run through my mind. Because her mother died—*died*—a month ago. And aside from that one bout of sniffling in the boat after her second day at the Glass House, as far as I know, she still hasn't cried.

Not tonight, Cooper. There's time for that later. "It's my guest suite. I'm putting you up in here. I don't like that your bedroom has a door that leads outside."

She tsks her tongue playfully. "Worried I might

get away?"

That's not what I'm worried about. At all. But I agree anyway. Because all of tomorrow's problems can wait. "Yeah. I am."

"Well, you don't have to worry about that." Then she sucks in a deep breath. "I've missed you, Cooper. And not just these two weeks, either. I don't even think I knew I missed you until you knocked me over that day on the steps. But ever since then…" She shakes her head. "You're it, Coop. You're my *it*."

I want to do things to this girl. So many things. And I want to do all those things *right now*. I reach for the light to flick it off, but she grabs my arm and says, "No. Leave it on."

Then she reaches for the hem of her t-shirt and pulls it over her head. Just stands there in her pretty yellow bra and looks at me. Not at my body, like most girls when we get to this part of a night. But me. My eyes. She pops the clasp between her breasts and then her bra falls open, baring her to me.

I reach for the lacy edges of it and slide it down her arms. She's already moved on to the button of my shorts, hastily pulling the zipper down and reaching inside to pull my cock out.

My eyes close involuntarily, but I open them again just as quickly because I don't want to miss a single moment of Cadee Hunter dropping to her knees in front of me.

I think I hold my breath when she begins sliding her hand up and down my shaft and when those perfect lips part and the tip of my cock slides past her lips, I have serious doubts about my ability to stay standing.

"Fuck, Cadee."

Her eyes are locked on mine as she seals her lips around my head and takes me deeper. Her tongue dancing along my dick.

I fist her hair with both hands, and enjoy the feeling of her breath tickling across my balls. And then her hand is there, cupping them.

She knows just what to do. She knows exactly how I like it. "*Fuuuck*." It just feels so good.

I dreamed about getting Cadee on her knees in front of me for months back when we were sneaking around my senior year of Prep. And she held out for a long time too. If there's one thing I know about Cadee Hunter, it's that she doesn't easily give in. She would watch me jerk off though. And it's like she took notes. Like she paid attention to how I would get myself off. And then, when she finally did put her mouth over the top of my cock the very first time, she gave me the best blow job ever.

And then I realize this is the first time we've been together without Lars or Ax. That's why she was asking about them. It wasn't her rule back then, it was mine.

All those times I insisted she be shared equally between us, she liked it.

She pulls back, lets my cock slip out of her mouth, and stands up.

"What are you doing?"

"You're thinking too hard."

"How do you know?"

She unbuttons and unzips her shorts, then wiggles them down her hips. It's super sexy, but I don't even think she's trying to tease me. She's just being Cadee. And then she's standing in front of me, as naked as I am.

She starts pushing me over to the bed.

But I'm done living in my head and I twirl her around so fast, she squeals as she flops onto the mattress on her back.

I grab her knees and open them up, grinning at her as I kneel down and ease my mouth up to her pussy.

She's already wet. And her breathing becomes ragged immediately as her fingers slide into my hair, urging me on. The other hand grasps onto my shoulder, digging her nails in as she arches her back.

"Cooper," she whispers.

I pull back, my cock hard and throbbing now, eager to be inside her. And the memories of times past flood through my mind and I can't help but wonder, as I kiss my way up her stomach, pausing briefly to squeeze her breasts and suck on her nipples, why I ever walked away from this girl.

I push her up the bed. She smiles and giggles as she brings her knees up to her chest, inviting me to take her however I please.

Then I'm kissing her mouth, letting her taste herself on my tongue. And I make a promise to myself that I will never let her get away again.

Her hand slides down her belly, the back of it dragging across mine as well. And she grabs my cock and directs me to her entrance, sliding the tip of my dick back and forth across her wet clit before finally letting me slip inside her. We moan in unison as I push myself deeper inside her until she winces and sucks in a sharp gasp. I ease back, then forward again. Getting our rhythm going as she rocks her hips up to meet me. Digging her nails into my back.

I can't stop kissing Cadee Hunter.

I never want to stop kissing Cadee Hunter.

And when we climax together, the deal is sealed.

She's mine now. And I'm not sharing her with anyone.

CHAPTER TWENTY-EIGHT

Cooper and I lie in each other's arms, my back tucked up against his chest, his face pressed against my neck, him gently kissing me while his hand cups my breast. And the sigh I let out in this moment is monumental in nature.

It is one of tremendous relief.

It is one of settling.

A feeling that I haven't experienced since my father died three years ago and then, shortly after, my mother and I moved into the attic in the inn and my life started unraveling thread by thread.

I lose myself in the settling.

And suddenly Cooper feels surreal. Being here in his house. The scholarship at the end of the summer. The new friends, the new clothes, the new everything.

Then comes the guilt.

What kind of terrible person loses her mother one month ago and just slips into a new life like this? A new life filled with privilege. Pool parties, and champagne toasts, and lakeside mansions that hold angsty bully kings inside.

And let's not forget that you might actually be looking forward to going to High Court College. Even though your parents lived on this campus since you were born, and they never wanted that for you.

Is this rebellion? Do I have some secret desire to erase everything they taught me?

I don't think so.

Then why?

Why am I doing this?

I should not be looking forward towards the future. It's too soon. I should be stuck in the past. At least for a little bit.

And I should not want to go to this school or get involved with their weird secrets.

But… I do.

I have wanted to be a part of High Court since I was a little girl. Oh, how I wanted to wear the prep-school uniform. The mustard-yellow pleated skirt and the perfectly-tailored navy-blue blazer with those fighting lions embroidered in gold on the left breast pocket. The crisp white shirt and the navy and gold striped tie. Don't even get me started with the white knee socks and those gold tassels bouncing along their calves as the rich girls walked through the beautiful central gardens that my father created like they owned the world.

And they did. At least in my mind.

I do love who I am. But is it so wrong to want more? Is it so wrong to grab the golden ring when it's in reach?

Cooper turns over and I slip out of his arms. He's sleeping hard. And for the first time in years, I wonder how Cooper is really doing.

I turn too. And I study him in profile. His mouth is open a little, his breathing slow and even, but a little bit loud. Like he's tired.

That's what he told me that one night we were talking in his boat. *I'm tired, Cadee.*

And he is. I can tell. He wants out so bad.

And I only want *in*.

I swing my legs out of bed, put my clothes on, and leave his room. I don't know where I'm going. Maybe Mona is outside smoking.

But then, when I get to the bottom of the stairs, I hear noises in the kitchen.

I silently creep down the long central hallway and enter the great room to find Ax leaning against the large soapstone island. His back is to me, and even though there are no lights on, the moon is shining through the French doors.

His back. I don't think I've ever seen it before, because Ax never takes his shirt off. He hasn't been swimming in the pool once so far this summer. And even three years ago, when we were together for months, he never took it off then, either.

And now I know why.

Scars. Long gashes cover his back like… claw marks. But there is almost no animal alive that can make a gash like that. Maybe a lion or a tiger, but come on. That's just stupid.

So how did they get there?

He turns to the industrial-sized refrigerator, swinging the door open so I can't see his face. Then he takes a jug of milk over to the far counter, gets a glass from the cupboard, and stares at it in his hand for a few moments too long.

He uncaps the milk, lifts it to his lips, and drinks straight from the jug. And then turns again and sees me with my mouth hanging open.

Because he's got scars on his chest too.

"Cadee," he whispers, quickly putting the milk down. "Is everything OK?"

"Is everything OK?" I repeat.

"What's wrong? Why are you down here?"

"Ax," I say, walking towards him, unable to stop looking at the large, round burn marks where his fighting lions should have eyes. I reach for them with my fingertips, but he grabs my hand in his fist before I can touch him. When I look up he's staring down into my eyes. "What is this?"

He sighs, lets go of my hand and then shrugs. "Exactly what it looks like."

"Is this why you sleep in the boathouse? Does the Judge—"

But I can't finish. Because when I think about it, of course this is what the Judge does to him. The man is huge. Easily the tallest person I've ever met. And broad too. That's where Ax gets his build from, but his father is a whole other level of muscular. The Judge looks like he used to wrestle for the WWE. Or maybe he was some kind of mercenary in another life. He is that scary.

I've never had to appear before the Judge myself. I'm one of those good girls, after all. But I've heard the rumors. He doesn't give anyone three strikes. He throws the book at them the very first time.

Even Ax didn't escape his wrath in that department. He didn't go to jail, but I know about his stints in rehab. And once I heard he spent half a year in a psych ward. That was way before I knew him.

Ax sighs again, because my silence is long. And now I don't know what to say to him. He simply lifts the milk jug back up to his mouth and drinks. Then he wipes his lips with the back of his hand, caps the milk, and puts it back in the fridge.

When he turns back around he's smiling. "Don't tell Coop I did that. He fucking hates it."

Then he walks away. Like he's just going to leave.

I jog to catch up with him and grab his arm before he can get out of the great room. "Hold on. You're not leaving."

He grins at me again. "I'm pretty tired, Cades. I'm gonna crash. You mind if I take your room? I've been sleeping in there for two weeks and you're pretty preoccupied with Cooper these days." He shrugs, then smiles again. "I can smell your hair on the pillow. I kinda dig that."

I'm shaking my head at him.

"That's a no?" He laughs. "You're telling me no?"

"You don't get to walk out without telling me what all these scars are."

He cocks his head at me. "Come on. You know what they are."

"That bastard did this to you?"

"Actually, no. It was my mother. She's fucking

certifiable."

"Wait. You have a mother?"

"Cadee, everyone has a mother."

"Yeah, but—"

"You thought she was dead? No. I didn't get that lucky. My father keeps her locked up in a wing of our house. Every now and then, if we're having a big party, he'll drug her up and put her in a wheelchair and let her come sit downstairs for a while. But she's been out of it for so long now, so many drugs, I doubt she could sober up even if she wanted to." He pauses. Finds my eyes. Stares down into them. "And I don't think she wants to."

"How did I not know this?"

"That I have a mom? Or that she uses me for carving practice?"

"Both."

He shrugs. "You never asked, Cades. Everyone else knows." He turns again. Like this conversation is normal and it's over now.

I grab his arm again. "Wait. Ax."

He doesn't turn around. Just kind of side-eyes me over his shoulder. "What?"

"The burns on your tattoo. Those aren't old."

"No," he agrees. "They're not." He pauses for a few moments. "Anything else?"

I know he wants to leave. But I'm not going to let him. Because he and I are… more than this. I don't really have a word for it, we're just… *more* than this.

"Yes," I say, coming around in front of him. Then I wrap my arms around his middle and hug him.

"Cadee."

He tries to push me off, but I don't let go of him. I just shake my head and say, "No. I'm not letting you walk away without this hug. I don't even care if you hug me back. I just want to hug you forever and never let you go."

He takes a deep breath and I can hear his heart. He's a lot taller than me so my ear is right over the top of it. It thumps fast and erratic inside his chest. And then he wraps his arms around my shoulders and hugs me back. "I don't need the hug, Cades. But if you do—"

"Shut up, Ax."

We stay like that even after it gets weird. And I do not care.

"If Cooper saw this, he'd get jealous."

This makes me pull back a little. But I don't let go of him. Just in case he wants to walk away. "He didn't used to get jealous."

"Yeah, he did."

"What? No, he didn't."

"Cadee. Come on. Maybe you didn't see him when I was with you, but I was always watching him watch us."

I frown. "But… it was his idea."

"Yeah, well." Ax sighs. "Sometimes things change." Then he carefully pulls my arms from around his waist and backs up, creating distance between us again. He keeps backing up. Like he's afraid to take his eyes off me. "I think this is it, Cadee."

"This is what?"

"Goodbye, ya know? It was fun. And I do like you. I'll always be there for you. But…" He shrugs. "All good things must end."

Then he salutes me, turns away, and walks down the hallway towards my old room.

The next morning, I have a feeling. I can't explain this feeling and maybe it's just about Ax's midnight goodbye, but something seems wrong.

Cooper and I get ready separately, and even though I know I should bring Ax and Lars up, I don't. Not because I don't want to, but because my mind is stuck on those scars on Ax's back and the burns on his chest.

I don't know what to say. I just feel with all my heart that something needs to be said and I feel guilty for not saying more. Ax might not be everyone's dream man, but he's got a soul inside him. He feels things deeply. He just doesn't show many people that side of himself.

Valentina sees it though. She stuck up for him.

And this leads me down a rabbit hole of questions about Ax and Valentina. I've seen them together lots of times. Ax is a toucher, so I've seen them close. But aside from that kiss during day one of rush, I have never seen them together as a couple.

And even though Valentina didn't hint that they are a couple, she pretty much stated outright that they are partners. At least in the society.

Lars and Selina don't kiss, but now that I think about it, they do hang out a lot. Maybe hang out is the wrong word. They… gravitate to each other.

And of course, Cooper and Isabella *are* a thing. Just not an exclusive thing. She's not jealous of me, that's for sure. She hasn't made a single derogatory remark for weeks. So she's not in love with him. And he's certainly not in love with her.

But there's *something* there.

Cooper doesn't notice my distraction this

morning. He smiles, he talks, he opens doors and lets me walk through first. But something is definitely on his mind too.

"Wait," I say, pulling Cooper back to me before we leave the woods. "What do I do today?"

"Just..." He stares down at me. And his deeply disturbed eyes have a look of concern. "Stay away from Dante. Help in the kitchen, I guess. I don't care, Cadee. You can just hang out in the cabañas if you want. I don't think anyone is going to mess with you. Do you?"

"No. I don't think that." Then I shrug. "OK, then. Good luck with the challenge. I'm going to go help in the kitchen."

He smiles, then leans down to kiss me. It's not a make-out kiss or anything. Nothing spectacular. It's just very... natural. Like kissing each other goodbye in the morning before work is something we do. "Thanks. We'll talk later." And then he walks off towards the pool, where Lars is hanging out in a group with Michael and Jamie and I go inside the Glass House and make my way to the kitchen.

"Well, look who it is."

I find Victor's face as I'm searching for an apron in the locker room. "Hey. How's it going?"

He folds his arms and leans against the door. "Didn't expect you back."

"Why's that? I'm here for the summer just like you."

"Yeah, and you're certainly not going to walk out now."

I smile at him patiently, the way one might smile at an annoying child. "Listen, Victor. Thanks for the warning a couple weeks ago, but I'm fine. I filled in for Mona and now I'm just going to do my job, finish the summer, and then go to school like everyone else."

Victor stares me down for a moment. It's uncomfortable. But I finish tying my apron and keep smiling. "What do you need me to help with?"

"You know what my problem is with you, Cadee?"

"I could not even begin to imagine. But I'm sure you're going to tell me."

"You think you're doing us a favor when you decide to show up in the kitchen. Like you're a visiting family member asking if she can help with the dishes after dinner. And you're not. You're an employee, Cadee."

"Thanks for the update."

"You report to people here."

"I know."

"And it's not Cooper Valcourt."

"Is it you?" My tone is overly sweet now. I'm so

not interested in fighting with this guy.

He actually sneers at me. "No."

"Then who do I report to?"

"You can serve the coffee. But hurry up. The second challenge is today."

As if I didn't know that.

I don't know what Victor has stuck up his ass, but I suspect it has something to do with me not accepting my place and station in life. So I don't spend any more time thinking about it. I just get the coffee ready without speaking to any of the other servers, and try to control my nervousness about what's coming today.

And when I go outside and start setting up the coffee service in the tent, all the girls look pretty nervous too.

"Cadee," Sophie whispers as she comes up to me.

"What's up?"

"Do you know anything about the challenge today?"

Cooper knows what the second challenge is, obviously. But he didn't fill me in on it. "No. But don't worry about it too much, Sophie. You're going to be fine. Michael is on your side."

"Right."

"He didn't mention anything?"

"No. He didn't know."

Or he's lying. But I don't say that out loud. Sophie is a gentle soul. But not the same way I am. She's also… weak. Always on the verge of falling to pieces.

"Mona is in the house!"

Everyone turns to see Mona walk out of the woods, her hands up in the air, her trademark just-fucked hair piled on top of her head. Her lips are glossy red and she's dressed in head-to-toe *black*. I'm talking cargo pants, t-shirt, and combat boots. She looks like she's been cast as an enemy tart in the next *Mission: Impossible* movie.

"Yay!" I say, smiling at my new friend, but then realize—I'm the only one happy to see her.

Except Dante. "There she is, folks. My woman."

Mona makes a face. I wait for her bodyguards to appear, but she enters the tent alone and there are no men in black coming out of the woods.

Dante is approaching Mona, but she puts up a hand and walks right past him over to me.

"Hey, where's Meat and Chatter today?" I ask.

"Ask your boyfriend," Mona says.

"What?"

"Cooper said I couldn't bring them anymore."

"Why?"

"Because they fucked up my challenge, that's why," Dante says.

Mona turns to Dante. "You got your way, asshole. But if you think the scariest thing about me is my troop of bodyguards"—she lifts her sunglasses up so she can stare him in the eyes—"you better think again."

Dante mumbles, "Bitch," and then walks off.

"He really told you they couldn't come?" I ask Mona.

She sighs. "Yes. Apparently, Dante's father called the Chairman complaining about the bodyguards and managed to get them banned from the rest of the challenges. So we're on our own."

I look around at the other girls and figure the bodyguards probably aren't needed anyway. Elexa and Ivan are best friends now. Sophie has Michael. And Maddie, Natasha, Jamie, and Roland have settled into some kind of foursome. But they look happy. They're sitting over at a small table laughing and smiling at least.

"But don't worry, I'll be fine." Mona smiles at me. "I know how to handle Dante."

I catch Victor shooting me a dirty look from across the tent at the other side of the service table. And when Dante wanders over to grab some fruit, Victor leans in to whisper something in his ear.

Dante's eyes immediately find mine. "Fugling!" he yells. "Get your ass to work before I let the Chairman know you've been fucking off this whole time."

Mona and I roll our eyes at each other. "Go. I'll take care of him." She saunters off, calling Dante's name, and I gather up trash and straighten the glassware.

Cooper's hand slides over my hips and he leans in to whisper. "Don't let him get to you. Just ignore it. He's just pissed because he knows I'm looking for a way to cut him."

"I'm fine. I'm actually looking forward to working today. I've had enough sitting out by the pool."

He kisses me on the cheek and this time when I look around the room, I catch Lars staring at me. I give him a little wave and he returns a half-hearted smile.

Yeah. Cooper and I need to have a talk with him.

Maybe Ax is OK with how things are shaking out between Cooper and I and doesn't need to have a conversation about it. But Lars definitely does.

But then everyone is interrupted by Ax. "Hear ye! Hear ye!" he belts out from the front of the tent. "Line up for challenge two, ladies!" He's wearing a pair of faded jeans with lots of holes today and a white t-shirt that says 'Crybabies are Losers.' His wallet chain flaps against his leg as he paces back and forth, those evil eyes of his searching the tent like he's looking for a victim.

It doesn't quite have the same effect on any of us this time. I think we all know that Ax is dangerous and will beat the shit out of you if you cross him, but deep down he's got a really soft heart. Especially for girls.

And I have to give him props for that. If my mother had wounded me the way his did, I might harbor some deep-rooted resentment of women.

All the girls look at each other nervously, wondering what this challenge might be.

I sigh and lean against a chair.

"Get. To fucking. Work."

I look over at Victor, startled. "What is your problem?"

"You work here, *Fugling*. And we need help in the kitchen. You're not here to enjoy the show."

"Whatever." I push off the chair and walk towards the Glass House, cursing Victor under my breath. And once inside, everyone seems to have a job for me to do. Starting with scrubbing the floors on my hands and knees.

They have the curtains open today. And the other servers are setting up for what looks to be an elaborate luncheon, but the door is closed, so I don't hear anything that happens outside in the tent.

All I see is Sophie crying hysterically as the other girls do their best to console her.

One of the servers comes through the door from outside and I stop her before she can retreat into the kitchen. "What happened to Sophie?" I ask.

The girl—no clue what her name is—smirks at me. "She was traded."

"Traded? What?"

"Yup. Dante bought her right out from under Michael."

"Yes!" a boy says behind me.

"What's good about that?" I ask.

He laughs. "We have a pool going and they were my picks. I just won a thousand bucks! Drinks on me tonight, people!"

They all whoop and holler, enjoying Sophie's fear and sadness.

I want to go out there and console her—tell her she will be fine. I made it, she can too. Even without the bodyguards. But I hesitate. Because the only reason Dante didn't make my life a living hell was because Meat and Chatter had their eye on me every second of the past two weeks.

Then he's there. Dante is standing in the doorway to the Glass House. "Fugling," he barks. "I need you to massage my feet. Get your ass out here. Now!"

CHAPTER TWENTY-NINE

"Calm down!"

But Michael isn't capable of listening right now. "Don't you tell me to calm down, Cooper! When your girlfriend gets bought by a sadistic asshole, you send in bodyguards. When mine gets the same sentence, you send them home!"

"You're overreacting," Lars says.

"Am I? Am I really?" Michael swings his gaze to me. "Then why did you feel the need to send in thugs to protect Cadee? And why aren't you doing the same thing for Sophie?"

I let out a long breath. "Michael, it's not my call. Dante's father called the Chairman and he put an end to the bodyguards. Otherwise—"

"And you don't care! You do not care! That stunt you pulled to help your nobody girlfriend? That just made things worse! *You*! Made things worse!"

I can't say he's wrong. Dante is gloating like a fox who just got handed the keys to the hen house. And he is bad. I knew that from the beginning. Then I went and put him in charge. Which was a stupid thing to do because Dante took that shit seriously and used it against me when he had his father talk to mine. *If he's such a bad guy, Cooper, why did you put him in charge?*

"Michael, Sophie is going to be fine."

"She's not going to be fine! She has no protection because she knows she can't walk out! You made sure of that too!"

"I didn't have anything to do with that! Don't you get it? I'm just following orders!"

"Then you're worse." We all turn to find Isabella standing a few feet off with her arms crossed over her chest and a deep frown. "Or at the very least you're just like them. Just like your father. Just like mine. You knew the second challenge was a trade. If the boys aren't happy"—she throws up her arms—"then they get to trade us. Find a better, more compliant girl. You could've at least warned Michael so he could've brought enough money to keep his girlfriend from being sold to the devil."

"You knew too, Isabella. And so did you." I point to Valentina and Selina. "We all knew. So any one of you could've warned him too. But we didn't. Because we…"

"You didn't because you all underestimated me." Now we turn to Dante. "You're no King, Cooper. I don't even know why you bother pretending. You don't even want to be here. You should be the one to go home." He looks at us. All of us. And even though I knew he was evil from the very start, he's not even trying to hide it now. He takes a step forward towards me. Leans in a little, like we're about to share a secret. "And make no mistake. I hold grudges, Cooper Valcourt. You think you put one over on me when you sent Cadee to my house with bodyguards? You didn't. I was planning the minute I saw your little girlfriend had joined the party. I planned this, Cooper. And make no mistake, my game is far from over."

He turns, his gaze wandering over the crowd until it lands on Sophie. "Come on, Sophie. We're gonna have some fun together today, girl. Where's that Fugling?" He looks over his shoulder at me. And I swear to God, I think I see a glint of red in his eyes when he smiles with satisfaction. Like he really is the devil. "My father told the Chairman all about how Cadee Hunter was shirking her duties and the staff was pissed. He's going to take it all away if she doesn't spend the next six weeks doing *exactly* what she's told."

He turns back to Sophie. "I'm gonna go find the Fugling. You just concentrate on putting your bikini on for me."

"I don't have a bikini!" Sophie objects.

"Oh, you do now, Sophie. I brought one especially for you."

Fuck. I run my fingers through my hair and spin around, seeking out Lars. He's off to the side now, his arms folded across his chest. *Don't look at me*, that's what he's saying. *Your deal, dude.*

I turn back to Dante. But he's gone. Already heading towards the Glass House to presumably start making Cadee's life miserable too.

"OK," Ax says. "That's enough. No one is getting hurt on our watch, you got it?" He's looking at Sophie. "If I need to break into his house every night to make sure you're safe, I will."

Sophie is crying in a weird way. Not sobbing. Tears, for sure. Her face is wet and she's breathing fast and heavy, but no noise is coming out of her mouth. She nods at him and wipes her face with the back of her hand. "OK."

"Yeah?" Ax asks. "You're good? Just… put on the bathing suit, Sophie. Then do what he says. Only say no if he hits a hard line."

She hiccups a little. Probably imagining all the

various hard lines she has.

"OK, then. Go change. He has to hang out here every day from nine to five, Sophie. You're gonna be fine. I promise." Then he looks at Michael. "It's only two weeks. Then… we buy her back. All of us, if necessary. He's doing this to divide us. We're not going to let him do that."

Michael looks over at Sophie, then back at Ax. "We'll buy her back?"

"No matter what it takes," I tell Michael, thankful that Ax is here standing in for Lars as the voice of reason. Because Lars sure as fuck isn't doing anything.

Michael nods, placated for now. The idea that we can buy her back is a good one. He walks off after Sophie, talking softly to her as they go.

"Well, this is a fucking shit show," Isabella says.

"Yeah, thanks for your support, by the way. I really don't appreciate you fanning the fucking flames, Isabella."

She looks at me with… what? What is that look? It's not hate. It's not loathing.

It's… disappointment. I recognize it. My father shoots me that same look all the time.

"I'm doing my best, Isabella. We will protect her."

She just…*stares* at me. Finally, Selina and Valentina step in and lead her away, talking about bathing suits and a nice day at the pool.

It's not a nice day at the pool. Or a nice week, for that matter. It's seven straight days of Dante humiliating Cadee by making her massage his feet while he gets a hard-on and doesn't even try to hide it. Or making her fan him with a leafy branch she had to hunt down in the woods. He made her go back six times before he was satisfied. Then she had to stand in the hot sun for hours, waving that useless branch like a fan.

On day three it rained and he made Cadee and Sophie mud-wrestle in their bathing suits. I thought Michael was going to lose it after Dante got the staff to come out and place bets.

I think Ivan and Ax both enjoyed that day a little too much. And honestly, even though Cadee and Sophie were muddy, they managed to have fun and no one got hurt.

In fact, everything was just childish things like that until this morning.

Day eight.

Cadee and I spent the nights together and we

didn't talk about Dante at all. But it was clear she was too worried to think about our new relationship status. And tired, too. Dante just refused to let up on her for a moment during the day.

Ax wasn't staying in the house because he was stalking around Dante's mansion, trying to keep an eye on Sophie. He gave her a little panic button device, and she pushed the first night. Enter Ax, via a window, and then the sheriff was called and that was the end of Ax's inside access.

I had to call my father on day two. In fact, we had a conference call with the Legosis and the Bettingtons. Lars did all the talking because I was too pissed to speak.

After about two hours of Mr. Legosi bitching about how much money his family has donated to "the cause" and the fact that Sophie was taking home in excess of two hundred thousand dollars at this point, we all agreed she could keep the panic button. But if she pushed it without good reason, she would forfeit her right to be traded again at the end of the challenge, and Dante would get another two weeks with her for free.

She sucked it up after that.

But she's not happy. At all.

And neither is Michael.

As far as Ax goes, he was told to stay away from Dante or the next time his father would step in and take care of things, i.e. Ax will probably go to jail and be made an example of. Which would probably be fine with Ax, except his father is known for coming up with very creative punishments.

Ax sucked it up too.

Isabella has been drunk every single day and I'm tired of her shit. Even Selina and Valentina are tired of her shit. But Isabella is… weak. That's the best word to describe her. And pushing her does no good. She doesn't rise to the occasion, she shuts down. She's a lot more like Sophie than anyone wants to admit.

So day eight.

I'm sitting at the pool fully clothed because the idea of sitting at the pool lost its novelty about five days ago. It's hot as fuck, everyone hates me, including the fucking servers, because Lacy Pendleton made an appearance two hours ago throwing a fit about how Cadee stole her scholarship and demanding that I find a place for her.

I have no place for her. I'm not even in charge here and everyone knows it. I'm a fucking babysitter. So I told her to tell her father to call my father and they would work it out.

Lars escorted her home and when they turned to

leave, I caught Victor English snickering like an asshole near the back of the Glass House where the servers hang out during their breaks.

I'm ninety-nine percent sure he was behind Lacy's sudden appearance.

Then Dante made a rule that Cadee couldn't walk all day. She had to crawl everywhere.

Fine. He wants to be a dick? That's his prerogative.

So I go over to Cadee to remind her that she's here by choice—and yeah. That was not what she wanted to hear.

Every single girl ganged up on me and now… I'm the dick here. Not Dante.

Could it get any worse?

Yes, it can always get worse.

Because I get a cryptic message from my father's assistant, Laurie, telling me she needs to talk to me—in person, mind you. All the way across the fucking lake—and this meeting needs to happen today at three PM.

Cadee was pissed about that too, because she wanted me to wait until five when she could leave the rush, and come with me to see if her cottage was OK because one of the other servers told her this morning that Victor was living there. So even though I am perfectly capable of checking in on her cottage myself, she's mad at me because I won't wait.

I can't wait because Laurie was only stopping in for a day to handle some things for my father and she needs to leave campus by three-thirty so she can catch a plane to wherever the fuck she's spending the rest of the summer.

I wish that were it, but it's not.

Lars is definitely pissed at me about something. What this something is, I'm not quite sure, because he won't talk to me. But it's probably about Cadee.

I sigh. Because I'm being killed slowly by a thousand papercuts and this fucking summer is only half over.

But it's two-thirty now and I need to leave to make the appointment with Laurie, so I force myself to get up and wander over to Ax. "Please," I say to him. "Please do not let anything else happen today while I'm gone. Can you do that for me?"

"Sure." He doesn't even look up at me. He's playing cards with Elexa and Ivan, who, to everyone's surprise, seem to have hit it off because they show up every morning wearing smiles declaring themselves to be the happiest couple alive.

What the hell is happening? is now my new favorite phrase.

I would like to kiss Cadee goodbye before I take off and tell her I'll see her at home tonight, but she's currently crawling over to Dante's feet, getting ready to massage them, and even dumbfuck me knows how to read a room every once in a while.

So I just leave.

Thirty-seven minutes later—the boat ran out of gas seventy feet from the High Court Marina and I had to coast in. I'm probably being written a ticket right now by security for illegally parking my boat. I'm also wet, didn't quite make it to the dock—I almost run Laurie over as she's leaving the admin building.

I flash back to three weeks ago—how the fuck has it only been three weeks?—when this very same scenario played out with Mona and Cadee, and then say, "Where are you going?"

"Walk with me, Cooper. I can't be late. I'm not missing my vacation. My mother had surgery two weeks ago and I had to spend my entire summer so far listening to her tell me how worthless I am. I *need* this vacation."

I put my hands up in surrender. "I'm cool walking

and talking."

"So I got a phone call this morning. Apparently, they've been calling for two weeks but no one has been answering. Do they not understand this is a school and we have lives in the summer, Cooper? Lives that involve vacation?"

"Who?" Jesus Christ. I don't think I can do people today.

"Some self-storage place out on Highway 54 near Poplar Creek."

"OK. Is this supposed to mean something to me?"

"Yes, it is. Because they were looking for your father."

"Can you get to the point, please?"

"They're calling because he paid in full for one year's worth of storage, but the facility has been sold, someone's going to turn it into a 7-11, and they need everyone to clear their crap out by next week."

I sigh. I don't think I can do life today. "So what? I'm supposed to clear this shit out?"

"I guess so. They need you to come up there today to sign some papers."

"That's like an hour and a half away. Does it have to be today?"

"Today."

"This doesn't make sense."

We're in the staff parking lot now and Laurie is busy click-click-clicking her key fob to unlock her car. "Well, Cooper, I just wanted to let you know." She pauses. And it's only now that I realize she's carrying a box of stuff because she's hiking it up on her hip to pull the car door open.

A box of stuff like… "Did you quit?"

She takes in a long breath, lets it out, and smiles at me. She sets her box down in the back seat, and then extends her hand. "Goodbye, Cooper. I always did like you. But…" She shakes her head. "I think I've overstayed my welcome. Here's the key to the storage unit. And just in case you decide that self-storage unit can wait and my excuse to get you up there wasn't enough, do not wait, Cooper. You're gonna find something very interesting in that unit."

"What?"

She gets in her car, starts it up, waves her fingers at me through the window, and drives away. Leaving High Court College forever, apparently.

Then my phone buzzes a text.

Cadee: *Well?*

Me: *Well, what?*

Cadee: *Is that jerkface fuck Victor living in my cottage?*

Me: *Hold, please.*

I turn towards the prep side of campus, leave the college side by way of one of the wall gates, and then walk all the way down to the opposite end of campus, go into the freaking woods, stop in front of Cadee's cabin to peek in the windows, and decide not to answer her back.

Because yes. That jerkface fuck Victor *is* living in her cottage.

I turn my phone off so I can have time to go back home, find keys to the fully-restored 1954 Ford pickup in my father's small-but-mighty classic car collection, and go up to Poplar Creek Self-Storage to see what fresh hell awaits me behind a dented-up metal garage door.

Poplar Creek isn't really a town. It's an intersection you have to pass in order to get to Poplar Lake. And Poplar Lake is pretty much just like Monrovian Lake, except it's not surrounded by mansions and a private school. Just cabins. Ordinary, everyday, family-friendly vacation cabins.

The intersection consists of a gas station mini-mart, a bait and tackle shop, a pizza place, and a Tastee

Freez. The sign for the self-storage facility has been living on a billboard over the gas station for decades. It looks more like a prop or a thing forgotten than an actual advertisement for a business. A landmark.

I'm pretty sure no one who drives past that sign ever seriously considered it an option for storing junk.

Except my father, apparently.

It takes a minute to get past the front gate—five, actually. I don't have the code to get in, Laurie didn't give me that. But once I say the name Valcourt, the woman on the other side of the crackling speaker decides to buzz me through.

The key did come with a number on it, so I find the building, go inside, and stand in front of the metal roll-up door, unsure if I should be doing this.

Whatever secrets are in there, they don't belong to me. They belong to my father. And I'm not sure I want his secrets.

I pace up and down the hallway for a while, trying to decide what I should do.

Walk away?

Or face whatever truth is inside?

I have never pretended to be something I'm not. I have never called myself smart, or motivated, or polite. In fact, my father's litany of complaints about me—*Cooper, you are an inconsiderate little prick who thinks that this good life you've been provided is a right instead of a privilege. You are also greedy, stupid, lazy, and will never amount to anything*—is all pretty much dead on.

I am all those things.

So fine. I deserve his litany of insults. I've earned them.

But I'm not a coward. At least I haven't been up until now. I know that whatever's going on in the upper levels of Fang and Feather is bad. It doesn't take a genius to figure that out. That's why Lars, Ax and I are trying to walk away.

Trying, Cooper? There is no trying. Either you walk away or you don't. Enough with the excuses. Because that's what they are.

I have one more year of college and then I can walk away. I've been saying something along those lines since I found Cadee Hunter in a crying heap up in her Alumni Inn attic bedroom by accident three and a half years ago.

The key is sliding into the lock on the door before I even realize I've made a decision. I toss the lock on the ground, roll up the door, and stare at the room filled with neatly labeled boxes.

Cadee's name is on one of the boxes in front, but hers is not the only name on a box in this storage unit.

There are dozens of them and even though I

should not be able to find the connection between them so easily, it's there and it's easy.

I don't need to open them up and see what's inside.

I know.

Because I am invested in this cover-up.

I am, in fact, an accomplice.

It takes me about an hour to transfer the boxes to the back of the truck, and then another couple hours to drive them to a place far enough away to feel safe when I drop them off in another storage unit. Then three more hours to get back to High Court.

It's after midnight when I get home and by the time I close the door to the garage and walk down the long hallway towards the stairs, I know she's not there. I don't need to check her bedroom, but I do anyway.

It's empty.

I pull out my phone to call her and remember that I turned it off this afternoon after I checked on her cottage.

Seven messages from Cadee ranging in anger level.

But the only one that matters is the last one.

I'm with Lars.

CHAPTER THIRTY

Cooper didn't call, or text, or even show up at Lars' house in the morning to walk to the Glass House with us. And this walk in the woods with Lars is just as quiet as last night.

Lars is not pushy like Ax. He's not going to get in my face and annoy me to death until he makes me talk something out. And his silence isn't an indication of building resentment like Cooper. Lars is just patient.

I sigh loudly as the Glass House comes into view. And when I look over at Lars he's watching me closely. I was so pissed yesterday afternoon, I couldn't see straight. Isabella was so drunk by the time five o'clock rolled around, Ax had to help Valentina and Selina walk her home. So I finally asked Lars if he could take me across the lake to check on the cottage.

"Lars," I say.

"Yup."

"Thank you."

"Cadee, it's no problem. I hope you know I'm here for you. I know we walked away three years ago, but I was a different guy back then. I kinda just followed Cooper's lead. And I don't know what happened between you two, but it wasn't my decision."

"I know that."

"Well, what you don't know, because I have never told you, is that I missed you. I really did. And I'm glad you're back."

"Thanks."

"I know that year started weird. You were Cooper's… I don't even know what to call it. Target? Obsession, maybe? But I take full responsibility for how we treated you that first semester."

"You know, at the time I *felt* very targeted. But by the end of the year you guys were my best friends. My only friends pretty much ever, aside from my parents, until this summer. So if the bullying keeps you up at night, keep that in mind, Lars. You're not a bad guy. None of you are."

"I'm still sorry about how we got here. And if you ever need to talk—"

I stop listening. Because *that's* what this is about.

He knows. Maybe not everything. He can't know

everything. If he did, he wouldn't be so calm. But he's heard rumors.

"I will, Lars," I say. Because he's stopped talking and he's waiting for an answer.

"Anything, Cadee. I'm here."

"I know." I smile at him as we enter the Glass House clearing. And I immediately start looking for Cooper. But he's not here yet.

"Did he ever call you last night? Or text?" I don't need to say who. There is only one person I could be talking about.

"No," Lars says. "He never did."

"Do you think he's OK?" But just as the words come out of my mouth, Cooper exits the Glass House and stops in his tracks when he sees us.

There's an awkward moment when none of us speaks or moves. And then Ax is there, blocking our view of Cooper, and I just give Lars a wave and head towards the kitchen area to grab my apron.

Inside the kitchen people are rushing around busily. Like something is happening that I have no clue about. I scan the room for Victor, because I have a lot to say to that guy today. How dare he move into my cottage?

Lars wouldn't let me confront him last night. He said Victor is there for a reason. Everything around here happens for a reason. And confronting him isn't the way to handle things. Maybe the Chairman gave him that cottage when he figured out I wasn't using it?

So I agreed and bit my tongue. But Lars isn't here anymore and he was the real source of my self-control last night.

"Cadee!"

I turn to find Dante in the kitchen. Jesus Christ. If he's looking for me already, this day is going to go bad fast. I've spent the last week being his little Fugling bitch and I'm just about done.

"Yes, Dante," I say, smiling as he comes towards me. "How can I help you this morning?"

"Sophie is sick."

"What?" I look over my shoulder at the kitchen door. "Where is she?"

"Lying down out there. I need you to take care of her today. I have things to do and I won't be around."

"OK. I mean, yes. Of course, I'll look after her." And thank God for small favors. At least I won't have to see his face.

He stares at me for a moment and I start to get uncomfortable. There are more than a dozen other servers in the kitchen with me, so we're not alone, but I suddenly feel very outnumbered. "Is there anything else, Dante?"

He pushes past me without saying anything and I roll my eyes, then glance over my shoulder just before I reach the door and find Dante and Victor talking conspiratorially, and looking straight at me while they do it.

Something about this request is wrong. I just don't know what it is.

But he wasn't lying. Sophie is lying on one of the couches with an ice pack over her eyes. For a moment I wonder if he hit her and she's hiding a black eye, but Valentina takes it off her face and gives her a fresh one and I let out a breath of relief when there are no bruises.

"Oh, good," Selina says. "You're here. We're on Isabella duty today, Cades. Can you just look after Sophie?"

"Sure. But what's wrong?"

Valentina sighs. "She's just…"

"I'm sick," Sophie says. "I need to go home and be in my own bed."

Oh. I get it. She's sick of Dante.

"There's less than one week left, Sophie," Selina says. "You can stick it out. Trust me. We've all been there."

Sophie sits up suddenly, her face red with anger. "You've been there? No! You haven't!" She points to

Valentina. "You were with Ax." Her finger migrates over to Selina. "And you were with Lars. Being with Dante is nothing like what you two went through. So don't tell me you get it. Neither of you have been here, OK?"

"I have," I say.

She directs her anger at me next. "You had bodyguards. If anything, you made it worse for me."

"What's happening?" Valentina asks. "Did he… force you to do something?"

"No, he's just a sadistic dick. He insults me. Puts me down. It's a constant barrage of emotional abuse. He's not touching me. But he's hurting me. I should not have to put up with this. This whole thing is crazy!"

"Did you try to talk to your father, Sophie?" I ask. "Because he's the one who put you here, not us."

"I *have* talked to him. And he says I just have to suck it up. That his child is the *offering* this year and there's nothing he can do about it."

I recoil at that word. "What the hell?"

"Sophie," Valentina says in a stern, soft voice. "You need to shut up. Right now. Cadee"—she looks at me—"no offence, but you're not one of us. She can't be talking about this in front of you. And it's got nothing to do with who is better than who, or who has money and who doesn't. It's just… secret."

"Hey." I throw up my hands. "Fine with me. I don't want your secrets."

"You should've left," Sophie says. Then she plops the ice pack back over her eyes and sighs. "You are the dumbest girl alive, Cadee Hunter."

I'm starting to agree with her.

"Cadee?"

I turn to find Cooper scowling at me. "What?"

It comes out angry. Because I am angry with him. I thought we were making progress. Like on the verge of having something real. But he ignored me last night. I texted him repeatedly and never got a response. And he either didn't go home at all, so he didn't even know I was missing, or he did and didn't even bother to call and check up on me.

"I need to talk to you. Now." He grabs my arm and starts tugging me across the room. I yank it out of his grip and he doesn't do it again. Just leads me outside and into the woods.

"Where are we going?"

"Just… right here. Away from there."

We stop under a large tree and both of us fold our arms defensively. "Well? What do you want?"

He sighs and scrubs his hands down his face. He hasn't shaved in days. It looks good on him though. "Did you tell Lars anything?"

I squint my eyes at him. "About?"

"You know what about. Senior year. New Year's Eve. The abortion. Any of it?"

"No."

"You're sure?"

"Of course I'm sure. I'm not an idiot. Don't worry, your secret is safe."

"No, it isn't."

"What do you mean?"

"Look, I know you're mad at me for ignoring you yesterday, but…" He stops. Turns away. Sighs. Scrubs his face with his hands again.

"What the hell is going on, Cooper?"

"Listen, I don't want to tell you everything right now, but we have a problem. You're caught in something… bigger. Bigger than either of us realized. And I'm sorry I ignored you last night, but I need my eyes on you. All the time. Until I figure this out. Do not go home with Lars tonight. Do you hear me?"

"Is that an order, my king?"

He scoffs. "Yeah. It is. We're only halfway through the summer. All we have to do is make it three more weeks, then you're done."

"But what about the fourth challenge? We have five weeks left, not three." It makes me sad just thinking about it. Five more weeks of this? I can't do it. I'm not gonna make it.

"The last two weeks aren't spent here at the Glass House." He looks around nervously, like he's checking to see if anyone is close by. "I'm not supposed to tell you this, but the last two weeks are just getting ready for the rite."

"The *rite?* Would that have anything to do with Sophie being an *offering*?"

"What? Who told you that?"

"Sophie."

"Jesus fucking Christ. That girl—" But he stops and just turns his back on me.

"Cooper. What the hell is going on?"

He turns back to face me. "You don't want to know, OK? You don't. And I can't tell you. But even if I could, I wouldn't. Because once you know things, Cadee, you can't unknow them."

"Well, thanks. I feel so much better now."

He comes towards me, puts his arms around me and holds me close. "I'm just trying to protect you. I want to get you out. I do. But I think you've been *in* this entire time. I just didn't realize it. And I'm not going to tell you anything else. So you have to trust me to do the right thing and take care of it"—he pushes me away from him just enough so he can look me in the eyes—"so I can protect you. You just need to trust me."

I see fear in his eyes and my stomach sinks suddenly.

"Will you trust me, Cadee?"

I nod, but find I don't have any words. Things suddenly feel very dark and serious.

He places his hands on my cheeks. "Three weeks. That's it. Just don't ask me anything for three weeks. Just…" He sighs. "Help me, Cadee. I really need your help right now."

I place my hands over his. "OK, Cooper. I do trust you. Just tell me what you need me to do."

"Do not agitate Dante."

"I'm not agitating him!"

"Shh," he says. "I know he's the problem here. Believe me. I know. And I'm going to have this talk with everyone, not just you."

"Sophie isn't going to go for it. She says she's sick and she needs to go home."

"She's not going home. And don't fall for her innocent act. She knows everything. We all know why we're here. Pull her through this week. That's what I need. Get Sophie through this."

"How? We're not really friends."

"Sit with her. Talk with her. Pat her fucking hand like she's a child. Do whatever it takes to keep her calm.

One more week and we're going to buy her back, remember?"

I nod. "OK."

"We'll buy her back, force Dante to take Mona because she can handle him, and then we're done." He smiles his charming I'm-Cooper-Valcourt smile. "Done."

He's already admitted that there's more, so that's not even the truth.

But I get the feeling that Cooper is standing on the edge of something right now. Barely holding shit together.

"OK, Coop. I'm on your side. I'll make sure she's OK."

"Thank you." He sighs. Then he kisses me. It's not long, or passionate, or even a little bit romantic. But it does feel like a real thank you. "I'll make it up to you. At home. You're coming home. Every night. Hear me?"

"I'll be there."

"OK," he whispers, looking over his shoulder at the clearing. Everything looks normal over there. Maddie and Natasha already have their feet in the pool and are chatting. Jamie and Roland are sitting at a nearby table playing cards like all these crises aren't happening. Mona is sitting with Isabella, having what looks like a one-way conversation. And everyone else is inside with Sophie. "Be nice to Dante today. That's all we need."

"Dante isn't going to be here today."

"What?"

"Yeah, he came up to me in the kitchen and said he was taking off and I was in charge of Sophie."

"Where is he going?"

"Didn't say. But I did catch him talking to Victor and it looked like they were cooking up a conspiracy."

"Great." He pauses. "Well, maybe that's good. If we can keep him away from Sophie, maybe she'll come to her senses." He pauses again, distracted. "OK, then. Let's go."

We part ways by the pool. Cooper stays outside and I go back in to the Glass House and sit next to Sophie.

Selina and Valentina leave me there with her and that is pretty much my day.

Nothing else of consequence happens. Sophie brightens up a few hours later when she realizes Dante is not around. And then, at four o'clock, her phone buzzes a text from Dante.

He wants her to sleep at home tonight.

She just stares at the phone screen in utter disbelief, unable to believe her good luck. Then she jumps up and goes outside to tell Michael.

I follow her, but I don't have the same level of enthusiasm.

Dante is up to something.

This same situation plays out the next day. Sophie is sick. Dante tells me to watch her. He disappears, then texts her at the end of the day, and tells her to go home for the night.

Day three, same thing.

Day four, ditto.

And by the morning of day five, Sophie is back to normal. She's not even pretending to be sick anymore. She sits with Michael out by the pool and even laughs a few times over the course of the day.

I have to admit, it's been a good week for me too.

For everyone, actually. Dante's absence didn't really register that first day. It felt like a plot twist. But by day five, we're all pretty much thinking Dante is trying to make Cooper kick him out.

And Cooper is too smart to fall for that. He wants to kick him out. The whole group even talked about it, urging him on. But Cooper refused. He wasn't convinced that Dante gave up.

I go home with Cooper every night. We make dinners together. Ax is usually there. Lars, sometimes. Ax stays in my old room, but Lars goes home at night.

And even though Cooper and I are absolutely sleeping together, he plays it down when Lars is around.

I already know how Ax feels about Cooper and me, because he told me in the kitchen that night. But Lars keeps his opinions to himself. And Cooper goes out of his way not to make our new relationship a point of contention between them.

I get the feeling this underlying tension is about to snap—probably soon, but definitely after this whole summer rush crisis is over—so I'm not holding this against Cooper. He's stressed. That is very clear. And he never did tell me where he was that night he disappeared.

I decided to drop it for the time being as well. Because I feel like we're all holding hands. Walking along the same edge. And at any moment, one of us could lose our balance and fall, taking the others with them.

At four o'clock, right on time, Sophie's phone dings a text. We're all playing cards under the thatched-roof hut. Even me. The servers in the kitchen are all pissed about this and they don't hide it. But I went to work in the kitchen this morning and Cooper came in and told me I was spending the day with him. And he made sure the whole staff heard his command.

So they can't really hold it against me.

I'm following orders.

"No!" Sophie exclaims, looking at her phone.

"What?" Valentina asks.

"No!" Sophie says again. "He can't do this! He says I have to go to his house tonight!"

"Fuck," Cooper says. "I fucking knew it."

"She's not going," Michael says. "I won't allow it. He's playing a game."

"Michael," Ax says.

"No!" Michael says. "I will not—"

"Then you're out," Cooper says.

"What?"

"You're out, Michael. We're so fucking close. She has one more night. One. Tomorrow is a free day and then the day after we will have the third auction. Everyone here is putting up money to make sure we get her away from Dante. We have all gone out of our way to pull Sophie through this week. You will not fuck it up at the last minute. Do you hear me?" Cooper is growling at him. "Either you help us help you, or you're out. And that's my final word. Sophie, get your shit together. You're going to Dante's. Ax will walk you. Michael, you're going home with Mona and you will stay the fuck away from the Legosi house tonight. Do you understand me?"

Fuck. The bully king is back, I guess. And everyone knows it.

Because Michael says, "Fine."

And no one else says a word.

Not even Sophie.

The next day Sophie doesn't show up at the Glass House. But Dante does. He's standing at the edge of the pool with his hands in his pockets and a smirk on his face.

"Where the fuck is she?" Michael is livid. "She's not yours anymore. You can't order her around. Where is she?"

"Oh, make no mistake, Michael. She's still mine until tomorrow. And even though she's not very fun and she's a frigid fucking virgin—well, not a virgin anymore"—his sadistic laugh makes the birds take flight in the nearby trees—"I am going to buy her again. You see, Sophie is getting through this High

Court shit show no matter how difficult she is. And I already know that Cooper wants me out. So she's my little insurance policy."

"Where *is she*?" Cooper demands.

"Who? Oh, Sophie?" Dante mocks. "Sophie tried to kill herself last night and she's in the hospital."

I don't even know how to describe the utter shit show that happens next. There are fists, and screams, and fingernail scratches across Dante's cheek and he's bleeding from the mouth. The sheriff comes, puts Ax in handcuffs, and he disappears in a squad car. Isabella loses her mind grabs a huge rock, then makes an announcement to everyone—including the sheriff—that she's done here, and then jumps into the deep end of the pool. Cooper and two deputies fish her out screaming, and she is taken away in an ambulance.

And then the rest of us are forced into squad cars and taken down to the station to give statements.

CHAPTER THIRTY-ONE

Two days later everyone is back at the Glass House except Sophie and Isabella, who are both locked up at a nearby psychiatric center on a seventy-two-hour hold because… *attempted suicide.* And Ax, because he's being held in the county jail for felony assault on Dante.

The Legosi family is pressing charges.

Sophie downed a whole bottle of pills that were conveniently left out in Dante's bedroom and Isabella has a long history of self-harm and she was telling the doctors that she was checking out for good this time.

So. Here we are. Challenge three.

Yet another auction.

Even Michael showed up. I told him not to, but he's in it to win it now. His exact words to me when I called to ask him to stay home today were, "No fucking way am I leaving Sophie to live in that hellhole alone. I'll be there."

So that's just fucking wonderful. And I know this sounds like I'm only thinking about myself—and if people want to see me that way, I guess that's their prerogative. Lars, anyone?—but the auction starts in five minutes and even though Sophie isn't here, she's still up for grabs.

And Dante has already promised to buy her just out of spite.

It gets better. Cadee is now her stand-in.

"We're still buying her?" Mona says.

"What choice do we have? We're not letting Dante get away with this. Not on my watch. How much cash did everyone bring?"

"Us girls brought what we've earned so far. And the boys have some too."

"What's the *total*, Mona?"

"Four hundred and seventy-five."

"Good." I breathe a sigh of relief. "Should be more than enough."

Famous last words.

Dante buys Sophie for a million dollars.

Only he didn't buy Sophie, did he?

He bought Cadee.

And this time there are no bodyguards and I have been told, in no uncertain terms by the Chairman, the Judge, and the Mayor, that I will not interfere with Dante Legosi in any way. If I even *speak* to him for the next two weeks, they will take it out on Cadee.

In fact, after the auction I got a call from my father telling me to go home. He has forbidden me from going to the Glass House again until the third challenge is over.

Lars has been put in charge of everything.

And even though Lars and I have been best friends for the better part of two decades—which is saying something since we're only twenty-one—when he shows up at my house after the auction, I'm not at all sure we're still actually friends.

He enters the living room and sits down on the couch opposite me.

"Well," I say. "What happened?"

"She went home with him."

"I cannot believe how badly we have fucked this up."

"We?" Lars laughs. "I didn't do shit, Cooper. And

if you try to blame this on me—"

"Relax, Lars. You're still the good son. Your future is intact and promising."

"You're just jealous."

"Of you?" I scoff.

"Yeah. Of me. You and Ax both. You hate that I don't have family problems like you guys do. And you know why, Cooper?"

I side-eye him with some fierce fucking anger. "Because you're a sellout?"

He laughs. "You want to believe that. But you know it's not true. I'm not a sellout, Cooper. I just play the game so much better than you two do, it's sad."

"Sellout."

He studies me for a moment. "Well, at least I'm not a fucking baby-killer."

"What?"

"I know what you did to Cadee, Cooper. People have been talking about it all summer."

"What people?"

"Everyone in the kitchen for one. Dante. Victor. Hell, even Selina came up and asked me about it. I cannot fucking believe you forced her to have an abortion without even telling me and Ax. What the fuck is wrong with you? It's not me who's buying in to this whole kingmaker thing. It's you. You're the one who fell for it. I've always had a way out."

"With or without us, right?"

"My father is already working on the Judge about Ax. He'll be out on bail after his arraignment. And he's already offered to pay off the Legosis, because God knows, the Judge won't do it. Even if it was just about politics, and we both know it's not. So no, I'm not going to sit around at your pity party and put my father in the same category as the Chairman and the Judge. And even though you've lied to me, pushed me away so you could have Cadee for yourself, and took my rights away when you forced her to get that abortion, I've still got your backstabbing ass, Cooper. That could've been my baby."

I laugh. So loud.

"And I'm not going to sit here and listen to you criticize me or ruin Cadee's life any more than you have. At least I understand why she was so sad that spring. And why you wanted to kick her to the curb so fast before summer rush."

"You don't know shit, Lars. You have no idea what I went through with Cadee that year."

"Because you lied about it. And I'm done here. I just wanted to stop by and let you know that I'll be taking care of her from now on. You've done enough."

CHAPTER THIRTY-TWO

Sophie was right when she called Dante a sadistic dick.

He doesn't need to touch people to hurt them.

Dante Legosi is all about psychological warfare.

And he's good at it.

He didn't take me to his house after we left the Glass House. He took me out to dinner at the Rib Shack in nearby Monrovia, a family place with red-checked plastic tablecloths, cheap beer served by the pitcher, and paper napkins.

It's packed with people. Lots of kids running around with broken crayons in their sticky fists, and parents who order the family meat plate, with a soundtrack of country music and pinball machines playing in the background.

I don't quite know what to think about this. And

he can tell. Because he hasn't stopped smiling since we sat down in the booth.

"What's wrong, Cadee? You don't like ribs?"

"I like ribs." I decided on the way over here that I wasn't going to let him win. And I wasn't going to be meek or pout about my situation. My bank account is *insane.* I have over a million dollars in there now. Because the first thing Dante did was transfer the money to my account. "Sophie doesn't deserve this money," he said. "You do."

And… he paid me for the stand-in I did for Mona too. Plus, I still have the money from the Chairman.

I'm fucking rich.

And no matter what happens, no one can take it away from me. Even if I walk out right now, what is he going to do? I didn't sign a contract. I'm not even obligated to be here in this restaurant with him.

I get it. I didn't need to come here and play this game with them in the first place, but there is really no reason for me to be here now.

So why am I?

"So what's the problem?" Dante asks. And he's being so reasonable. I mean—the Rib Shack? It's all very normal. So what *is* my problem? "I didn't pay you enough?"

"My problem, Dante, is that you can't buy people.

And I know you probably think that's funny, and the rules don't apply to you, but freedom isn't a rule. It's just a God-given right."

"That's why I paid you first. If you don't want to be here, walk out."

"So you can torture Sophie instead?"

"I don't give a fuck about Sophie. I don't want her to kill herself, and that's why I let her go home all week. She started threatening me with suicide that very first night. And I'm just not gonna deal with that shit."

"You left pills out for her to find."

"Says who? Sophie? The girl in the psych ward right now? Listen, I'm sorry I tried to suck your tits that first day. I was wrong. OK? I was… caught up in the moment and Ax taught me a lesson. And I'm sorry for bullying you this summer. But I didn't do anything worse than Cooper Valcourt did. In fact, my brand of bullying doesn't even come close to his."

He's got my attention now. And I hate that. Because I've never seen a rational Dante. I've only seen… well, what he's *wanted* me to see.

"Do you accept my apology, Cadee?"

I shrug, then sigh. "Sure. Whatever."

"I'm not your enemy. I'm trying to figure this shit out, just like you."

"That's not true, Dante. You've been against all of

us this summer."

"Really? What did I do? I got caught up in a moment with you in front of the wrong guys. It's obvious that Cooper, Ax, and Lars still like you. Fine. I'm not here to lure you away from them. And I made the first mistake. I own that. But Cooper turned me into his little scapegoat. I don't understand how you can even look at him after what he did to you."

I turn my head away. "You don't have any idea what Cooper Valcourt did to me."

"No?"

"I've heard the rumors." Then I look at him again. Right in the eyes. "They're not true."

He sits back in the booth and shrugs. "Whatever. I'm not here to make you spill your secrets. It's none of my business. I'm here because I want to tell you the truth. And then you can judge me all you want. You can walk out, Cadee. Walk away. You have more than enough money. If you need a good financial planner, I know a guy who can stretch that money out for twenty or more years if you live frugally. I can help you make this all go away. I can help you get the life you deserve. But you'd have to walk away never knowing. That's the catch."

"Never knowing what?"

"The truth. I just told you, all I want to do is tell

you the truth."

I hesitate, unsure if I should even be having this conversation with him. It feels a little bit like making a deal with the devil.

But it also feels like he has a bird's-eye view of a very big picture. And I hate to even think this, but this Dante sitting across from me in the Rib Shack seems to know exactly what he's doing. He's dripping with confidence. "What do you get out of it?"

He smiles. "Power. Cooper is on his way out. He doesn't even want to be King."

"And you do."

"And I do." He laughs a little. "A freshman King at High Court? It's unheard of. Four entire years of power."

"I find that to be a little bit sick, Dante. I'm not gonna lie."

"That's because you're a good person, Cadee. And I'm not. I'm Dante Legosi. My lot in life is pretty much set. And that's fine. Whatever. But if my family—if all these High Court lake-house families—think I'm just gonna settle for table scraps?" He shakes his head. "They don't know me at all."

I'm starting to think no one really knows Dante Legosi.

"Did you force Sophie to have sex with you?"

"What?" He laughs.

"You said she's not a virgin anymore."

"Yeah. Because she let Michael pop her cherry on Tuesday. She told me that. Threw it in my face." He huffs. "Like I wanted her for *that.* Please. Sophie is a cute girl. Very sweet. But so not my type."

Could this be true? Did we all… *misunderstand* Dante?

"Listen," he says. "I'm not gonna sit here and pretend to be a good guy. I'm not. I'm a total dick. And I'm fine with that. Someone has to play the role of villain. But if you want to hate me for it, at least get the facts straight."

"What are you asking, Dante? Specifically?"

"I want you to tell Cooper about my plan."

"You want me to *tell him*? Why?"

"Because he's part of it."

"Why don't you tell him?"

Dante laughs. "Cooper's had it out for me since day one. I knew he was going to cut me. And the only reason I'm still here, in the game, is because I played hardball all summer and he pretty much checked out three years ago after his rush was over. Cooper Valcourt doesn't give a fuck about me. What do you think he would say if I walked up to him and told him I had a plan to get him and all his friends out, but in order to do that I get to take over his spot as King?"

I scoff.

"Exactly. But if you tell him"—Dante eyes me—"he'd listen to you. Cooper has to be on board. Because this threat I'm planning? To get us all what we want? It has to come from him. Everyone has to play their part for it to work, Cadee. Even you. So I'm gonna lay it out one more time. You can take your money and go. Just walk away from this fucked-up world and never look back. And hey, I'll throw in a bonus. If you ever run out of money—if that million isn't enough? You look me up and let me know. I'll shoot you another one."

I laugh. "Right."

"I'm dead serious. Money? Who gives a fuck about money? Real money, Cadee? That's a byproduct of power. Power is what matters. So take your money and walk away. Leave the deep dark secrets for us lowlife lake-house people. It's a smart move. But if you want more than money—if you want to be a player in the game of life? Then stick around and help me out. This is a win-win for all of us. Me. You. Cooper, Lars, Ax, Sophie. This plan will get her out too. Isabella. All of them. If they want out, they're out. If they want to stay, they'll stay under my rule. But we'll have to remain teammates. That's the catch. You get one chance to walk away from me, but if you choose to stay, we play ball forever."

I think about this for a few moments. "So… we're basically making up our own secret society."

He points at me and clicks his tongue. "Bingo, babe."

"OK."

"OK?" He laughs.

"But I want to know one thing."

"Truth was part of the deal."

"Right. That. OK, I'm in. Tell me the big secret."

"Are you sure?"

"I just said I was. Tell me." I need to know what he knows. Especially if it's about me and Cooper.

"Cooper's engaged to Isabella."

"What?"

"Yeah. Lars is engaged to Selina. And Ax is engaged to Valentina."

"But… they're not even really dating, are they?"

"Of course not. Arranged marriage. Why do you think Isabella is so sad? Come on. She doesn't want to marry *Cooper Valcourt.*"

"You act like he's a disease. He's not. And you don't know anything about us. He's not a bad guy."

"Hey, he's fine. I get the attraction. But Isabella is a lesbian."

I laugh. "Shut up."

"I swear to God. Her family is having none of it. They're gonna make her marry him and have babies. Be a good little wife." Dante frowns. "They're gonna tear her down and make her surrender to Chairman Valcourt. The real King of High Court Castle. They made that dark place inside Isabella. They are the reason she tried to kill herself during rush. Not Cooper. They're bad, Cadee. And I get it. I'm bad too. But I will cut her free. She doesn't have to live like this. My plan will cut everyone free."

"Free from them but not from you."

He shrugs. "You gotta trust someone. Do you want Cooper and Isabella to get stuck playing their game as a legacy? Or do you want to invent a new game and be a founding stakeholder?"

He's got a point. "OK. But is that it? Is that the only secret you have?"

He smiles. And the old Dante is suddenly back. I get a little nervous, but he reaches across the table and grabs my hand. "Relax, Cadee. We're on the same side now. I'm gonna protect you. Forever. As long as you protect me. Same deal goes for everyone else."

I pull my hand away. "Look." I sigh. "I'm tired. My head is spinning. I feel like I was just dropped into a Dan Brown novel mid-plot, and I don't want to beat around the bush anymore. What do you know?"

He gets a little glint in his eyes when he grins. "I know what really happened to you. I know why you got that abortion. And I know it had nothing to do with *Cooper* Valcourt."

CHAPTER THIRTY-THREE

Once upon a time I met a girl in the woods.

A gentle little girl who likes to wear dresses and peek out from behind trees to giggle at me and my friends. She always had a book, often had a paintbrush, and sometimes she talked to us.

She made hyper-Ax calm, quiet-Lars chatty, and selfish-me generous.

I wanted to give her everything. Rocks. Sticks. The crumbling cookies in my pockets.

Just… all the things.

Cadee Hunter makes us better.

I think that's why I like her.

Because when she's around I am *better.*

I spend the first four days of challenge three absently flicking through various streaming services, moping on the couch, and generally thinking about why I am such a fucking fuck-up.

I count up all the ways this summer has gone wrong. How I failed everyone who needed me. How not even Cadee Hunter could make me good enough to save Isabella, or Sophie, or Ax.

I think about how I let Lars and Michael down, how Valentina and Selina will just have to surrender at the end of the year, and how I should've spelled out the consequences to Maddie, Natasha, Roland and Jamie.

Because that's what the whole point of rush was about.

Consequences.

And their indifference won't save their souls once they're sold.

I think about how maybe it's just time to admit that I can't win.

My father really does run this world and there is no hope for me.

I am an utter and total failure.

But that's not even the worst part.

The worst part is that I'm taking everyone down with me.

I'm dreaming about the girl in the woods when my phone buzzes and wakes me up.

"Yeah," I say, still imagining Cadee Hunter.

"I'm coming up to your room. I just didn't want to scare you and make you scream."

"What?" I laugh and sit up. "Cadee?"

"Are you expecting someone else?"

"Did you just say—"

"Knock, knock." My bedroom door opens and there she is. My dream girl.

"What are you doing here? Jesus Christ. Dante is going to lose his mind."

"Dante sent me." She stalks towards me, taking her shirt off as she crosses my room. Then she pulls my covers back, takes a moment to admire my body in the moonlight, then straddles my legs and hovers her upper body over mine.

"What the fuck is happening?" I laugh.

"Cooper Valcourt. I would like to save you."

"What?"

"Save you. But first, I would like to kiss you." Then she leans down and presses her lips to mine.

I'm so stunned, it takes me a moment to kiss her

back. But once I do, I forget all about her offer to save me, and this fucked-up summer, and what might be waiting for me when my father finally gets home, and I just enjoy her.

The kiss starts soft, our lips meshing together as I wrap my arms around her back and release the clasp on her bra. Our tongues doing a little dance as her hair sways across my bare chest. Our heartbeats picking up as she flicks the button of her shorts.

I immediately start tugging them down her legs. And when I get them over her hips, she squirms and wiggles until she's naked too. Then, breathless, she hovers over me once more, her heart pounding against mine. I smile up at her, dragging her hair behind her ear so I can see her face better. And I'm reminded of easier days. When she was younger. When we were both younger. And I would spy on her in the woods and she would pretend not to see me.

I'm just getting ready to miss that girl—her innocence, because she's not innocent anymore and that's what bothers me most about what happened to her three years ago—but I stop myself. Because she's still here and she's strong now.

I sit up, bring her with me, and then lay her back on the bed so I'm on top now. She giggles at me. And there it is. That innocence. It wasn't lost. Just hidden.

Waiting for the right opportunity to bring it back.

Or the right person.

And that right person is me. I vow it.

I bend her legs and push her knees up to her chest as I kiss the inside of her thigh. She shivers with anticipation underneath me. My kisses travel upwards and then I place my fingers on either side of her pussy and gently open her up so my tongue can slide in and caress her sweet spot. She wriggles, her fingertip caressing a line from my neck to my shoulder, so softly that I shudder under her touch as I memorize her taste.

"Please, Cooper," she begs. "Now. Please."

I want to eat her out forever. Just lick her until she comes. But I don't want to deny her anything either. I made a lot of mistakes with this girl. Enough for several lifetimes. And now… all I want to do is everything she tells me.

She is tight when I enter her. And her back arches up, her fingernails no longer gentle as she digs them into my upper arms. Like she's clinging to me. Like I am her lifeblood and we are meant to be together like this, always.

It's a slow fuck. With lots of kissing, and eye contact. I never want to stop looking into her eyes. We don't talk. There's a lot to say, but it can wait.

We just move against each other, drawing our

togetherness out in a way that makes me want to stop time and stay like this forever.

But the climax is too tempting. The release necessary.

And when it comes, everything feels new again.

We didn't sleep afterward. Just stayed still for a little bit. Then she got up and started ordering me around like a queen.

No. Not just any queen.

My queen.

"Where are we going?" I didn't want to go anywhere. Least of all to meet Dante. But Cadee insisted. And she promised I would be very happy by morning.

"Will you just relax?" She's got my hand and she's dragging me across High Court College campus via the woods. We pass the old cottage that Lars, Ax, and I called home for the past three years. I can barely remember the anger inside me that day.

Over what? A couch? A dorm? It makes no sense now, but it felt like the end of the world at the time.

We pass through the wall and enter the prep side

of campus. And we keep going. "Are we going to the inn?" I ask, trying to figure this out.

"Trust me," Cadee says, glancing sideways at me.

"I trust you. Hell, it's not every day a queen climbs up into the king's tower offering to slay a dragon. You are gonna slay a dragon, right? I'm expecting something big like that. Something very cinematic. Is Dante the dragon? If so, I might slay him myself."

"Keep talking, tough guy."

"Seriously. We're nearly to the parking lot. Where are we going?"

"What do you usually find in a parking lot?"

"I could've just stolen my father's truck if you wanted to drive somewhere."

She drags me through the parking lot. There's only one car out here. It's two-thirty in the morning. And it's a piece-of-shit blue Camaro that probably ran out of gas on the main road and coasted in here, because it's parked all crooked.

But it soon becomes clear that we are making our way towards this heap. And we're about twenty feet away when the engine roars to life.

"What the—Ax?" I laugh. "What the hell is happening?"

He grins evilness. But it's an evilness I recognize as happiness on my best friend. Then I see Lars in the passenger seat wearing mirrored sunglasses that glimmer from the street light overhead.

Ax gives the Camaro some gas and it backfires, then roars with the threat of a V-8 engine.

Ax winks at me. Then his door opens with a loud creaking squeak, and he works an ancient switch on the side of the seat to make it flip forward. "Like my new ride?" Then he nods to the back seat. "Get in. We got people to see."

Lars is out of the car too, and Cadee is sliding into the back.

"I don't think I can fit back there," I say.

"Pussy," Lars says.

"What the hell is happening? Where did you get this car? And where are we going? I've been at home for four days, not four years."

Ax claps me on the back. "A lot has happened in those four days."

I squeeze in the back and Ax slams the front seat back, hitting my knees. The space is so small—like what the hell were car makers thinking in the Seventies? Two-door cars that seat four has to be one of the dumbest ideas ever.

Then he punches the gas as the car lurches forward. Lars laughs. "I think you just ate ten dollars' worth of gas to do that, dumbass."

"Where did you get this car?" I ask again.

"From me," Cadee says.

"What. The fuck. Is happening?"

"I bought it with my million-dollar take-home from Dante." Then she leans over and whispers, "I bought a house too!"

"What?"

"Well, it's not a house. It's the old Alumni Inn."

"Why the hell would you buy that piece of shit? That place went out of business ten years ago."

"Because it matches the car," Ax laughs. Then he screeches the tires around a corner, slides the Camaro into the gravel driveway, and skids to a stop in front of an old rickety porch.

Everyone from rush is waiting for us. Even Dante. And… "Victor? I'm so lost."

"Jesus." Cadee laughs. "You are really bad at surprises."

"I just don't get it."

Ax cuts the engine and then he and Lars are both out, flipping the seats back so Cadee and I can get out.

"OK. Someone want to explain what's going on?"

Mona comes forward and stands on the top step. Everyone else flanks her as she plants her hands on her hips and grins. "Welcome to the ruling class, Cooper Valcourt. You are about to be officially crowned the

King of Nothing."

And then everyone is talking at once. And their plan—*Dante's* plan—comes spilling out like a stroke of royal genius.

With one exception.

Dante is asking me for the truth.

And it's not my truth to tell.

It's Cadee's.

The six of us sit in the office of the old inn—me, Lars, Ax, Cadee, Dante, and Mona. I didn't want Mona here, but she has agreed to stay on campus with Dante next year. So she needs the truth.

"OK," Lars says. "Do you want to explain why we're all in here?"

"And not out there getting drunk, like everyone else?" Ax laughs.

Dante already knows Cadee's secret. She told me. So he's just leaning against the back wall with his arms folded over his chest. Giving us space to do this our way.

I look at Cadee. "You sure you want to do this?"

"Do. What?" Lars is losing patience. "What are we

doing?"

"Lars, can you just stop talking?"

He shoots me a dirty look. "If we're having the conversation I think we're having—"

"We're not." I cut him off. "What you think happened never did."

"What?"

I look over at Cadee. "Do you want me to tell it?"

She takes a deep breath, then shakes her head no. "I can do it."

Ax walks over to her and bends down. Then he looks up at her with very soft eyes. "What's going on, Cadee?"

She takes another deep breath. "I know there's a lot of rumors going around about me." She glances at me. "And Cooper too. I did have an abortion three years ago. Cooper was the one who took me to the clinic. But it wasn't his baby." She looks over at Ax, then Lars. "It wasn't yours, either. It happened before we… started doing any of that stuff."

"What's that mean?" Lars asks. He looks at me. "What does that mean, Cooper?"

Cadee sucks in a deep breath and I squeeze her hand to give her courage when she lets it out.

But she doesn't need my help.

She's always been stronger than me. Always.

She puts up a hand and waits for silence and then she starts talking in a soft, low voice. "Cooper found me. By accident, actually. It was the first night my mom and I were living in the attic apartment, remember?"

She looks at Ax and Lars. They nod. We were all together that New Year's Eve. And it really did feel like a new beginning. We were laughing outside in the woods. Drinking a little. Not Cadee, she wasn't drinking that night. But I was.

And it was such a good night.

We had fun that night.

We kissed her, and made her laugh, and we laughed too.

And I remember thinking… *I think I could love this girl forever.*

And then it all went black.

"But my mother was new to the catering team," Cadee continues. "So she was busy with the party and wasn't thinking about me. But I was thinking about her. I told you guys I wanted to go inside and find her so I could give her a kiss at midnight." Cadee's chin begins to quiver and then her eyes are filling up with tears. She wipes furiously at them as they ride down her cheeks. "I just wanted to give her a kiss at midnight. Because my father…" She pauses again. Shakes her head. "Was gone. So I went inside…"

She stops and stares off at nothing. And I want to make her stop. I just want all the words to stop. I don't want to hear what comes next.

And it's like she reads my mind, because she skips ahead.

"Cooper came back. He was very drunk by then and…" She looks at me and her next words come out as a sigh. "I don't really know. I don't know why you came back. I'm just glad you did."

"I was looking for you. It was never an accident, Cadee. I felt so bad. I knew my father kicked you and your mom out of the cottage—"

"He told me you wanted us to move out so you could have it for your lacrosse team."

"What?" Lars says. "We never used that cottage for lacrosse."

"So he lied," Cadee says.

"He lied," I sigh.

She frowns for a moment. Her brow furrowed. "It was all lies, wasn't it?" She looks at me. "You were right. He never cared about me at all."

I squeeze her hand again, and this time I think she really needs that support.

"OK," Ax says. "But what's that got to do with anything, Cooper?"

"When I went inside to find my mom," Cadee

says. "I found Dane instead."

"What?" Lars asks.

But Mona sees where this is going. Because she comes over to Cadee and sits down next to her. Pulling her into a hug. "Oh, Cadee."

And now Cadee is really crying. And it's not just what happened with her and my evil asshole of a brother. It's all of it.

All the shitty fucking cards she has been dealt over the past three years finally catch up with this girl.

"What the fuck is happening right now?" Ax asks. He stands up and starts his pacing. "Dane... what? What are you saying? He… *raped* you, Cadee? Is that what you're trying to fucking say here?" Then he looks at me. "And you covered for him, didn't you?"

"It's not like that, Ax."

And my heart fucking cracks in half when I realize Cadee is about to make excuses for me.

"I did," I whisper, talking to Ax.

Total silence in the room.

"Why?" Mona asks. "Why would you do that, Cooper? You don't even like Dane. I've seen him kick your ass so many times over the years. So why would you cover for him?"

"I don't know."

"Fuck that!" Mona says. "Fuck you, Cooper!"

"Today, I wouldn't. I know better. But back then, I was just…"

"You were just a fucking coward," Mona says. Stating the truth.

And what can I say? "Yeah." I sigh. "I was just a fucking coward. A selfish fucking coward."

"So that's why Cadee suddenly became important to you." Lars is sneering at me, disgusted. "First semester she was a target. We bullied her, and messed around with her a little, and made her feel like shit. And then…" He pauses. "Then, after New Year's, she was all you thought about. You were obsessed with her. Like… in love with her, almost. But it wasn't love, was it, Cooper?"

I look at Cadee and she's squinting her eyes at me. I want to deny it. But it's pointless now. "I wanted your secret, Cadee. I needed it. I needed something to hold over Dane so that when the time was right, I would have it in my back pocket and I could use it against him."

"Did you?" Ax asks.

"No" I say. "No! I didn't tell him. I didn't tell anyone."

"That's the fucking problem, Cooper," Mona hisses.

"So…" Lars is thinking things through. "That's

why we walked away from her at the end of senior year. You were done with her."

I can't even answer. Because this is still only half the story.

I glance at Cadee and find her frowning. Her eyes find mine for only a moment, then she looks down at her feet. "I knew I was pregnant almost immediately. I just felt it"

Lars stands up. "Oh, my fucking God." He looks at me. "It's true. You made her get that abortion so you could keep the whole thing secret."

"Lars!" Cadee says sharply. "You don't get to have opinions about this. OK? You just don't. You weren't *there*."

"I *was* there!" he says. "All fucking semester." He glares at me. Then he looks back at Cadee. "Why didn't you come to me? I would never—"

"That's why," Cadee says. "You would've let me make the decision. And you know what, Lars? I wasn't able to do that at the time. I just wasn't. I couldn't think straight. So Cooper sat me down and started asking me questions. And when I said no, I do not want to have my rapist's baby, and no I didn't want to tell my mom and break her heart—again. Right after my dad died. He said, "Then you don't really have any choices.""

"That's not what I said." The words are out before

I have a chance to think them through. And I'm glad. Because this is the only chance I'll ever have to try and make this right. It is not the time to lie or omit the facts to save face.

I deserve this.

And Cadee deserves it too.

"I said, "I think I can rectify the situation.""

As if her problem at the time was a situation to be rectified.

Ax just stares at me. But he doesn't need to say anything.

I know exactly what he would've done to Dane if he had found Cadee that night instead of me.

He would've *killed* him.

"I thought… I thought you guys really liked me. I don't know. It was dumb, I guess. I thought being with you would make it all better. And it did." She shrugs. "It did."

"I did like you, Cadee. I was just—" I look at Mona. "I was just a fucking coward. I wanted to skate through life. I wanted it to be easy. And then there you were. Like a gift. I had a secret and everything in our world runs on secrets. I felt rich. Like a fucking king." I take my shirt off and point to the tattoo on my chest. "Because they tell us we are kings. They want us to believe it. And I did."

"And then"—Dante finally speaks—"you threw her away. You got what you needed out of her and you threw her away."

I want to hate him in this moment. I really do. But he's not wrong.

And I think I'm probably a little bit jealous of Dante. Because he always understood the game. He always knew how to play it. Like someone gave him a rule book. Like he was cheating.

But he's not cheating. He's just… *smart.*

And I'm not. "I'm an inconsiderate little prick who thinks that this good life I've been provided is a right instead of a privilege. I'm also greedy, stupid, lazy, and will never amount to anything."

Mona sighs. She's the only one who knows what these words mean.

"My father was right about me," I say. "He saw it a long time ago and that's why he didn't like me. That's why I was never the favorite. I was weak. And he hates weakness. I was all those things for my entire fucking life. And then one day…" I look at Cadee. "One day another secret was dropped into my lap like a gift. Only this time, I wasn't going to be a coward about it."

"Now," Dante says. "Now we're getting somewhere."

I narrow my eyes at him. "Did you know?"

He nods. "Yeah, I knew. Laurie is my aunt."

"What?"

"Yeah. She really did get a call from that storage unit. There was a flood. A pipe burst. And they called saying someone needed to come check on things in case they needed to add it to their insurance claim. I was there when the call came in and told her I would take care of it. I had already been up to Poplar Creek. I had already been through all the boxes."

"Then why did you need me?"

"Listen, Cooper," Dante says. "You're not the only asshole in this room." He looks at everyone in turn, lingering on Lars for some reason. "We all know things." He nods his head to Lars. "You know why Ax doesn't sleep at home, Lars. And you do nothing. You just let it happen. And you have been letting it happen for years. So if you're starting to feel special and righteous, you better take a good long look at yourself first." Dante looks back at me. "I needed you, Cooper. The only way my plan works is if you're the one who makes the threat."

"What are we talking about?" Cadee asks. "What storage unit?"

I explain that day. Tell them what I found in the boxes.

And that's when they all begin to understand the

full extent of Dante's plan.

I show up at the tomb wearing a pair of faded jeans with rips in the thighs, a white t-shirt that says 'Your hole is my goal,' and a pair of black Docs. I raided Ax's wardrobe for this and I like the look so much, I might keep it. I even like the chain wallet. Lars let me borrow his mirrored sunglasses for the occasion. Because this is one for the books. And I only get one chance to do it right.

Dante is dressed in a tux like everyone else. And Mona is hanging on his arm looking like a queen in a red silk gown.

They are the only pledges here aside from me.

The rest of the party is all old guard. Parents and siblings. Lake-house people who invented the game, I guess, and think it's going to last forever.

It's not.

My father spies me as I exit the woods and I allow myself a wave of pure satisfaction when his face contorts into an expression of controlled rage.

He's crossing the narrow clearing and then he's got me by the arm and is yanking me back into the trees. "What the fuck are you wearing? And where is everyone? You're ten minutes late."

We stop far enough away from the tomb that no one can hear us. And that's fine. They don't all need to be threatened, he'll do for now. "I'm on my way to a party, *Dad*." I smile when that word comes out. "So I'm dressed for the occasion."

"The occasion is black tie, *Christopher*. And where the hell have you been? We got home three days ago and you haven't been there once."

"No." I laugh and wave my hand in the direction of the tomb. "Not this party. And I don't live at home anymore. I moved out three weeks ago."

"You moved—" He laughs. "This is it, Cooper. I'm done playing with you. You will get nothing from me. Nothing, do you hear me?"

"Oh, I'm so over your money, Dad. So you can save your breath. I'm only here to explain how things are gonna go down from now on."

He laughs again, still not getting it. "You're going to explain something to *me*?"

"Yup. And you're going to listen."

"I hope you're not counting on a college degree to get anywhere in life, Christopher. Because you won't be returning to school next month."

"Well." I scratch my neck. "You're wrong about

that. I will be in school. And all the other pledges will be there too."

"Where are they? What did you do with them?"

"*Do* with them?" Now it's my turn to laugh. "I got them out, that's what I did with them. Just like that girl at the graduation party that night you had me arrested. I bet her father is still pissed off about that night, isn't he? Anyway," I wave my hand in the air. "My pledges aren't coming tonight. Those two assholes over there?" I nod my head to Dante and Mona. "That's the cream of the crop. And the extent of your new Fang and Feather members. Everyone else is out. Including Isabella." I glare at him. "So you make sure and tell her father she's done. She's with me now. While you assholes were all out here tailgating before the big event, she was moving her shit out of their mansion. And if her father tries to come get her, or Ax's father gets any big ideas about letting his crazy mother beat him as punishment, or any of the other families even speak to my pledges, they're gonna have to answer to you."

"What are you talking about?" He guffaws. "You've gone crazy, Christopher."

"No." I sigh. "I've finally wised up, old man. You see…" I lean in and smile. "I found your little storage unit this summer."

He backs up a little.

"Yup. Went through every box. I have spent the entire three years since Dane raped Cadee telling myself it was a one-off thing. Telling myself that it was a secret only I knew about. Wow." I huff. "Was I ever stupid. You know I get it now, Dad. Why you always hated me. I was pretty fucking dumb." I narrow my eyes at him. "But there's a cure for stupid. It's called the truth. And I found a whole lot of truth about Dane in that storage facility. Cadee wasn't the only one. She was just one among many, wasn't she? And when her father found out about one of the other girl's Dane raped and didn't take your bribe—"

"That's enough!"

"Oh, no. I'm just getting started, *Dad.* You killed him. You killed Cadee's father. And then somehow her mother found out too. They really were moving, weren't they? Because she knew and she was done. And you know the funny thing? Well, it's not funny. It's really fucking sad, actually. She was never going to say anything. You didn't need to kill her too. She was taking her daughter and moving far, far away. But you jumped the gun, didn't you? Got a little scared. Thought you could bribe Cadee. And that almost worked. If I had just. Done. *My job.* She'd have been your quiet little minion."

"What are you doing?" He says this with a straight face too. Like… wow. The balls on this man. They are bull-sized.

"What am I doing?" I laugh so loud, he looks over his shoulder to see if any of his cronies heard me. "I'm threatening you." I take a few steps forward and lean in to his face. "If you come near me, or any of the missing pledges, or any of the people who are now part of my new on-campus society—all that hush money you spent will be for nothing. Because your secrets—all those secrets—will go out into the world and finally everyone will know who and what you really are."

I say it like I've been practicing this speech and waiting for this day since my mother died when I was five.

Dane wasn't the only secret in those boxes.

That place was my father's vault.

We now have dirt on all of them.

I leave that last part unsaid. He knows what I found.

"I wish I could say it was nice knowing you, *Dad.* But the truth is the last twenty-one years were practically unbearable. You make me tired. And I'm done dealing with you."

I spit his own words right back at him.

And I even give it a little time to sink in.

Then I slide my sunglasses down over my eyes like I'm some hotshot with power, and walk off into the sunset.

Cadee, Ax, and Lars are waiting for me in our new piece-of-shit Camaro on the blacktop road in front of my family mansion. I walk around to the passenger side and get in, then smile at Ax and say, "It's done."

He nods, puts the car in gear, and we roar away towards our new home at the Old Alumni Inn.

Meet the new ruling class of High Court College.

Our motto is: *They can't ruin us if we ruin them first.*

And that's exactly what we're going to do.

Welcome to the End of Book Shit. This is the part of the book where I get to say anything I want about the story. It's not edited and there will probably be some typos, so please ignore that shit. This is mostly just about the message.

I started writing an EOBS for this book a few days ago because I need this final chapter before I can put the paperback up and then order author copies. And I was a little bit stuck on it. I had maybe a thousand words. But they didn't feel like meaningful words, so I put it aside and did something else.

It's always a good idea to put writing aside when the ideas aren't flowing. You can keep going. I've done it before. And in the case of some writers, you can actually do a whole book like that. You really can pull words out of your ass and hit publish.

But it's almost never worth it.

The real reason I was writing the EOBS that day was because I was working on book two, Ruling Class, and I was stuck. It wasn't writer's block. I don't do writer's block. I just didn't have a good scene set up for the next chapter and I've been doing this whole writing thing long enough now to take a break when that happens and do something else.

But the EOBS for Bully King and the next chapter of Ruling Class are related. Same story. So neither of these projects were going anywhere.

It's stressful to stop writing a story (or an EOBS) because everything I write has a deadline. And I'm constantly counting days and words to make that deadline. I'm on a tight deadline for Ruling Class so taking time away from it isn't helpful. And I had already taken a whole week off because I got injured and needed to recover.

But… there is no point in forcing the writing. Even if I want to.

So I decided to proof the audiobook for Bully King instead. It was a two-day job. And it helped a lot because I literally had to read and listen to every single word of Bully King.

It was nice though. I don't normally produce my own audiobooks, I have a publisher. So I don't proof them, they do all that for me. This was the first book I've done outside my publisher since 2015, I think. But it gave me a lot of time to focus on the story and the characters, which was very helpful for Ruling Class and I was only about two hours into the proofing before I had all fresh ideas for book two and was eager to get back to writing.

But I was still stuck on this EOBS. I figure if I'm going to write them then they should say something. They should carry some weight, add to the story itself, and be meaningful.

I've haven't been on social media a lot lately. Deadlines, and the injury, and then, of course, I loathe politics. But I went to Facebook like an hour ago and saw two posts. One was something about current events (that nobody even knows is true or not, but people were all angry about it already) and the second one was about a reader who was upset that her favorite author unfriended her (presumably over some opinion she posted.)

And both of these things made me sad.

The first one because posting that current event (that might not even be true) was only about taking someone else down. It was a hateful post masquerading as self-righteous indignation.

And the second one because I felt for that reader. She is allowed to have an opinion (and I don't know what she posted. Maybe she deserved that unfriending) and in a perfect world we would all be able to respect each other when we disagree.

But our world is far from perfect.

So then, even though I don't like to make public statements of any kind, I decided to put up a post making a public statement. It was a very simple post that said: I don't understand why people waste time on hate. Hate is such a waste of time.

And then I started thinking about people I have hated in the past. I had very good reasons for this hate. Like… I'm talking what happened to me was fucking Lifetime Movie of the Week kinda shit. I will put my past suffering up against ANYONE.

ANYONE.

I do care how fucking bad your life has been, MINE can compete. I might not win in the end, but no one would laugh, that's for sure.

And then I started thinking… well, how did I get past it? How did I let it go and move forward?

And that memory of how I moved on came back to me in an instant.

Someone stole something from me. I'm not going to say what, but I will say it wasn't a WHAT. It was a WHO. And it wasn't about some girl stealing a guy. It was, as I said, Lifetime Movie of the Week kinda shit. It involved lawyers in two states, me making a fifteen-hundred mile road trip alone with a hundred-and-sixty-five dollars to my name, standing in front a judge crying and begging for help, and then finally, resolution and a very long drive home.

And when I got home, and things were calmer, I got a phone call from the asshole responsible for all that shit. And before he could even talk, I said, "I forgive you."

That's it. That's all I said.

He was stunned, to stay the least. So I expounded. "I forgive you. It's over. And I'm not going to waste one more second on what just happened. I'm going to forgive you and move on. Goodbye."

And that was the end of it.

Because there is nothing else to do when something that horrible happens.

There is nothing else to do but forgive and move on.

The only other options and hate and anger.

And everyone who has ever been angry knows, deep down, that you're an uglier person when you're angry. And hate is the fuel for anger.

Yes, this terrible thing happened to me. But I was not going to waste another second of my life on hate and anger.

And I will say, right now, that wasn't the end. It would take a few more years to really get away. And I did actually get revenge for all of it. No one was assassinated. lol It was a very legal revenge plan. So I'm not saying I'm like super evolved or anything. I'm human.

But that forgiveness was real. Everything that came after I didn't control. That was all him.

The only thing I could control was how I reacted to him.

And as long as my reactions weren't based on hate and anger, I would be fine.

And I was.

I win.

So this EOBS is about forgiveness.

It's so fucking powerful.

Once you forgive—truly let it go and forgive—you're free.

And that's what Cadee decided to do in this book. She hasn't articulated it yet because she's still in denial. But she knew instinctively that letting things go was the only way forward.

I don't forgive Cooper yet.

Lars certainly doesn't.

Ax—maybe. Because he's well-versed in hate and anger and he knows it's a trap.

But we don't matter. If Cooper was a real person and not just some character in a book, the only thing that would matter is that he is able to forgive himself.

And that's a LOT harder than forgiving someone else.

We don't forgive ourselves very often. Our mistakes stick with us for years. Decades. Sometimes a whole lifetime. The stick with us and manifest as guilt. They color us in a new way and unless we're very aware that we made a mistake that led to this moment, we don't often get off that path of self-destruction.

It is so much harder to forgive yourself. (Unless you're a sociopath, that is.)

So if you're thinking Cooper didn't earn Cadee's forgiveness—he doesn't have to.

Her forgiveness isn't about HIM. It's about HER.

And if Cooper can forgive himself, that's not about Cadee. It's only about him.

And just like me when I forgave the asshole, it didn't really make anything better in my life. The only thing that got better was my opinion of myself.

Because forgiveness isn't about the person being forgiven.

It's about the person doing the forgiving.

It is a magnanimous gesture. And the greater the sin, the more noble the act of forgiveness is.

You just have to let it go.

I respect Cadee Hunter. Obviously, she still has a lot to deal with. This is a duet. Neither Cadee nor Cooper are at the end of their road yet. So we'll see what happens in book two.

But I hope, if you're holding in some past anger and hate, that maybe you take some time to forgive whoever hurt you. You don't even have to tell them. Just as long as you believe it.

Anyway, that's it for me. This EOBS is done.

Two books. That's it.

If I ever revisit these characters (I kinda love me some Ax and Valentina) it will not take place on this college campus. But I could see a standalone book about Ax a few years in the future.

Ruling Class releases September 2 (so a short wait) but to make it all easier I will be releasing a PREQUEL to Bully King on August 19th. If you're craving a little sexy history between Ax, Lars, Cooper, and Cadee you can get your fix with a novella. If you're not in to that—skip it. Ruling Class will not be a reverse harem. Just getting that out of the way now.

Thank you for reading, thank you for reviewing (please go leave me a review! I really love it when you do that!) and I'll see you in the next book!

Julie
JA Huss

JA Huss never wanted to be a writer and she still dreams of that elusive career as an astronaut. She originally went to school to become an equine veterinarian but soon figured out they keep horrible hours and decided to go to grad school instead. That Ph.D. wasn't all it was cracked up to be (and she really sucked at the whole scientist thing), so she dropped out and got a M.S. in forensic toxicology just to get the whole thing over with as soon as possible.

After graduation she got a job with the state of Colorado as their one and only hog farm inspector and spent her days wandering the Eastern Plains shooting the shit with farmers.

After a few years of that, she got bored. And since she was a homeschool mom and actually does love science, she decided to write science textbooks and make online classes for other homeschool moms.

She wrote more than two hundred of those workbooks and was the number one publisher at the online homeschool store many times, but eventually she covered every science topic she could think of and ran out of shit to say.

So in 2012 she decided to write fiction instead. That year she released her first three books and started a career that would make her a New York Times bestseller and land her on the USA Today Bestseller's List twenty-one times in the next five years.

In May 2018 MGM Television bought the TV and film rights for five of her books in the Rook & Ronin and Company series' and in March 2019 they offered her and her writing partner, Johnathan McClain, a script deal to write a pilot for a TV show.

Her books have sold millions of copies all over the world, the audio version of her semi-autobiographical book, Eighteen, was nominated for a Voice Arts Award and an Audie Award in 2016 and 2017 respectively, her audiobook, Mr. Perfect, was nominated for a Voice Arts Award in 2017, and her audiobook, Taking Turns, was nominated for an Audie Award in 2018. In 2019 her book, Total Exposure, was nominated for a Romance Writers of America RITA Award.

Johnathan McClain is her first (and only) writing partner and even though they are worlds apart in just about every way imaginable, it works.

She lives on a ranch in Central Colorado with her family.

www.ingramcontent.com/pod-product-compliance
Lightning Source LLC
Chambersburg PA
CBHW022017050726
47499CB00004BA/1038

* 9 7 8 1 9 5 0 2 3 2 5 2 9 *